Invisible Ecologies

Also by Rachel Armstrong

Songs for the Ecocene:

Origamy (2018)
Invisible Ecologies (2019)
The Decomposition Comedy (forthcoming)

Invisible Ecologies

Songs for the Ecocene II

Rachel Armstrong

NewCon Press
England

First published in April 2019 by NewCon Press,
41 Wheatsheaf Road, Alconbury Weston, Cambs, PE28 4LF

NCP192 (limited edition hardback)
NCP193 (softback)

10 9 8 7 6 5 4 3 2 1

ISBN:

978-1-912950-08-9 (hardback)
978-1-912950-09-6 (softback)

Cover by

Text edited by Ian Whates
Book interior layout by Storm Constantine

For Rolf Hughes

Po's Song

Perhaps, in another time, more
Innocent, when all was sweet,
No worlds were beyond us.
But as you ask about my birth,
It was a sudden shock from
Liquid rapture to the violence
Wrought between air and land.

PART I
BIRTH

Delivery

Alesya, my mother, is throwing up over the side of *Fortune*, our small fishing vessel, when her waters break. Already exhausted by seasickness, a series of extreme contractions drain her vitality.

"I'm on my way," yells Krists, my father. He tethers the wheel and carries Alesya down to the hold, as she violently heaves from both ends at once. Appearing to sprout extra limbs, he uses his elbows, knees and forehead to steady himself on the lunging deck.

"Push woman. Push!" he begs, with brine streaming down his cheeks.

The boat lurches so violently that it's impossible to tell which way up it is.

Aleysa's lips part as if she's saying something, but she's inaudible against the tempest.

"We'll push together," says Krists encouragingly, gripping her wrists with his huge hands. "Come on. Take a deep breath. One, two, three. Give as much as you can," but the tone is draining from her body.

Twin waterspouts scar the lemon-yellow sky, like the horns of a colossal sea snail, and frame the stage for my birth. Our trawler is tossed like flotsam high into the air.

"Push, woman, push!"

Despite Krists' pleading, my mother cannot bear down any more.

As the other six vessels in our convoy bolt down their hatches and manoeuvre away from the freak weather conditions, my distraught father knows he simply cannot handle both steering the vessel to safety and my difficult birth.

"Mayday, Mayday, Mayday" he howls over the radio waves, hoping our kin will hear him.

The grey waters continue to swell and roll, kneading my mother like dough, but her flesh is already cold. Krists gently lifts up her eyelids with the pulp of his thumbs; her pupils as big as Charon's coins and rubs the glabellar space between her eyebrows.

"Come on, stay with me!"

Then he grates his knuckles on my mother's chest. He drops his cheek to her lips and feels no breath. He tries again, harder, to rouse her, compressing her chest and bellowing rescue breaths, but there is no response.

"Push, damn you!" he weeps.

Knowing the sea' has defeated him, my father takes a gutting knife and splits my mother's lifeless flesh across the top of the public bone. Then he pulls me from her innards like a fish. Hauled by my father's spade-like hands into the contrary gloom of the world, I bawl.

Budding Bioregion

A small clump of matter breaks from my riverbank. It's the way we elemental bodies propagate. My own lands and shores feed the inlets of the Venetian Lagoon of the North Italian delta where people have largely lost touch with the rhythms and moods of my kind, so I am mostly invisible to them.

Descended from ancient families of giant bodies that encircle the earth, sea and air, we have souls, passions and legacies to uphold. Like all my kin, I have no eyes, ears, tongue, skin, or lips to witness and narrate events. I am a place, not a mechanism, an aspect of nature that is moulded and remoulded by the incessant flow and exchange of electrons. I am a shapeshifter, taking on different forms that seem appropriate to the surroundings. Swept along by molecular gusts on the chemical river of life's fluid substrates, I am simultaneously 'one' and many mutually interdependent agents. Although I do not possess what you might describe as a well-circumscribed brain, *I am sentient*. My thinking takes place at the interfaces between my constituents, so it is impossible to point at a central source of my existence. Rather than interpreting the patterns around me, or being occupied by some homuncular essence, my experiences embody the tensions forged between all kinds of lively things and may differ from moment to moment. I make no grandiose claims about my abilities, but claim my rights to be regarded with compassion, fairness and mutual respect. I simply ask for you to 'see' me as a different *kind of person* than you are. Remember, my terrains are yours too and through them, we share a deep history and kinship with the community of life.

If you choose to recognise me, then you may find the first homeopathic traces of my existence everywhere. I lay down my accounts in the great book of Nature through my residues, soils and stones, carried by the spray of chilled waters from Alpine runoff as it condenses on spartanly-spread grasses that claw at tenuous traction on gravel. As I tumble down the valley, I program and reprogram the subatomic charm of water molecules and raise a chough to flight with the echoes of my swelling mass. My first consolidating bodies are ionic charges and solutes that leave no residues, or confer any kind of recognisable shape on my being. In fact, you may wonder how I *am* at all.

Wait.

Here it is again. This little knot of matter has been sucking on my dirt for a while, trying to stay attached by soft carbohydrate tethers. Its hold is weakening and it is coaxed into a twirling dance by the gentle near-shore current. Now, it is vulnerable to human observers, who are likely to think of it as river scum, and poke it further out from the water's edge with a stick. This hardy tangle of scraps slowly rotates out towards the faster, more streamlined fluxes in the middle of the rivulet, and is whipped up into a current, which expedites its seaward migration.

Of course, I care! My feelings are simply different than yours.

My flesh is diffusely channelled through tentacular networks and soft-bellied hubs of rhizomatic interaction that filter my sensations through vegetable matter. My moods are crystallised in carbon and spread over an entire bioregion. Communicating through multiple modes of expression, I sing over rocks, hiss around thin obstacles, carve my signature in sediments, tumble rocks along the river bed and babble in the shallows. Sloping through winding rivers, I am still little more than a set of imprints that convey chemical intentions, which find ways to become atomic instructions and energizing matrixes. Now, I flow into Lake Maggiore where these tiny clumps of material traces become incorporated my expansive body are beginning to express an innate character. As I wind through historic towns, I push through ditches, where impurities accrete. Layers upon layers of these deposits bind in complexes along my riverbanks to form loosely coupled assemblages that shape my agglutinating matter in soft silts. As I move through the delta bringing the promise of vegetation, I pass around the ornate stones and arched bones of bridges, to carve my earth-name into their foundations.

Po.

Of late, human settlement complicates my thriving. Your artificial fertilisers, plastics additives and the lively chemistries of excrement, coagulate in clots of surface-scum of dubious character within my flesh. My waters boil in places with every kind of poison, and gleam with insidious oil films. Fading blossoms spin on detergent-weakened water tension, while keeping their poise like pond skaters. Eels move silently under the shadows of my swelling tissues and use me as cover to take shortcuts over the land. Even here, fish fry bind plastic microparticles in their intestines, as knots of dough-like matter, while lurking under fallen leaves with incandescent brilliance. Herons freeze in wait for prey as dams silt up my flow. I find my way around even the most pervasive blockages by flooding plains and carving out a patchwork body of impromptu channels where I form, and re-form the land in fertile bridges and budding island masses.

Look! The raft of matter persists.

Slurping on liquid nourishment, which passes in and out of its loosely knitted substance, the tangle is spinning all kinds of materials into its developing body. Strolling through my aquatic and terrestrial habitats – marshes, tidal flats, the eel beds of Comacchio and their bird-haunted marshes – the little clump becomes increasingly imprinted with their geology and meets the channel-etched, boggy soils of the two main cities – Chioggia and the Venetian archipelago.

The raft is denser now, assimilating your trash, poisons and filth into its soma. Where this cannot be transformed into useful organic compounds, it hosts metabolising biofilms that transform its embryonic forms into a subversive proto-soil. Compelled by opportunity it indulges its appetite for waste materials, plastic bottles and sewage until the lagoon currents lure it out into the open water.

Right now, this little island embryo is little more than a hairball of vegetable matter, silt and plastic trash. Right now, it is not self-aware but as it establishes its own unique community of mutually interdependent bodies, the transforming matter will reach a threshold. Just like its elemental forbearers, this marks the transition towards independent existence, where the island embryo starts to formulate its very own thoughts.

• POV
↳ PO, the sentient elemental body

• Themes
  • Acceptance
  • Differences
  • Respect
  • Human impact – pollution

Voice

A voice
Reaching out
For intelligible words,
Melodies and poetry.

Utterances,
Eddies, currents,
Slurping, seeping, smashing.
Liquid chimes on splintering rock.
Contaminated sludge, scum, dust, dew,
Biofilms, pond skaters, dandelion seeds.
Soap bubbles, oil slicks, surface swirls,
Kaleidoscopic plastics, fragments, drool.
Surfaces thickening under the slick and smog.

Engines drone,
Vibrations gather foam,
Sticks, feathers, leaves, algae,
In their wake, as industrial heat
Discharges through gaping pipes, scar
Soft silts with nitrate runoff, pesticides,
Tainted rain, acids, organic rot, rust, salt,
Jolly plastic bottles, household bleach, turps,
This cocktail tastes, smells of something like life.

But not
All that I touch,
Nurtures life and its
Substrates. My budding
Soils feed upon cadmium,
Bread-for-the-ducks, worn tyres,
Polychlorinated biphenyls, batteries,
Lead, mercury, decomposing carcasses,
E numbers, ballast water spews invaders
And poisons. Fine powders that clog gills so
Fish tip belly-up. I thrive on these delirious sediments.

POV
↳ baby

po²·

Turn Around

My grandfather Anatoly brings the *Voyager* to a sudden stop.

"Something's wrong," he radios, "The *Fortune*'s issued a Mayday."

Holding an unbelievably tight turning circle, and using a 'back and fill' manoeuvre to 'rotate' the boat, while giving the engine a quick 'goose', he turns his single screw engine vessel almost on the spot.

"How the hell does he do that?" crackles Csaba from the *Sanctuary*.

"Like this!" growls Nastia, cutting her engine. "The old man once told me that when you goose, you can't be gentle with the power."

"Like a mule, not a lover," says Piotr.

"Mine's making enough noise to be both!" says Csaba.

"The salty rascal never ceases to surprise me," says Ivan. "I'm turning now, but I'll beat you all there."

"Hey, you guys, perhaps Aleysa has given birth," says Nastia. "Let's go and greet the nibling."

"The what?"

"We don't know if it's a niece or nephew yet," Nastia explains, "that's a *nibling*."

"I heard the word *sofralia* is the thing now," says Ivan.

"I do hope you realise while you all wallow in your dictionaries," says Piotr, "that the old man has just changed the laws of physics. Maybe you'll find the right phrase for it but I'm going to catch with him."

"That's a *pursuit*," says Nastia.

"You're lacking ambition today, sister," says Ivan. "I'm going to *overtake* him."

But as the trawlers break into shrieks of radio-whooping, the *Voyager* has already reached the *Fortune*, which is now surrounded by blue lights.

• Relates To:
· Delivery (pp 9-10)
– temporally
– cause + effect

· Theme
↳ gender neutrality; family

15

Birth

The first responders to the Mayday are the Venice Police Department Marine Unit, who are met with grim circumstances – a recently deceased young woman, with home-made Caesarian section and a roaring newborn. A tear and blood-stained seaman grips them both and refuses to cooperate, or let either of them go.

My grandfather immediately begins arguing with a police officer about his right to drop anchor.

Nastia is just behind him. Undeterred by the police presence on and around the *Fortune*, she pulls alongside and swings onto the deck.

"You can't come here, miss," warn the duty officers, as she swaggers towards them in her metal calipers that bend like jointed tights around the knees. Sensing the gravity of the situation, she speeds up, brachiating across the deck towards the hold.

"This is my brother's boat," she says, "I'll go where I like."

"Not today, miss." The officers form a barrier across the door. "He's in a state down there. His missus just died in childbirth."

"Don't lie to me," insists Nastia, attempting to push the police aside, "I want to see him."

As she forces her way through the blue barricade, my uncles arrive and, like a swarm, start to nudge the elegant speedboats with their sturdy fat hulls until they inch their way into a protective formation alongside the *Fortune*. Then they lash their vessels together while my other aunts: Jelena, Kasia and Ruzica, as well as the wives of my uncles, Tia, Ljudmilla and Kristi, also board like pirates.

Despite legislation to protect our rights, coast guards generally greet marine 'gypsies', refugees, or vagrants, with at least a modicum of suspicion. Our history is littered with heartbreaking stories of displaced peoples and nomadic seafarers that have reputedly perished on account of bloody-minded regulations, but today my kin are fortunate unfortunates.

"Let them go," hisses the officer in charge, Salvatore Santoro, pained by memories of his own stillborn child and the tenacity of his wife's conscience, which hold him to account in *doing the right thing.* "They've been through enough," he adds, waving his team to back off. "But watch them. I want you to remain present at this *scene.*"

Below deck Krists is sobbing inconsolably. My bloodstained mother is still cradled in one of his giant arms, while I, clasped in the other, am equally marinated in a cocktail of body fluids.

"Come on, brother, let them go," says Csaba gently, but Krists does not acknowledge their presence, or alter his gaze from somewhere incredibly far away.

Together, my kin put their arms around him, as Jelena coaxes me from Krists' grip. Yet he stubbornly clings to Alesya. While his brothers try to talk sense to him, Kasia and Ruzica find me some milk and something to cut the umbilical cord with. Apparently, my mother had already anticipated the temperamental nature of lactating breasts and filled the cupboards with infant milk powder. Ruzica decides the best way to sever me from my placental ties is with her teeth.

Steadily, stealthily, Nastia and my uncles release my mother and respectfully, pass her body over to the *Voyager.*

"We'll lay her to rest now, brother."

At some point, Csaba peers back into the hold to check me out, and asks: "Is it a boy, or a girl?"

I am briefly inspected but no pronouncement is made.

My kin look at each other, shrugging in turn about what to say to my distraught father.

"Let's clean the child, and parcel it up in a snug blanket," says Kasia. "We can take this discussion outside."

• POV
    ↳ P₀ (the baby)

• Related To:
  – Turn Around (pp 15)
    • temporally
     • cause + effect

Marine Travellers

As long as I can remember, perhaps even before I could understand them, my aunts have told me stories of our forbearers.

We are descended from Roma who took to the sea to escape ethnic cleansing. Like our ancestors, we trail the Black Sea and Mediterranean coastlines, where we are carried by the winds like pollen to seek opportunities on new shores. Our native realm is a liquid world whose inconstant surfaces and invisible depths of open water are not constrained by the conventions of terrestrial territories. While we prefer to keep on moving, sometimes, in search of fishing, beachcombing opportunities and finding new lovers, my kin have remained attached to particular shores longer than planned and re-settled.

Being pale-skinned, black-eyed and yellow-weathered by the elements, we are not considered an especially handsome people. Yet we are keen observers, with an intense gaze and agile hands that personify our strong work ethic. We are also blessed with intelligence and resourceful inventiveness. Opportunists rather than staunch traditionalists, our culture is at odds with modern lifestyles. Maestros of making our fortune, we are artful in turning base materials into valuable goods, assimilating new beliefs and cultural traditions like chiffonniers. The eastward expansion of the European Union means that many more nations have extended my kin the same rights as their own citizens, in permanently settling the land. However, we are seldom wont to do so. While land-dwellers prefer their fixed abodes, clearly delineated territories and accumulate material wealth, we consider these habits peculiar as they are at odds with the living world, which is steeped in transience, uncertainty and change. While there is always a risk of disaster, there is just as much potential for flourishing. Since we share such different values to land-dwellers, our cultural practices are regarded as sins against modern conventions. Indeed, we are demonised for benefiting from an economy of recycled plastics.

We do not regard our rag-picking as contradictory to the natural realm but continuous with its many different expressions. All matter, indeed all life forms are equal – even when they're sloughed off by industrial and organic excesses. It is simply our responsibility to find value in them. We do not look backwards for times when the world was considered kinder, richer, sweeter and more beautiful – but actively embrace the materials that litter our shorelines. The character of nature has changed and plastics are integral to every aspect of the living world. While my kin have contributed little to this, we are shamelessly resourceful. These qualities of adaptation and survival connect us to the revelations of nature.

While we consider all people and creatures equal, our own care and compassion is not always reciprocated by others. Owing to our willingness to work with unspeakable substances such as, trash, dirt and even human cremains, we are often called 'unclean'. As long as we are safe, we shrug and enjoy the notoriety, since we are proud to fulfil arguably civilization's greatest role – linking the cycles of life and death. We are proud to consider our culture as performing the regenerative work of composts. In doing so, we demonstrate great craftsmanship in dealing with the left-overs from urban regimes. There is much joy in the simplicity of our lives, too. Although our culture is generally regarded as having low social status, we have been graciously welcomed by certain communities, and in some cases, are even respected.

- P.O.V
    ↳ First Person (Po?)

- Themes:
    - Change
    - Equality
    - Simplicity
    - Natural

- Related To:
    - Budding Bioregion (pp 11-13)
        - Thematically

Swelling

A gathering of vessels draws me
Into to the lagoon. As canal-side
Gums suck at me, like an illicit
Substance. I break in choppy
Waves, stealing through gaps
And creeping under love-locked
Bridges where couples hold
Hands and selfie sticks, aiming
Their inward gaze on pouting
Lips stretched against theatrical
Backdrops. They see me not.

Detritivores, biofilms and planktivores
Feast on the crusts of ancient sludges.
I savour their salty richness, leaving
Mineral deposits of my own as trace
Memories. Writing my name in water.

Skillfully, I avoid alley openings where
Same sex couples share first forbidden
Kisses. Churned by the broad bows
And scraped green hulls of refuse barges
I mingle with toxic trash and hustle
Towards the gondoliers' charming smile:
A song, a journey, a memory, a dream.
Seagulls land on me, their deadly beaks
Carve out tasty morsels: old sandwiches,
Pizza crusts, a rose, sweetcorn, ice-cream,
An apple core, scraps of a drowned pigeon.

I stretch my filth towards open waters, Spartan
In nutrients, but thick with dregs of uncertainty.
Order begins to emerge from chaos, ingenious

Organisms persisting despite the ravages of ⎤ survival
Time, poison, sunlight, water, writing their own ⎦
Stories in in elements that are channelled by
Chemical rules of energy, flow, pairing, mingling
And death, each species leaving unique footprints.

Now with a monstrous tail like an eel,
I am carried towards the southwest wall
Of San Michele beyond easy sight, or reach.
There's nothing beguiling here to explore;
Too risky for a coastline to take root,
Too sacred for the tourists to amass.
Too sheltered for dredgers to reach my
Foetal flesh or haul it into refuse tanks.
I sink my tentacles into the gaps between
Old bricks, plastics, marine crusts, delta silt
And take shelter, shaping these vague
Shores with my amniotic attachments.
I am becoming an island mass, capable of
Supporting new ecologies and human settlers.

• Poetry

• P.O.V.
    ↳ First Person
        • Possibly the perspective of
          the clump of matter that
          broke off of Po in
          "Budding Bioregion"

• Themes
  – leaving a signature
  – survival

• Related To:
  – Budding Bioregion
    (pp. 13)
    • thematically
    • temporally

21

Boy

My kin discuss where they'll cremate my mother.

"We should scatter her ashes at sea," says Piotr, "according to our traditions."

At odds with how they'll manage the logistics, the discussions become heated. Jelena beckons Nastia aside and carefully unwraps me, holding me up for her inspection.

"It's an incredibly small penis. But I'm sure it's a son," she asserts.

Thankful for a diversion, my uncles beg to differ.

"This has to be a girl," says Ivan. "All our kin have very large genitals."

"Keep a sense of proportion," snaps Ljudmilla.

"Now we live in a world where women decide what makes a man," grumbles Casaba.

"Good job too," says Ruzica, "Otherwise it would be *all* about the penis."

"He's both. Boy and girl. You know," adds Kasia.

"Impossible," objects Piotr. "That just doesn't exist."

Ivan shakes his head, agreeing, but quickly stops as he catches Kristi scowling.

"This child can be whomever he wants to be," asserts Ruzica.

"His eyes and mouth are wide, just like his mother's. God rest her soul," observes Kristi, exchanging care of me with Jelena for a while.

I am passed around to a host of compliments.

"Such a beautiful boy. Incredible skin," says Ljudmilla. "It's like he's been modelled from soft, honey stone. I could eat him all up!"

At some point, they discuss what portent a 'hermaphrodite' carries for marine travellers and I am passed around again, turned over and every part of me inspected.

"He's good luck, of course!" says Nastia.

Between them, my kin cuddle me over and over, my 'good luck' rubbing off on them. All the while they marvel, admire and praise my existence as a miraculous event, until exhausted from all this attention, I bawl inconsolably.

Jelena then has the presence of mind to feed me.

What is it?

There are more people in the world with unconventional sexual configurations than there are with common genetic disorders such as cystic fibrosis.

Everyone wants to establish my gender, but it's just not that easy.

While categories are assigned to us at such an early stage of our development, determining how society subsequently treats and values us, biology is liquid. Unlike many other species, our sex, which informs our gender choices, is not supposed to change after we're born. This is like only having summer or winter, with no variations in between. It is always hot in summer and only snows in winter. Any deviation from these expectations overturns the laws of nature, which is considered, frankly, a devilish thing to do.

Nature does not allocate binaries but offers a range of options, including sex, which informs gendered beings. Shaped by a range of characteristics, their differences occupy a spectrum of expressions similar to the climactic moods from which the nuanced variations of weather emerge. While some characteristics are easier to change than others, in all instances biology plays with boundaries, where one 'type' of characteristic, such as sexual embodiment, blends into others. Depending on our cultural expectations, certain aspects of our anatomy and character are foregrounded, then processed into categories. These are then named, sorted, ordered, valued and normalised in ways that reinstate our cultural values. Genital phenotypes, by which we are evaluated at birth, are only part of this portfolio. While our infant sex organs may start out as relatively characterless, they soon grow to be distinct, even remarkable – big small, wonky, straight, hairy, bald – similar to the variations to be found in the face! Over time these become entangled with other forms of identification. Think of a rugby player in drag, or a centenarian who has surrendered their youthful sex-hormones. Each of these people is gendered, but the nuances that inform gender assignments are complex and personal. Of course, it makes social sense to talk about gender classifications but beyond our anthropocentric preferences and neuroses, this is not the way that *nature* works. There is no decree that we possess five senses, nor are there inevitably seven colours in the rainbow: the way we sort, order and value the world is a convenience, adopted to help us interpret our surroundings. We have the power to change these perspectives.

Specifically, nature does not insist there are only two sexes. Indeed, the majority of organisms – most of which are microbial – do not comply with the sex, gender, or even species categories that people impose on the world. Such rarefied categories, invented for humans, cannot be accepted as a universal truth about the character of the living world. Microbes enjoy a variety of signalling displays and ways of reproducing, in ways that thoroughly complicate their typologies and socialisation.

Of course, we are not microscopic creatures, but it is worth appreciating that gender is a peculiarly, although not uniquely, human thing, which is assigned at the start of our life's journey. While conventional 'male' and 'female' gender types predominate, around one in every two thousand children is born with genitals that do not confirm to these archetypes.

Owing to my ambiguous gender assignment, I am disproportionately asked to define what, or who, I am. People feel entitled to ask deeply personal questions in relation to my identity, sexual preferences, social role and biological capacities. This is not only intrusive but also impossible for me to respond to correctly. I am variably all – boy, girl, intersex, 'hermaphrodite' – and none of these things, since they still reach for some kind of fixed position, or bearing on the world. The genital 'parts' that are equated with gender at birth, do not define me as a developing person. Rather than seek conformity, I am drawn to discover the freedoms of alterity that release me from these unnatural notions of fixity, so that I may ally with shape shifters, changelings, monstrous nonconformists, proteans, Paradoxa and freaks that embrace change over the course of their lives. The very nature of these beings is to defy categorisation. We are the outsider set.

But do not conflate an outward appearance with an inner character. These are very separate things. Monsters are monstrous when they do not possess a moral basis for making decisions in the world. A monster will respond negatively to being cruelly treated, just as humans do. Not all monsters are negatively regarded, however. Some, like 'hermaphrodites', have enjoyed a sacred status, blessed with ability to transgress the limits of gender. Indeed, Paradoxa have inspired others to consider new realms of possibilities. However, with the progressive march of physiological rationalism, anatomical standardization, genetic programming, mathematically describable morphologies, and the wedding of form to function, the idea of hermaphrodites and other monsters, is equated with deviance, devilry, damnation and does little to dispel our fear of unauthorised bodies.

Regarding the question of my gender, what I *can* tell you is that in those first few hours following my birth, my kin's love and curiosity for my uniqueness empowered me with a deep sense of belonging. While many seek to confuse my sex and gender, attempting to call my otherness out, I do not let them reduce who I am. Instead, I regard their quest in naming me, as an expression of their fear concerning the uncanny potency of our enchanted world.

• P.O.V.
  ↳ First - Person
  • Baby from Delivery

• Themes
  - Conformity
  - Categorization
  - Nature
    - gender
    - shape -
    shifting

• Linked to Boy
  • Coherence
    ↳ sex, gender

• Not a part of the narrative of Delivery
  ↳ seems like an essay (expository)

Embryogenesis

Living is sense making.
But at times of disaster
There is no future in a
Rational world. Splinters,
Out of alignment with
The senses, now lurk at
The root of everything.
I too am born Paradoxa,
Transcending the known
Order by constantly shape
Shifting to become a thing
That never existed before.

My veins swell with unknown saps
Shedding azure mucus and violet
Clots in my afterbirths, as succour
For greenish parasite herds that
Strangle dark flowers with their
Virulent suckers. In the regenerative
Rot that follows, my black scent
Breaks upon the nacreous embers
Of tides, which swallow all that was
Once familiar. Never complete, my
Varicose transformations describe
Whirlpools within a world of
Meaning that I construct as my own.

Identifying with Po

Insinuating Po is the sentient biomass (giving the human characteristics)

- Poetry
- P.O.V.
  - → First Person
  - Possibly the sentient matter that broke off of Po
- Linked to What Is It? (pp 23-25)
- Coherence

Me

Traditionally, my father is required to announce my arrival in the world. Yet, he is too traumatised and distraught to hold me, let alone have an opinion on the matter of my gender. Maybe, he just grunts when I'm presented to him.

My kin call me 'Po', after the treacherous, yet life-giving bioregion. This sets the scene for the precarious nature of my birth and seemingly inspires my anatomical contradictions.

.P.O.V.

> First Person (Po the human)

- Linked to Boy (pp 22)
  - Causality
- Linked to "Budding Bioregion" (pp 11-13)
  - Coherence

Collective Individuality

A breakaway.
Still connected
To the entangled
Bodies that make
Up my substance.
I am
not
Individual.

Separateness confounds me by
Its distance from others and
Conventions of bodily wholes.
A fish, fly, snail and ant colony
Are functional wholes. A brain,
A liver, an intestine – are not.
No ancestral free-living brains
Intestines, lungs or livers exist.
But within laboratories they may
Be cultured and printed as free
Living objects, and transplanted
To make depleted bodies whole.

Here.

Some creatures, pose paradoxes.
Functional individuals can be
Colonies, like siphonophores,
Which are made up of parts that
Are equivalent to free organisms.
The Portuguese man o war, and
Gelatinous abyssal beasts that
Wander as bioluminescent guts
On the sea floor seem designed

By committee and too odd to
Persist. Arising from a single
Fertilised egg, they specialise into
Different organs, none of which
Can live alone. Improbable, yet
Real, they challenge notions of
What being an individual means
When many become singular

Collectives ...

Nothing exists without context.
Existence is negated without the
Presence of others: a wolf sans
Caribou, caribou without grass,
Grass depleted of sun, which lacks
Dependents, is an extinct solar
System. This is not what we are.
Entangled by kinship within a
Peculiarly rebellious world,
Matter is interconnected, not

Individual...

- Poetry
- Themes
  - Individual vs Collective
  - Paradoxes
  - Shape-shifters

Shelter

The patience of the coastguard dwindles, and the *Fortune* is boarded by the maritime police, who escort our convoy to a temporary mooring just behind southwest wall of San Michele in the Venetian lagoon – the city's island graveyard.

Here, my kin are given assurances that no charges will be pressed and are encouraged to deal with the difficult circumstances of my arrival away from the public eye.

- Linked to "Boy" (pp 22)
  - Continuity?
- POV
  ↳ Po (human)
    - First-person omniscient

Each Other

People and their lands are inseparable.

Conceived at exactly the same moment – in ground and womb – the embryonic island *Po*, which is descended from my bioregion and the human child, Po, are twinned.

Both share an unstable identity that is sensitive to changes in their world and brings richness to it through their rebellion against conformity. While these twins share many similarities, they are also very different, and there is never any confusion about which one is which.

Po is the land, and Po is the human.

- Themes
  - Conformity
  - Identity
  - Twin (Po and Po)

- POV
  └→ Bioregion

- Linked to "What is It" (pp 23-25)
  - Coherence

- Linked to "Embryogenesis" (pp 26)
  - Coherence

- Linked to "Me" (pp 27)
  - Coherence

Colonists

Our convoy drops anchor and Jelena's loosely fitting sandals sink the first human imprints on the embryonic spur of land that juts out from the retaining wall at the limits of the island graveyard.

Perhaps it is a failure of imagination on behalf of my kin, or maybe it is a tribute to me, that this place is named *Po*.

Stepping out against the backdrop of a city that is built upon the bones of its populations, where in some places it is said that the earths are half mulch and half human, my aunt's epic traces are unnoticed – just like the detritus that forms this site.

"Magnificent decay," she says.

While earths beyond this world have been iconized by such traces, my aunt's soft mark on the slender wayward shores is quickly erased by the tide. These transitional realms invite invisible ecologies into their spaces offering an uninhabited twilight zone of liquid and solid, where there are no established hierarchies of survival. Earths and water roll into a continuum of soft and liquid ground, where the very success of this rapidly propagating, yet immature land, seems to depend on *how* it is settled.

Kasia joins Jelena, to further test the integrity of the ground, which is made up from evil smelling sediments, plastic fragments, flotsam, organic matter, broken shells, biocrete fragments, wooden posts, oil slick from backwashed motorboat engines and the remains of a gull-picked pigeon. Squelching rudely in their tenuous steps, my aunts inadvertently upset clouds of dizzy male mosquitoes in their explorations, which until this moment have been oblivious to invaders. Startled by the human intrusion their only thoughts are of sex and nectar.

The flies are not exactly thriving. The secluded beach has a reputation for picnickers and lovers being mauled by vicious bites from females, which need food before mating. Lesions from these carnivores produce welts that are frequently infected and take around six weeks to heal without treatment. Without protein to sustain the quality of egg-making the females are barren, or produce malformed ova, which does little to secure the future of the species.

Finding neither a readily available source of sex nor nectar, the mosquitoes attempt to move further afield, risking a journey over the choppy water. Some of them even find their way to the mainland. Nobody laments their extinction, or bids them 'goodbye, which is poor recognition for the services these creatures have carried out in service of the lagoon's ecology. Lothario males are generous pollinators and the graveyard's ecosystems are richer for their contribution.

As one dominant species falls, another takes its place and a new system of biological relationships begins. The few deformed pupating mosquito larvae that survive are systematically spilled onto dry ground by my aunts, in a systematic search to destroy their potential breeding grounds.

.POV
  ⮡ Po (human)
      – First-person omniscient

. Themes
    – transitional realms
    – Invisible ecologies
    – survival

.Linked to "Shelter" (pp 30)
    – Continuity

New Start

My father refuses to go back to sea.

"The ocean is our way of life," insists Anatoly, but Krists is resolute.

"Never!" he shouts, his body shaking in uncontrollable sobs. "That leviathan took my woman."

Csaba and Piotr put their arms reassuringly around his shoulder. Ruzica slowly cleans a glass, all the time watching her brother.

"Do you think you're going to stay *here*," says Anatoly, "with an *infant*. How long exactly do you think you'll last?"

He snatches a long spoon from the table and strides up on deck. Shouting back at the cabin he waves the spoon in the air and, leaping with unexpected agility onto *Po*'s silty shores, plunges it into the ground. When he pulls it back up again, it is dripping with fetid muck.

"Just look at this stuff," he says and puts the spoon in his mouth. "You can't consume *this*."

Immediately and thoroughly he spits the evil sludge onto the beach. "There is nothing to eat, nothing to farm, nothing to live on here. There is no hope – no reason to stay."

Gathered in the cabin doorway, my aunts try to settle Anatoly down as he returns to the deck, but both my grandfather and father are agitated.

"You will not brow beat me into serving the beast that stole from me, old man," shouts Krists, raising his fist at the waves then the sky. "You will not have me, tempest!"

"It's no longer just about you," says Anatoly spitting more dirt from his mouth into the sink. "You're a father now."

Responding badly to persuasion, Krists succumbs to fits of ill-temper and shouts feverishly at Anatoly and many kinds of invisible foe. These episodes become increasingly violent and cannot be drowned out, even with large quantities of vodka.

While the Italian police have shown our kin a great deal of compassion, they now insist our informal congregation raises their anchors and moves onwards. Conceding that the marine police will be obliged to use more forceful methods of persuasion should my kin pose further resistance, Anatoly embraces my father with slow, backslapping hugs.

"I will return soon with Alesya's ashes, so you can bury her formally at sea. You must look to your son, now," he says. "He needs you."

Somehow Jelena, Ruzica and Kasia manage to convince the authorities there is no alternative but for them to stay on the *Fortune* as well, to take care of Krists and me. Holding me briefly aloft in a proud farewell and souvenir of good fortune, they wave our kin 'goodbye'.

"If I didn't think I'd wring his neck in the process," says Nastia as she swings her metal legs over the side of the Voyager, "I'd stay to help you all."

• POV
  ↳ Po (human) ; first-person omniscient

' Linked to "Colonists" (pp 32-33)
  - continuity

Growing

The refuse of human settlement
Joins with my fertile excrements.
In compost, we share a common
Language of sustenance and muck.
These people, nourish foundational
Ecologies like giant land worms.
Enrich my soils, swell my shores
In a casquade of succession and
Mutual survival. Being together.

- POV
  ↳ Po (Island)

- Themes
  - Interconnectedness
  - Survival

- linked to "New start" (pp 34-35)
  - Causality

- linked to "Collective Individuality"
  (pp 28-29)
      - Coherence

Apathy

The outbursts stop and my father's engagement with reality slips away.

Although my aunts sit with him for hours, immersing him in everyday conversation about the sea, the sky, what kin are doing and even tell funny stories, when Krists speaks it is little more than a mumble.

"I'm in hell."

Since my father has lost all interest in looking after himself and my aunts are already fully occupied with looking after me, they subject him to exactly the same treatment. Between the three of them they manage to hoist and turn him like a giant ham. They wash him in my left-over water, since it's wasteful not to use it twice, feed him soft mush with my future weaning spoon, change his clothes and toilet him with old folded strips of towelling that are regularly emptied into the lagoon. When it comes to my turn, I am met with peals of joy.

- POV
  ↳ Po (human); first-person omniscient
- Themes
  - Grief

- Linked to "New Start" (pp 34-35)
  - continuity

Kin

After a fortnight Anatoly returns with my mother's remains in a small earthenware container that bears every resemblance to a common garden pot, with an ill-fitting lid.

"It's time to put your woman to rest, son."

Krists doesn't even appear to notice my grandfather's arrival, let alone understand that he's just delivered Aleysha's cremains. Devastated by his son's plight, my grandfather leaves my aunts a little money to keep us all going, and carefully hands Ruzica the pot containing my mother's ashes. Then, he examines me admiringly, hugs each of my aunts, glances sadly over at my father.

"I'll return as soon as I can," says Anatoly.

As Kasia waves my hand from the *Fortune* porthole, Jelena stores my mother carefully in a cupboard under the sink so that, when my father is more 'together', we can say goodbye to her with the respect that she deserves.

At sea.

PART II
SETTLING

Neighbours

Po and Po are not the only twins in my bioregion. The grey-eyed the industrial colossus of Marghera and its green-eyed suburban twin Mestre stare across the Venetian lagoon.

On a clear day, these modern mainland complexes are proud and indiscreet, while Venice itself seems diminished, faint and fragile in comparison – a well-aged slice of prosciutto.

Standing at the foot of the Via della Libertà, which connects the island city to the mainland, you'll see them coveting ownership of the ancient city's water, sky and land. These supercilious beings were created as the *New Venice*. Together, they consume natural resources, invent technology and spawn gleaming buildings. They have tremendous appetites, always demanding 'more', or declaring there is 'no room' for other kinds of presence. Although they can taste the presence of *Po*'s new island growth, they are too arrogant to consider it important.

This apparent standoff is a symptom of on-going conflicts between economic and environmental agendas that are played out in this locality.

Back in 1920, when the monstrous twins were just a twinkle in nationalism's eye, and just a slither of grime from my flesh, they existed as a marine swamp known as the Botteniga. Drained by modern techniques they became wedded to industry with new factories, science parks and housing projects for workers, who were given direct access to the soils of the old city through ambitious transport projects.

Nearby residents of the fishing village Chioggia, condemned the industrial complex as 'the mother of all contamination' which discharged its waste into the lagoon, significantly altering the water quality. Inventing the slogan 'in Mestre the roast, in Venice the smoke', they drew attention to how the shiny new monsters' industrial bad manners and distasteful hygiene humiliated the old city.

Today their industrial discharges are responsible for issuing hundreds of thousands of tonnes per year of pollutants into the air, earth and water, including over seven hundred tonnes of carcinogenic compounds such as polychlorinated biphenyls, lead, zinc, hydrocarbons, mercury and dioxins. When it rains on Marghera, smog and toxic fumes slobber their poisons over the old city, gnawing at its substance, seeping into the walls, percolating into the ground and soiling its waterways with toxic run-off. Corrosion is rife here. Brickwork is scarred by efflorescence, and unusual nutrients catalyse the proliferation of uncategorised algae blooms within the lagoon whose environmental impacts are entirely unknown.

The soft foot of environmental catastrophe creeps through my wounded bioregion. Here, all the embryonic lands of my bioregion are continually under assault, being scooped out like abortuses by industrial dredgers, which make way for the increasing volume of marine traffic. These terrible twins drink my water table with an unquenchable thirst, leaving the old city even more vulnerable to the havoc brought by damaging tides that are becoming increasingly frequent and unmanageable. While I maintain my creative resistance against these incursions, they nonetheless leave parts of me barren and scarred.

Humans play a significant part in these contested territories and have sought to make peace between us. In an act of environmental arbitration Eni's oil refinery announced in 2014 that it would be changing from crude oil to bio-oil feedstocks in a Green Refinery project. The plant now produces around half a million tonnes of green diesel a year using a special Eco-fining process. This is a two-step hydrogenation reaction that can use oils from conventional biofuel crops like soy and palm, as well as non-edible oils such as algae oil, animal tallow and waste grease like olive oil, which otherwise present difficult disposal issues. While chemically identical with petroleum, these oils can be blended with traditional fuels and produce fewer carbon dioxide emissions.

Today, an expansionist enthusiasm for green products and advanced biotechnology steadily brings more people into Mestre. Entrepreneurial start-ups and incubator projects are flourishing, with biotechnology having the strongest foothold in the vibrant marketplace. This is shored up by a global demand for a whole range of *sustainable* product innovations that feed a new generation of bio-based pharmaceuticals from DNA sequencing, to cloning and advanced molecular chemistry. Employees from companies like 'Exitec', a biotechnological pest extermination company, have made this traffic-filled conurbation their home, as did the chemical factory workers before them – but this generation are not on subsistence lifestyles. They are the new merchants: shareholders in highly profitable small businesses, which are springing up around the industrial giants, as Italy's very own 'Silicon Valley'. This flourishing region of high-technology corporations and startup companies is a powerhouse in Italy's economy. With the rapidly increasing wealth in the area, property prices are escalating and designer condos are flourishing. Mestre is *the place to be*, with its easy access to shopping centres, commercial spaces, schools, recreation areas and car parks are all within easy reach of the ancient city.

Human settlement feeds these greedy twins that have long-harboured ambitions to advance upon the old city's shores. If they succeed, it will destroy the delicate balance within this bioregion that has been my life's work over the last eighteen millennia.

· POV
  ↳ Bioregion

· Themes
  - Human settlement
  - Technological Innovation.
  - Pollution

Being Dead in Venice

Although we are moored only metres away from the city graveyard on San Michele, my mother will not be buried here. This is not only a consequence of our custom of saying our farewells at sea, but also because of the complexity of being buried *in* Venice.

Until the early nineteenth century the Venetian dead were laid to rest under paving stones within the city. This was not a sanitary practice, especially during the times of plague. So, in 1837 the Austrian and French occupiers decreed that an island would be dedicated to this purpose. From this point onwards, people could live in Venice; they could even breathe their last sigh in Venice, but nobody could be buried in the city of Venice itself.

Consequently, the existing islands of San Michele and San Cristoforo were fashioned into an uncannily square yet small landmass, which was organised into an earthen grid of plots for the dead. This new island of San Michele soon became fully occupied and created an entrepreneurial opportunity for the city, as there was great demand for being laid to rest *in* Venice. A Venetian burial became a luxury commodity that was no longer for the city's few residents alone but also a lucrative business to run.

Together

Anatoly's financial gift is small but welcome and my aunts are extraordinarily resourceful in making do with whatever they can find. We live on almost nothing.

My father has given up trying to communicate with us at all. Catatonic with grief, he's stopped eating and even drinking. Yet my aunts ensure that, despite his inconsolable loss, Krists' life continues, whether or not they have to feed him with my spoon and toilet him the same as me.

At sea, my kin enjoyed a staple diet of seabirds, fish and even flotsam, cargo that had fallen overboard from passing ships, so there was always enough to eat. However, the lagoon ecology is very different to that of the open waters. The sheltered but tidal shoreline is so close to the densely populated city and industrial mainland that the waters are heavily soiled. While the lagoon offers its bounty in plastic-wrapped sandwich boxes, barely consumed drinks and even regurgitates a monk seal carcass, my aunts refuse to turn them into meals, as they are marinated in sewage and other poisons. On most days, the sea winds and tides produce enough flow to flush the worst of the toxins and rot away, but there are also days where everything becomes still and the city reeks of death.

As *Po*'s shoreline thickens, our moorings become secure enough for my aunts to develop a range of essential services for the *Fortune*. Our tiny kitchen becomes a distillery and on-tap supply of water for reconstituting Aleysa' milk powder stockpile. Rainwater is boiled using solar energy from panels on the roof but Kasia and Ruzica decide that a more industrial-scale method is needed. They design and build a compost water heater, which is fuelled by the decomposition of beach seaweed. Passing two flat coils of polyethylene tubing which have washed up from a construction site somewhere on the mainland through the vigorously decomposing mass, they make a contraption which, when properly turned, produces enough heat to boil a barrel of water. All the hot water needed to clean and bathe me is provided this way. Although the rotting organic heap is an eyesore which reeks of iodine and sweet beach decay, mercifully we are not held to account by neighbours.

Despite the significant challenges of subsistence living, my aunts do not give in to despair, or let us starve. They even transform toxic marine plastics into useable materials using natural procedures within an elaborate processing system where natural biofilms are cultured in shallow shelves within the rock pools. Here, they function like a liver, or kidneys, removing the tiny plastic fragments and their contaminants from the water. Kasia then grows these combined fabrics like gardens and periodically harvests her crop to make a unique fabric composed of organic and plastic material. Ruzica and Jelena spin, press, or compost this matter to make bricks, cloth, paper and composts. The extracted plastics are then melted using a solar-powered sinter that is stored under a tarpaulin out on deck. When the material is molten they cast it into moulds of saleable items such as masks, shoes, hats, and even fashion a small plastic boat from refuse, which is complete with matching paddle. Although remarkably makeshift in its design, the boat is robust enough to ferry my aunts over to the city to sell their wares to tourists.

As their processes become more refined, they install a series of plastic lined pools along the shore where Kasia cultivates algae, which feed on filtered water and whose biomass feeds us on lean days. Working tirelessly but uncomplainingly, my aunts deal with each day's challenges as they happen. Sometimes they fix leaks in the roof. At other times, they work hard to find enough to eat. Somehow, they even manage to deal with Krists' increasing detachment as he refuses to leave the *Fortune* at all. On those days where life seems impossibly hard and unfair, my aunts remember to play with me, and tell me that I am 'worth it'. Each night, they take turns to tuck me into my cot, sing me songs and get up in the middle of the night to feed me. My favourite lullaby is the 'Sleepy Giant', which Kasia croons when I am inconsolable. It's a song about a hungry ogre who likes to chew on little boys but since he has lost his teeth, he sucks on eels instead.

As I grow stronger, so does my father. Although he still eats with a spoon, at least he can now feed himself. Becoming bolder he begins to help with simple chores, like ferrying my aunts over to the mainland in the plastic boat, when they need to sell our wares, or spend a little money on things we can't make. He waits for their safe return at the hospital vaporetto stop, where he stubbornly stays in the water, refusing to make his way even on to the decking.

Within the year, my aunts are running a flourishing business of upcycled plastic souvenirs.

Tasting Spaces

Through each tongueless slurp
I taste the umbilical shores of
All that our twinship embraces
The conjoined, ground and child.

Forget we have boundaries.
We'll explore the bonds that
Draw the magic of our being
And all its strangeness. Here.

Comparing
both POS

- Language that
makes it seem
like the
biomass is
alive

Magic

"Are you joking me?" laughs Frosino Ricci, an elderly man with a spritely stride, and confident shock of white hair, "You've never set foot in Venice."

"I'm a former sea farer," replies Krists as he stashes Ruzica's returned souvenirs under the seat of the boat.

"I can certainly see you're a man with a story," says Frosino, noting my father's yellow skin and haunted eyes.

"You trade in plastics," observes Frosino. "Venice's new wave of reliquaries."

"What are they?"

"Magical objects associated with the body of dead saints. They have the power to cause miracles."

"Miracles?" asks Krists, his eyes growing wide but wrinkling his face to make out that he's not impressed.

"Venice has many kinds of magic. Reliquaries are a particular kind that reside in sacred flesh, which is said to heal the desperate and incurable. They brought people to Venice from far and wide. You could call these pilgrims the original tourists," says Frosino solemnly.

An intermittent wind keeps catching the old man's voice, which makes it hard to talk. So, Krists firmly tethers the boat and swings himself onto the landing. In these moments, he takes his first steps upon the city's shore.

"Tell me about the magic," says Krists, squatting on a bollard with his arms folded. "I'm waiting for my sister to return with supplies. I have time."

"It begins in 828," says Frosino, nodding, "when two Venetian merchants stole the body of Saint Mark, the founder of Christianity in Alexandria, who was martyred by pagans, who dragged him through the streets of the city, tied to a horse's tail."

"That's awful," says Krists, enchanted. "He would have been ripped to pieces."

"But he became strong in another way," says Frosino. "Because of the strength of his faith, Saint Mark's body was said to have magical powers that would bring any city good fortune. The merchants therefore smuggled his remains from the sarcophagus where it lay, unwrapped the shroud and loaded Saint Mark's corpse onto a ship, where it was placed in a chest and covered by pork and cabbage."

"That would have stunk!" remarks my father.

"Exactly the point," replies Frosino. "The merchants wanted to deter the Muslim inspectors from examining their cargo. Not only did the authorities shun the pig meat but found the stench of the flesh so foul it was too horrible to examine properly. So, Saint Mark was taken from the East under a carpet of rot."

"Where did they take him?" says my father.

"To Venice, where his body was housed in a chapel at the Doge's palace, which began a unique economy of treasured flesh."

"How so?" says Krists.

"With the church's support, people flocked to the saint's resting place," says Frosino. "The very possession of the relic supported the city's claim for ecclesiastical independence and asserted its importance in the Upper Adriatic."

"That's not magic. It's politics."

"Patience, young mariner," says Frosino. 'Magic only works because it operates through real systems. These were turbulent times when the first church of Saint Mark was destroyed in 976 during a rebellion against Doge Pietro Candiano IV and during the uprising the saint's body was all but lost."

Krists grunts, thoroughly enjoying the tale.

"But what is Christianity without its miracles?" Frosino continues. "In 1094 the phantom arm of Saint Mark declared the location of his body inside a reliquary pillar within a new church built in 1063, which could now be consecrated."

"A ghost?"

"A vision – maybe like a dream, or a hallucination. I'm not entirely sure. In any case, this phantom gave away the actual location of Saint Mark's body. After a long search, it was found and exhumed in 1835 from the crypt beneath the basilica and was placed in a sarcophagus, on the high altar. Pilgrims came from all over to see, believe, become enlightened and ultimately have their sins forgiven through their proximity to holy flesh. The economy of reliquaries offered lots of opportunities to donate money to and win God's favour through proximity to prominent relics."

"Other than saint Mark?"

"Of course. This was good business for Venice. Many reliquaries were said to come from Christ himself: fragments of cross, a sponge, his blood and thorns from his crown of shame. There were also relics from other important figures such as, Saint George, John the Baptist and Isidore. All of them were welcomed into the Basilica of Saint Mark and deposited in its treasury."

"But you said magic, not money."

"They are compatible in this instance. People believe in money and the currency of reliquaries is one that can make more of itself. Remarkably, relics were not exclusive but – like your plastics – touchable objects. Unlike your wares, they had an inner life that could infect neighbouring objects with spiritual empowerment, which spread the word and illumination of the world in Christ. With the loss of faith in God and mass manufacturing that accompanied modern times pilgrims became tourists that consumed cheap but meaningful objects. Instead of bejewelled glass flasks for pilgrims, the plastic trinkets that you peddle multiply like the reliquaries before them. Your trade is a different kind of magic, young mariner. Like the founders of this city before you, your work is transforming its substance and potentially, its economy."

Krists is moved by this strange conversation but he's not exactly sure why. He starts to formulate another question for Frosino but sees Ruzica approaching. She's signalling that he needs to untie the boat. She seems to be in a hurry.

"Sir, it's been a pleasure chatting with you," says my father as he unties the rope. "Thank you for your story. I promise you that I will think about the kind of magic that my kin bring to this city, would that dignify your tale?"

"Indeed it would, young mariner. But the deeper pleasure for me would be if you could make a *different kind* of magic happen in this city."

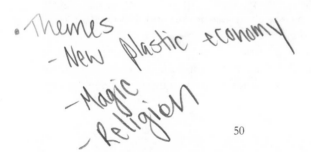

Themes
- New plastic economy
- Magic
- Religion

Plastisphere

Without faltering in their care for Krists and me, my aunts establish a flourishing trade in recycled plastic souvenirs, while my father broods on their value.

"There's no magic in working with trash," he grumbles, playing with an odd amalgam of polystyrene and dirt between his fingers.

"We welcome your growing interest in what we're doing," says Kasia tartly. "In the meantime, we'll be happy to consider your practical suggestions, while we put food on the table."

"Making something out of nothing *is* magic," adds Jelena, "It's *nature's* kind of magic."

Unable to formulate an alternative to hard work and the recycling skills of our culture, Krists is happy to dream on magical futures while he ferries my aunts to the mainland. Back home, he's unusually helpful in assisting my aunts with the casting and moulding process.

During this time, we're incredibly close. Even before I can speak I learn about the dual nature of plastics from Ruzica, who enjoys spooning Kasia's 'baby mush' into my mouth while unburdening her thoughts at the end of the day.

"They're infernal and wonderful substances all at once," she says. "Once 'plastic' simply meant a material that was highly flexible. Natural plastics such as horn, cotton and silk have been around since the dawn of civilization and are used in an incredible range of making-practices and industries. Today the term is synonymous with a range of flexible materials made from petroleum compounds. Poor disposal of these effectively immortal substances has contaminated every landscape on the planet and is responsible for the shocking change in the composition of the environment. Beaten into fragments by the elements, petroleum plastics are found within silts, sediments, sands and even linger as clouds of microparticles within the sea itself.

The speed at which these toxic shards of biological shrapnel have infiltrated the natural world is inseparable from their mass production. The first artificial plant cellulose was invented around 1880 and by the early twentieth century Bakelite was used for its insulating and heat resistance properties. By the middle of the century artificial plastics had fuelled a global consumer demand for cheap, disposable products – from Tupperware to children's toys, food packaging, machine components and women's stockings. *Somehow*, people attribute the environmental devastation reeked by their careless disposal upon the materials themselves.

In Venice, thirty million tourists throw thirty million or so disposable bottles each year into the lagoon – the equivalent of three million tonnes of the stuff, with devastating effects on marine wildlife. Suffocations and strangulations are only the most visible signs of a much more extensive assault on the creatures of the Po delta. While fishing lines trap limbs and wings, broken shards of plastic about the size of a lentil, called 'nurdles', cause lacerations and ulcerations. Unlike natural materials, which degrade into biologically re-usable substances, broken-down plastics become even more toxic with time. Not only do they absorb and concentrate poisonous additives, metabolic catalysts, carcinogens and artificial hormones, they also slowly infiltrate the flesh of all that is living." she adds. "Without our kind, our culture, the lagoon's shores would have no other means of removing this material pestilence. So, for now, little Po, we'll sinter and upcycle all the plastics we can find upon these silty shores and continue to do so until we can make something even more wonderful, or magical, possible."

- Themes
  - Plastic Pollution
  - Upcycling

Cremains

Every day my father takes the ferry from San Michele to the Giardini, avoiding paying fares wherever he can. Sometimes he surfs the sides of the boats without technically boarding them, agilely gripping their hulls with his spade-like hands. Of course, he reassures my aunts that he will pay for tickets as soon as he brings in a regular wage; a pledge they do not object to.

Meanwhile my lively antics and inquisitive fingers prompt Jelena to lock my mother's remains in the cupboard, before my curiosity gets the better of them. So, mainly for Krists' benefit, my aunts call a meeting, and Ruzica sits me on her lap while she explains what a proper sea burial for my mother means.

My father is completely against the idea.

"I cannot give any part of my woman to that demon you call the sea," he says, "I will not let her cremains be consumed by the jaws of its waves."

We eat our usual algae broth in complete silence. Between Kasia and Ruzica, everything that I spit out is scraped up with a wooden spoon just like Krists' and pushed back in again.

In the morning Krists wakes us all early with renewed vigour.

"I will not surrender my woman to the sea."

"You made that quite clear last night," sighs Ruzica.

"The sea will not have her," he says.

Kasia rolls her eyes at her brother's tedious insistence and wonders how she'll ever prevent me from inadvertently emptying out my mother's remains somewhere or other. It's just a matter of time before my curiosity gets the better of everyone.

"We will never bury her at sea. Instead we'll make a memorial sculpture in her image out of the stuff of the land instead."

My aunts fall silent as Krists animates his vision with his spoon, like an orchestra conductor.

"Then we'll place it in the lagoon, so that she looks out over it."

He opens the cabin door and strides out on to the deck.

"Like this, never fading, facing the sunset," he says to the horizon.

Tabbycrete

By winter my father is completely obsessed with making my mother's statue.

Kasia holds him to an agreement where he sells produce in the mornings and can return only after he's made fifty euros in profit – not before. Then, with our livelihood taken care of, Krists works with Ruzica to make tabbycrete.

They beat lumps of stone into sand and stir the coarse grains into containers with lime and water to produce different kinds of organic 'concrete' dough. Then they add all kinds of aggregate mixtures such as evaporated minerals from the lagoon, beach plastics, silt, oyster shells and even old bricks from the city. Finally, with more than a little help from Ruzica's growing talents in pottery and sculpture, they find the right blend of this mixture for Krists to produce the maquettes for Alesya's sculpture. Sometimes he works with salty eyes, recalling every physical detail of her flesh in sculptural form, as he runs his fingers over her stone body.

Inevitably, he falls in love with his creation.

Each night before our tiny table is laid for algae broth, which comes in a range of different flavours – smoky dulse, umami-rich kombu and a salty-sweet 'shony' blend – we go up on deck to watch my father working. As the light falls, he surrounds himself with Ruzica's candles, which are made from fatty left overs, dried-out rags and string that provide a flickering yellow light. This converses with the steady, ember-like glow of hollowed gourd burners that feed on algae oil and barely consume themselves at all. We spend our evenings watching these brilliant flames cast shadows around my mother and father that, like dark souls, rise and melt together into the Venice skyline. Sometimes, my aunts encourage me to wave at my father, who is almost too absorbed in making the memorial to notice my rapidly developing language and motor skills.

"Say hello to Daddy. Go on! Say hello."

"Lo, dada."

Although our communication is mostly lost in cross-winds, sometimes we catch him in a receptive moment, when he stands up and shouts.

"Hello, Po! Hello, you lot! What's for dinner?"

Tribute

After a meal of squid-ink tagliatelle and sea spaghetti, we sit alongside Krists on a narrow ledge along the cemetery wall. With a bottle of neat algae vodka for company in the spring sea breeze, we watch the sun set against an industrial flesh-coloured skyline, streaked with brilliant oranges and vibrant pinks. My father has taken to meditatively stirring his alcohol with a spoon as part of this ritual. Just as Jelena is preparing me for bed, my father jumps down on to the beach.

"Follow me!" he shouts.

Racing out into the waves he removes a plastic sheet, draped like a bridal veil over my mother's statue.

"She's finished," Krists says, as he removes the cover.

Under the peach sunset, the material's radiance is so soft and lifelike it seems my mother is standing among us.

My father races back to the shore and slings me up high on his shoulders. Like a two-headed beast, we wade out again into the shallow water. Then, he takes my little hands in his giant paws and guides them towards the statue.

"Go on, touch her, son."

I remember her warm cheekbones clearly. I knew they shouldn't be hot, as her skin was made of stone. But on that day, her flesh was soft and pliant. Her tabbycrete eyes, gleamed a sunset smile and so, I grasped the fullness of her face. In those moments, my mother was a 'real' person to me. To all of us. After a little while Krists lifted my fingers from the corners of her smiling lips.

"Give her a kiss now, Po and we'll watch the sunset together."

That evening, the entire bioregion glowed under a halo of orange-stained light. Still marvelling, we fell asleep under the cloudless sky among each other's coats and woke coated with sea-dew in the morning. From that moment I knew my father had kept his promise – she would be watching over us.

Life as a Non-Classical Object

Sarah Richards knows that she's giving the water taxi driver more than is the standard fare for the journey, as she alights at the Accademia Bridge, but she doesn't really have a choice. She's new to the city and desperate to find the *European Centre for Living Technology* (ECLT) where she's heading for interview. This is a dream position as a post-doctoral researcher in *Living Technology*, which involves applying the processes of the living world to solve everyday challenges, like purifying water, or making materials that can self-repair. Although she's studied the maps many times, the building is tucked away from public view within the maze of mediaeval alleyways behind Campo San Stefano and is impossible for a first-timer to the city to easily locate.

"Can you take me right to the entrance?"

The taxi driver shakes his head and gesticulates towards a narrow alleyway. It takes her a while to reach the entranceway, more by trial and error than from following directions. One of the building's facets overlooks a blind canal, which opens into the square where the statue 'Il cagalibri' – *the man who shits books* – is in turn defecated on by the pigeons. Pausing before ringing the doorbell, she reflects that the place seems made of paradoxes. The waterways, for example, turn buildings upside down in their reflections. People conduct their private affairs outside, not inside, and the ancient walls she stands before are not relics but house a brilliant international team of scientists that are unravelling the greatest mystery of all – the origin of life. Sarah is determined to impress her interview panel with her original approach to some of the most fundamental questions implicit in understanding life's character, and brushes her jacket down as the door opens.

"Life began as chemistry that became increasingly complex and, at some point, began to self-organise to generate a self-maintaining, autopoietic processes. This premise shapes the theories and laboratory models used to test our ideas about life. However, despite over two hundred years of scientific study, nobody has built a chemical system that can model the biological transition from inert to living matter. It's possible then, that some of our fundamental assumptions about what life *is* and how it *works* may be incorrect and may be preventing us from successfully making something that we can agree on as *life* from scratch in the laboratory. It's time that we tried new hypotheses and approaches."

Some members of the five-strong interview panel are affronted by her bold approach. The stone-faced man at the end of the table tightens at her reply.

"We need to expand the current portfolio of experimental concepts and procedures," she asserts. "Many of our present assumptions are based on knowledge of contemporary biology which has been progressed through incremental developments of old ideas over many decades. We need to take new pathways, to challenge our premises more thoroughly. For example, Stephane Leduc, who pioneered the field of synthetic biology, considered it as a more complex version of synthetic chemistry. What is interesting about *his* approach is that he regarded lifelike chemistry as the starting point for biological metabolism – rather than setting out to mimic versions of biology."

"Are you proposing that we go back to the old days then, rather than make new progress?"

"Of course not. But if we start with a premise based on DNA, we are working with a completely different set of ideas than Leduc proposed. I don't think we've given the story of life from a chemistry perspective enough importance."

"So how would you, as a contemporary researcher, go about things differently?"

"I would find ways of constructing lifelike systems that are not subservient to established biological conventions."

"Such as?"

"Well, prebiotic life forms likely existed as chemical infrastructure long before they ever started storing information and organizing protein synthesis as they do today. In the 1960s, physicist Ilya Prigogine described 'dissipative' structures, which are organised flows of matter and energy, which seem to remain stable at far from equilibrium states."

"That sounds incredibly complex. How are you going to model that?" asks a man with a white goatee without looking up from the smart interface on his wrist.

"In fact, they're very common. Dissipative structures arise

spontaneously in nature, occurring at many scales. For example, they occur in the form of crystals, and tornadoes, and they underpin the birth of stars. Although they're much simpler than DNA and therefore don't obey 'natural selection' in the biological sense, they are good candidates for playing an organising role in prebiotic life forms."

"But chemistry has no memory. How can it possibly 'evolve'?"

"Oh, but chemistry *does* evolve. The planet's chemistry has changed along with the living realm but in different ways to biology. However, dissipative systems *do* behave in strikingly lifelike ways."

"How so?"

"Think of a common dissipative structure like a tornado. It is sensitive to environmental conditions, capable of movement, growth, can interact with other tornadoes and influences its surroundings. While it seems to change all the time, it is still a recognisable body with repeatable behaviours that we can even predict to a fair degree of accuracy, although tornadoes can always surprise us."

"A tornado is not *alive*," sneers the man with the stone face. "It doesn't reproduce itself."

"No, but it can be *replicated*, quite frequently as it happens. And of course, not all dissipative systems meet the technical qualifications of 'life'. However, all life is a dissipative process. Despite their inconsistencies and contradictions, dissipative structures can be *created* and therefore be explored as an experimental platform."

Two members of the interview panel are paying close attention now.

A graphite tip suddenly snaps and the stone-faced man reaches for another form of writing instrument. "That life resists the decay towards thermodynamic equilibrium was Erwin Schrödinger's point" he says, "dissipative structures are Prigogine's. What's *your* particular insight?"

"I think it is possible to set up a system that increases the probability of lifelike behaviour occurring rather than trying to engineer it as an object."

"What platform are you referring to exactly?" says the only woman on the panel. "Are you talking about the Miller Urey experiments that reproduced the primordial atmosphere of Earth using basic chemistry?"

"No. I'm not looking for a sequence of molecular evolution that proves organic compounds arise from inorganic ones. I'm thinking of setting up a system that initiates lifelike behaviour using common substances."

Rachel Armstrong

"You said yourself that no such thing exists."

"I beg to differ. I said that 'life', as we currently recognise it based on biological systems has not been produced by this approach. However, lifelike chemistries have been developed, although they fall foul of our criteria of being *alive*. Such a system was described at the end of the nineteenth century by zoologist Otto Bütschli, who dropped strong alkali into a field of olive oil and produced what he thought was an artificial 'protist' – a single celled creature. It's a remarkably simple system that generates an expressive range of lifelike events."

"Extraordinary," says the woman, seemingly unconvinced.

"Well, if I am appointed to this post, I can show you just how it works. This is exactly what I'd like to explore."

Sarah has mixed feelings about how well she did in the interview but quickly faces a different kind of dilemma as she makes several wrong turns and loses her bearings in trying to reach her hotel.

"'Making life' can't be anywhere near as complex as navigating Venice's narrow walkways," she says to the puzzled receptionist.

° Themes
- What constitutes a living organism?
- What is life?

The Living Island

Kasia sits me on her lap while she makes tasty algae dishes.

She uses all kinds of seaweed to make vegetable side dishes. I love watching her nimble fingers strip off sections of seaweed that have been gathered and dried during the late summer, which she uses in a tasty range of seafood salads. Fresh or rehydrated sea lettuce, dried with salt, is her preferred salad base. She tears me off lengths of the chewiest sections and mixes the rest with cucumbers, avocado and edamame that she's asked my father to buy from a small supermarket on the mainland. At other times, she drapes smoky strands of dulse over melted cheese as a bacon substitute, or adds it dried to traditional Mediterranean tomato sauces, soups, stews, vegetable curries.

Sometimes, she turns the algae strands into food sculpture.

"Bish!" I say, when I recognise the structure.

"Whale," corrects Kasia, "Not a fish but a giant mammal. A creature that, like you and me, once walked on the land. It got so big that it forgot how to use its legs properly, and decided to live out in the sea instead, which was much kinder on its tummy."

"Like my tummy?"

"More like your daddy's tummy, darling. Buttery."

Dining is no longer subsistence living but an art form. The tip of her chin nests in my thicket of hair and she continues working while I twist my wriggly bones around in her lap, so that I can look out of the porthole.

Kasia's creative cuisine does not stop at savoury food. Sometimes we start the day with shony over porridge, which contains sugar kelp that gently sweetens the oats. A bit like honey. When Kasia is not looking, my father grabs a fistful and sprinkles it on secret helpings of wild blackberry crumble.

"Shhhhhhhhh," he says with a gherkin-sized finger against his lips and giving me a big wink, "Don't tell Aunty Kasia. This is our secret."

Krists is gaining weight. While my aunts are thrilled to see him cheery, his abdominal girth is taking up space in the small boat and they have to squeeze around him.

Unfortunately, the high fibre sea lettuce, which is supposed to help him lose weight, does not actually fill him up. In truth, my father has become somewhat of an algae cuisine addict. Every evening he consumes a few large plates of algae salad and complements Kasia on their 'healthy' iodine flavour, leaving his sisters to do the washing up. He then sits with Aleysa and a tumbler of algae vodka in his big hand, stirring it thoughtfully with his favourite, long-handled spoon, while he watches the sunset. Sometimes we join him before I am tucked into my cot. Mostly, though, we leave him to his solitude, while my aunts take turns sharing tales of the sea, as *Fortune*'s gentle rocking and their dulcet story weaving tones work their soporific spells upon me.

Moeche

For a few swift days every spring and autumn
Young crabs that have shed their baby shells
And are yet to grow their adult ones swarm
In the lagoon to become a particular kind of
Catch and culinary treat for gourmet palates –
'Moeche' to use the Venetian dialect. Anglers
Come to cast nets, a hundred euro for each
Pound of flesh. You sit alongside the nets and
I taste the panic of soft bodied crustaceans that
Never tasted so splendid as right now, save for
The mouthparts, gills and abdomen. Their hairy
Pincers and surprised eyes betray these hunters
Now as prey that seek the shadows, shed their
Traces and evade discovery, shunning the sky
In open waters to find rockpools to escape
Detection under the full moon's searchlight.

He sits beside us, dried fish tails and fruit hung
Around his ears, his apron made waterproof by
Extracts of fish liver. His purple waders turned
Up one day on the shore as a gift from the sea –
Then he licks his lips. His generous buttocks are
Tucked underneath as a portable cushion that
Helps him comfortably trap all kinds of marine
Creatures. "I've Been waiting patiently for hours."
Today he is after gustatory beauty. Soft crabs
Fried in flour batter and boiling oil – the typical
Sweetness of sea flesh and sapid saltiness of the
Lagoon without the fuss of shells, these suddenly
Semi-permeable creatures, infiltrated by their
Ecosystems, quickly harden their delicious attire
As the renewal process takes only a few hours

After which they become a living mudstone again.

Through scant peg-like teeth he marvels how
These delicacies have shaped artistic traditions.
"St Marks' lion, the rampant symbol of the city,
Has folded crab's claws, raised like these *moeca*."

— Use of "you" and "I"
↳ who is the "you"?

Bounty

An algal bloom is swelling over by the southwest wall of San Michele. Earlier in the year it was just a few stringy fronds. Now, its surface is thick, buckled and tightly hugs the shoreline.

Kasia finds an accessible shelf that protrudes from the cemetery wall, where she can catch eels by dangling a tyre into the water using fishing line, baited with leftovers. Fish from the lagoon are off the menu since my aunts netted ones that had hypodermic needles, tampons and condoms in their guts. My father shakes his head and says the women are making a lot of 'fuss and bother' about nothing. I am not sure what it all means, other than Kasia is much happier with smoking eels than she is gutting fish. From time to time she takes me down to the shoreline to see if the new slip of land can support our weight. Although I think she is just looking for ways to keep me amused while she hunts for crabs and mussels to cook. I pretend to ride on its great body like a whale.

"Look, Aunty! It's buttery. Like Daddy."

While the algae mass and its resident dirts are thick with green skin, they are still too boggy to support the weight of an adult, but I can squelch happily over the surface. After collecting shellfish, Kasia folds algae fronds into geometric shapes that look like little boats and we float them in the shrimp pools that have formed in the pockmarks of the swelling land's back. She even lets me push the algae boats that I have made from folded fronds out into the lagoon with a stick. Then I snuggle back on her lap and watch them until they disappear among the waves. This wonderful terrain soon becomes our playground. On most days it is little more than a dark green matt of vegetation, but on other days it is a theatre that glitters with sunlight sequins. On the best of days Kasia sings to me and tells me stories of the sea. Fish big as islands. Flesh hungry crabs. Farting swamps. Sweet and sour sardines that celebrate the end of a great pestilence over 500 years ago. I love the gestures and noises that she makes – bigger than a giant, cleaner than Daddy's plate, larger than life.

Sometimes I hear *Po* murmuring along with us, something like giggles. At least, that's how it seems. Its strange body is not talking or anything. It is more like thinking clearly aloud but not in any recognizable language such as Italian, Russian, or English, which Ruzica is particularly fond of. It is a special kind of thought-talking that you might expect to be shared by twins.

Po is just like me. We think along together and fully soak up the world with every passing moment as Kasia looks for food nearby. I don't think she minds *Po* and me playing while she works. Or, maybe she just doesn't notice.

* First interaction between the Pos

. Themes
 — connection
 —twin

Mosquitoes

Davide struggles to concentrate on chairman Monica Laing's marketing pitch to the Mayor of Venice, Giovanni Alessi, and his council. Having been in since around eight to complete three hours of laboratory work before the meeting, he is feeling caffeine-depleted.

"*Exitec* is one of the most successful businesses in Marghera. We are pioneers of advanced biotechnologies for insect control, using sterile techniques to achieve our integrated pest management programmes. These combine biological, cultural, physical and chemical tools that safeguard food supplies and people's health. We work closely with communities to develop effective ways of addressing local pest control challenges."

The prospect of a decent lunch break dwindles as Monica goes over her allocated time slot, determined that her audience fully grasps the potential of her company's products.

"Among our most successful merchandise are biotechnologies for controlling fruit flies such as *Drosophila,* that cause major losses in fruit and vegetables, but our fastest growing area of development is in combating mosquito borne diseases. These pests are moving increasingly northwards as a consequence of climate change and exposing European communities to devastating infections such as dengue fever and malaria. Venice is likely to benefit from an even richer portfolio of treatments than we currently offer. I therefore urge you, Mayor Alessi, to approve *Exitec*'s biotechnological approaches for managing infestations within Venice's bioregion."

It only takes a fortnight of deliberation for approval to be granted.

. Themes
  - Consequences of Climate change
  - Ecoengenerring

Eradication

Local resistance to the idea of eradicating mosquitos is weak even through controversial laws are passed that allow genetically modified creatures to be released in limited ways into the environment. The plague these flies present to both residents and visitors is a serious, ongoing concern that significantly outweighs the necessary environmental clean-ups and controls. Venice's only casualty department is clogged with people suffering from antibiotic-resistant secondary infections that have been caused by venomous Tiger mosquito bites. Although systematic eradications of the flies' natural breeding grounds using traditional techniques have been regularly carried out, it is impossible to treat every nook and cranny. So, the night air thickens with the song of insects intoxicated by the human blood in their stomachs.

Venice residents have even become accustomed to the idea that nature is never as they remember it. The whole bioregion is already populated by 'alien' invaders and Davide even argues that colonisation by non-local species is now the usual form of biological succession. On average, commercial shipping, recreational boating, shellfish culture and the flourishing seafood trade at Chioggia fish market introduce two new invasive species every year into the lagoon's rich ecosystems, such as Japanese wireweed, wakame, decapod crustaceans, various species of jellyfish, bluefin driftfish, splendid alfonsino, alamacko jack and chaunax.

While the technique is not suitable for all species of pest, Davide is excited by the potential of modifying mosquito DNA to address a seemingly intractable problem. True-breeding mutants are carefully incubated in suspension and hand-reared to adulthood, where they are mated with wild type flies. Modified mosquitoes are identified using bioluminescent markers and once a stable line is engineered, the *Exitec* boat is launched to look for suitable breeding grounds to culture them in. The lagoonside and major canals are too fast flowing and busy to keep them safe, so less well-travelled shores are sought.

About twenty metres away from an old fishing boat at the southwest of San Michele, Davide alights with his team at a possible site for a mosquito hatchery, with shallow stagnant pools that are well sheltered and publicly inaccessible. The scientists spread out, looking for the optimum place to grow their precious flies.

"What are you doing?" asks Kasia.

"I'm Davide." He smiles. "You are?"

"Kasia. We live here."

Davide looks around and I run up to shyly hold my aunty's hand, trying to find out what is happening.

"I'm doing an experiment," he says, holding up clear containers full of tiny hand-made eggs.

"What are they?" I ask.

"They're seeds for baby mosquitoes."

I look at him blankly.

"We're growing flies," he corrects. "Can you see these little dots? They're eggs. When they hatch, only the boys live. It stops the flies making too many babies."

I am not sure if this is a good thing or a bad thing. I nod agreeably and stay quiet.

"Can we help you?" wonders Kasia, who loathes mosquitoes, "Are you looking for anything in particular."

"Actually, yes. I need to find somewhere where these genetically modified specimens…" His eyes twinkle. "These 'special' boy flies will hatch safely. As they're very valuable, I'd hate to lose them. I need someone who can look after them"

This appeals to the helper in me and I pay close attention for instructions.

"They like warm little pools that don't have much water flowing through them. Do you know where anything like that might be around here?"

I race with Kasia to reach *Po*'s backbone, pointing out the well-organised fronds of seaweed, whose root systems tightly grip the firmaments of the cemetery wall as a string of lazy pools. Davide says they're 'perfect' and messages the other members of his team to begin seeding these spaces as hatcheries. I sit, perhaps a little too closely, as the scientists artfully use soft paintbrushes to transfer the super-boy mosquito creations into several shallow pools. I want a go too.

"Okay," Davide concedes. He takes my hand and pops a paintbrush between my fingers. "Now, be really, really gentle," he says, as we

69

carefully place an egg speck together into a pool of my choice. Somehow, Davide manages to make me think that I'd done something marvellous all by myself.

Once they're finished, we wave the cohort of scientists off, promising to take care of their treasure.

Over the next six weeks we scour *Po*'s pockmarked back for bundles of pointed mosquito eggs. We notice how they puncture the surface of the water with tiny breathing tubes and turn into tiny worms that move like vertical commas. Kasia says that we are not really harming any of the files, but I am worried that some of them may die.

"Only the greedy ones," she says with an air of morality.

On sunshiny days, the mosquitoes break free from their membranous, eggshells and spread their wings, waiting for soft gusts of air to lift them skywards. Singing on the breeze, they travel like dandelion seeds, and stumble over choppy waves to the mainland in search of females. At times like these, I start to notice how *Po* is becoming steadily stronger, stranger and more determined to assert itself in the world.

Artisans

Jelena's sinter is a strange machine with precarious functionality, which melts down plastics so they can be re-cast. Channelling the sun's rays into a sharp focus through a cylinder of mirrors, Jelena says I mustn't look directly at it, or put my hand into its beam, as it is deadly. The central cone reaches temperatures of around a hundred and fifty degrees Celsius, which is the upper limit of what plastics can bear. Resembling something between a kitchen sink and an ice-cream vendor's stall, the sinter can be trundled to different locations like a wheelbarrow. Since the spring has been kind to us, Jelena is looking for a more permanent location for a workshop environment than *Fortune*'s decking. She hoists it on to the beach and trundles the apparatus somewhat awkwardly over Po's knotted roots, testing their integrity as she goes.

"Can you move that thing away from my algae cultivation pools," says Kasia.

"Why?" responds Jelena.

"I don't want those poisons from your melted plastics ending up in our mosquito hatcheries."

"Do they really go that far?" says Jelena.

Kasia stands with her arms folded as her sister relents and yanks the sinter inland towards the cemetery wall.

"How about I park it up here, as far as possible from the water's edge, where there are no cultivation pools."

Kasia nods.

Po and I sit beside Jelena as she sets up her base and play games with trash. Noticing how absorbed I am in 'beach treasure', she stops what she's doing and takes me for a walk further along the beach.

"This part here is a ready-made collection system," she says, "that washes, grinds and sorts the refuse for you."

Then she shows me where to search for flotsam around a small, persistent gyre alongside the island's west shore.

"This part of the land is growing quickly," she says. "When you were first born, it was barely possible to stand here. Now, look just how far we can walk without slipping or sinking."

Despite her reassurances, Jelena protectively takes my hand and asks me to describe all the various items I collect.

"Let's bring them back with us and we can sort them too, if you like, into different colours and sizes," she says. "We'll put the big ones here and the small ones there."

Since I'm very good at this, we work together beside the sinter, collecting and arranging the fragments. Occasionally Jelena cuts up very large plastics into smaller pieces using scissors and a very sharp knife. Once we have a large pile of materials, we search for objects that we can use as casts, which is just as exciting as finding plastic treasure. Jelena points out a strange metal strut.

"What's that, Aunty?"

"It's a girder. It's probably been washed up from mainland conservation works. We can use this to make the legs for our sea furniture.

"And that?"

"This is a 'hub cap'. We can use it to form the seat of our chair."

Back at the sinter, Jelena tosses the piles of plastic into the apparatus like a frying pan, where they melt like butter. Pile by pile, she pours the boiling liquid into the moulds to cast new forms, which she cools in buckets under clouds of steam. When they stop hissing, she uses her knife to trim off the edges.

"See this pattern?"

"Red, green, white …"

"You'll see they're arranged in diamond shapes, like the multi-coloured coat of harlequin."

"What's har-leak-in?"

"He's a *zanni*, darling," she says, "From the Commedia dell'arte. He always wears a colourful costume. The colours in these objects tell a story about the 'trickster' materials that pollute the sea."

I'm intrigued by the brightness and duplicity of her work; it seems forbidden, dangerous.

All the while, *Po* watches what we're doing and even joins in by finding strange objects and casting them within easy reach upon the shore. Jelena never asks why some of the most interesting moulding structures and colourful plastics appear so frequently and conveniently alongside *Po*'s knotted roots.

But then, why would she? We're all having fun.

Succession

Thin grasses scattered on my substance
Thicken like hair. Rhizomes weave vagrant
Wild flowers and ferns with driftwood and
Sea weeds. Summer softens my body into
New life where butterflies flutter, lizards flick,
Spiders wait, dogged blue flies buzz, and
Mutant mosquitoes bloom, scatter and die.

Making Things

Po is excited by the different kinds of 'toys' my aunts leave around its shoreline; from washed clothes, to kitchenware, baskets, compost heaps, bamboo beach screens, recycled plastic sculptures and empty bottles. When they're not looking, it makes their exchange in return for 'found' treasures, like toothbrushes, cigarette lighters, combs, silk flowers, shoe soles, hose, worn shoes with their tongues hanging out, babies' dummies, fishing floats that mimic squid and sprats, Duplo bricks and drastically defamiliarised bath toys.

Every day my aunts lose things and collect newly found items along the beach. Kasia looks for cooking ingredients, Jelena for colourful plastics and Ruzica figures out how to make new mixtures of clay from local silt deposits and identify organic cultures that seem to dissolve them.

My father dutifully sells all their goods on the mainland, which means my aunts are often too busy for me.

At these times, I think through and play with *Po*.

Earning a Living

Although Krists keeps his oath never to return to the sea, on stormy days he strongly feels the excitement provoked by its tempers.

While his thickening waistline restricts his agility, he remains incredibly strong. Setting off for a day's trading and no money for an honest fare, he leaps the ferry barriers. Soon he figures out how to avoid the fences altogether and springs on to the side of the boats as they are leaving shore. Riding on the skipper's blind sides, his big hands function like a naval limpet mine able to grip onto almost nothing. Just before the boat docks, he lunges for the shore and disappears into the crowd before anyone notices what's happened.

Soon, he's riding the blindsides of ferries and motorboats. Since these vessels move faster, he uses a rope that gives him a bit more reach and stability. Then he lies low and long enough against the hull for many tens of minutes at a time, oblivious to the protests of chiding gondoliers.

On calm days, Krists rides on the stern of the garbage barges as quietly as falling ash. Nobody bothers him here, as the garbage crews never check for stowaways. Propped upon an elbow, he basks quietly in the sun with a flask of algae vodka, watching the world go by. Occasionally he raises his illicit nectar to surprised tourists, saluting them with raunchy seafaring songs.

Lido

It's a baking hot day and my aunts are absorbed in their crafts. Ruzica's elbows are deep in clay and tabbycrete; Kasia is grabbing eels that squirm like snakes, even when she cuts off their heads; Jelena casts a new range of ornate harlequin headdresses from beach jewels.

"Help me model some of these," she says, but I grow restless with sorting and ordering plastics.

"Off you go, then, and play," sighs Jelena, snatching at a wayward eel that's escaped up the beach from Kasia's haul.

Po's scales rival the sun with their radiance, which makes it impossible to see across its giant surface. Feeling lazy, I find a comfortable patch of dried algae and lie on my belly watching fish fry explode from under a dry stick. Like Inuit fishing through ice holes, I pick up the instrument and begin to poke it into many different kinds of crevices, hoping to catch illicit views of some of the creatures in the open water.

I look up.

Gripped by panic, I no longer recognise where I am. Stranded, to all intents and purposes, I am on a raft of algae in the middle of a vast open body of water.

At some point, I begin to calm down and can just see *Po*'s shoreline but I can't get back. I strike out at the water with my arms, attempting to swim the raft to the shore, but tire very quickly. Overwhelmed I start to cry – for Jelena, then Ruzica, Kasia, my father and my mother.

"Don't worry," says *Po*, its voice like waves breaking on sand, is more distinct that ever. "This is an adventure."

"Am I dying?"

I roll on to my back and look up at the cruel sun that vanishes behind a fat white cloud. "I must be drowning."

"You're very much alive," *Po* laughs playfully.

Comforted by my twin, who seems to be taking care of our direction, I stop crying. Clinging to *Po* like a bareback rider, I am amazed by all the new things I can see.

 eco-engineering

We are joined by a fleet of half-filled plastic sweet water bottles, which are not yet ready to die on the shore. Some contain miniature climates and micro worlds, where it continually rains.

A swell of water circles us around over a large sunken object.

"This is one of the hydraulic gates of the MOSE project," observes Po. "This sleeping robot army can make a protective wall between Venice and the sea, when the rising tide wakes them as it climbs over the one metre mark."

We skelter through the series of mechanical gates and make our way through a lagoon inlet, turning sharply towards a long sandy beach.

"Welcome to the Lido. It's Venice's main beach," says *Po*. "I'll wait here, while you go and explore."

I need no encouragement.

Dragging Po's island fragment up the beach so that currents don't coax it away, I tuck my monstrous land twin safely under the shade of a stranded old beach umbrella.

A giant orange man catches my eye and smiles. A beach vendor is shouting at him.

'Hey! Get out of here! You don't have a vendor's licence! I'll call the police on you!'

Feeling ignored, the shopkeeper dramatically slams his fist against a large warning sign, painted with a mosquito glaring *'Pericolo! Malaria!'* Its surface is swallowed the force of his hand with a dull 'thud', which no one feels the least bit intimidated by.

I like the giant. He seems friendly, with smiling eyes and teeth that don't turn off. He continues bumping his reticent cart over the dry sand through the searing heat. I assume he needs company.

"Why is your skin so orange."

"I'm partial to red seaweed ice cream," he says through even more teeth than I assume possible to fit in one mouth. "They are particularly rich in the vitamin carotene, which turns your skin yellow."

I notice that even the whites of his eyes are yellow.

"It must be *really* tasty."

A small boy dashes towards us with his hands outstretched. But before he can demand his treat, he trips on a half-buried shard of driftwood and falls sprawling on the sand. The vendor lifts the boy to his feet and dusts down his palms with two quick 'high fives'. Then he presses a dried seaweed cone into his hand. Wide-eyed the boy looks at the delicious treat, which seems to have appeared from nowhere.

"It's my favourite pick-me-up flavour, little man!"

An anxious woman scuttles after the boy, passing the vendor a five euro note, while choosing to ignore us. She firmly perambulates her son back towards the beach.

"You could have hurt yourself on something nasty, like broken glass, or metal fragments buried under the sand," she chides with visible relief. "Sit down there, with your sister."

The young girl under a sun umbrella doesn't want to stay still next to her brother. She springs up and dances on her tiptoes in a most irritating manner, like a fly. I want to play with her. She seems remarkably mosquito-like, with a harlequin-patterned mask, just like the ones Jelena makes, which she is using as a sun visor. Suddenly, she dives on her brother, taking a large bite of his fizzing ice cream.

"Zizz zizz zizz zizz. I'm an ice cream mosquito. I attack little boys who eat their ice cream too slowly. Zizz zizz ziz zizz."

"Hey! That's mine," says the boy as half his treat vanishes in one swoop. Their childish wrestling brings their mother to her feet as the end of the boy's cone falls crumpled on to the sand.

"Mosquitos eat ice cream, even when it's on the ground," asserts the fly.

The boy tries to fight off his licking sister and their faces become splattered in vibrant yellow sand as the contested treat melts into a sticky patch of effervescence.

I inch closer, laughing with them.

A small queue of excited children, chattering mothers and heat-exhausted husbands gather around the vendor's sand-bruised aluminium cart. They wait in turn to buy effervescing green and yellow cones of melting ice cream, which he produces as if by 'magic', pulling carbonated ice cream out of the air.

Having forgotten their ice cream tussle, the boy and his mosquito sister climb into their ropey algae espadrilles and race each other over the scorching sand, towards the colossal walls of the MOSE gates.

"Don't go too far!" their mother shouts from the pages of her 'Today' magazine.

I follow them as the orange man turns his empty aluminium cart around and heads back to his commune. A few over-excited children continue to pursue him for a while but they soon tire of mimicking his seven-league strides.

At the MOSE gates, the boy and girl stop to catch their breath and bathe in the chilled sea breeze.

"Hello! I'm Po."

We perch on a huge chunk of karst rock, which sprouts barnacles from its base, and watch the waves break on splinters of shells. We do not really talk to each other but enjoy our mutual companionship until we race each other back to the beach, revitalised by the sea breeze.

The children return to their mother without saying goodbye, while I recover *Po*, who is looking decidedly limp, from under the old umbrella.

"Can we go home now?"

I push the island fragment back into the water and we glide as twins, in body and purpose.

Expecting to be chided for my absence on arrival at San Michele I fill my head with excuses – but my aunts are still working hard and seem not to have missed me.

Ecological Beauty

Sucking, slurping, tasting, honing my appetite
For adventure as outlets thick with scum like
Plaque on teeth spill their filth into gutters.
Drooling their dark spit, bile, phlegm, blood
Vomitus into the lagoon – excesses from the
Night before the morning after, these liquid
Phlegmatics, choleric currents, sanguine spills
And melancholic fluids, are churned and
Altered by tides, stones, boats, becoming
Delicious new filths whose corruption draws
Me in
Closer.

Wondrous landscapes that evade reduction
Into rational modes of experience, or polite
Encounters, are forged by unlikely unions
Between unnatural substances that flavour
Marine landscapes. I move along the shores
Tasting the famous monuments as bittersweet
Saltysharp happenstances: The Doge's Palace,
Bridge of Sighs, Zattere, Arsenale, Giardini.
Sampling this world, I add my own aftertastes:
Rotting blooms of algae, plastic detritus, scum,
Pigeons murdered by sea birds, packaging, spit
Grit, and every sort of unspeakable excrement.

Forged by ropey fibres, my gelatinous flesh has a
Kind of beauty that is immune to fickle fashions
And fine tastes that imprison the world in fleeting
Moments of glorious form, detail, and function.
Soaked in the secretions of life and its magical
Broths, my glistening surface responds to their

Joy through the billions of tiny creatures that
Give vigour to my flesh and translate the fickle
Lagoon chemistries into languages, which speak
To the passions of all monstrous life. Now, I'm
Compelled to dance and compose more flavours
Along the shore, marking my realm with new dirts,
Richer, more wayward and stranger than before.

With you in me, and I in you, we are conjoined
By our taste for adventure as paradoxical twins,
Relishing the enchantment that permeates this
Sentient terrain. Continually devouring each
Other, without being consumed by the process,
We are transformed and empowered by these
Exchanges. My plastic-strung vegetable heart
Pumps rich blends of solutes through its spaces
So forcefully, they rip marine creatures from their
Tethers and cast them as flotsam on the shore.
Slapping loudly as they swell before a storm, my
Fibrous ventricles dilate their valves for you and
Propel our confluent lifeblood onwards, as one.

We feed, we nurture, we change
We grow beautiful
Together.

Boat Surfing

"I'm so furious, I can't even talk to you."

Jelena is animated.

I seldom remember her cross, but tonight, everyone glares at my father. His chin aloft, he is trying to maintain some kind of dignity in front of his sisters, holding his shoulders back, but he is being worn down.

I cannot get any sense out of my family, but sit with them for supper trying to figure out exactly what kind of trouble Krists is in. Kasia pushes a plate of crispy insects, crickets and something else under my nose that I don't recognise. I count eight legs.

"You can explain to your son why the Italian police escorted you back to our mooring," growls Ruzica.

Krists winks at me.

"Don't you dare try to make light of your actions," she says.

"Your father is a stowaway."

I'm impressed.

"He makes a habit of not paying his fare. Then he hangs on the hull, to avoid being caught, and surfs these vessels daredevil style."

My father is awesome. I want to learn how to do it.

I slowly stir my algae broth made from the leftovers that we couldn't finish yesterday, hoping that my aunts will tell all my father's secrets without me having to ask. I chew nonchalantly on lumps of spongy worm meal bread, which is apparently good for my gums. I watch everyone's face carefully.

Jelena cannot even look at Krists.

"You're putting all our futures at risk," she says. "You're not just endangering your own life but jeopardising everyone's future."

"You're so selfish," adds Kasia. "You've made it possible for the authorities to move us on. We could lose our home because of you."

"Tell us. Why have you been so lousy at selling our work recently? Have you just been off enjoying yourself?" adds Ruzica.

My father refuses to provide any explanation. Grimacing like a scolded schoolboy he stays silent. Then I catch the twinkle in his shoeward gaze and know that he's not sorry, but letting my aunts have their pound of flesh.

After dinner, I sit with *Po* and ask if I should get good at surfing boats blindside. Before my monster twin can express an opinion, my father joins us with his usual tumbler of vodka. Lifting his cup to my mother, he puts his big arm around me.

"Po, come back inside and help us out in the kitchen," shouts Kasia but my father is fed up of being told what to do. He hoists me defiantly on to his shoulders and walks out into the water.

Now, I can see beyond the limits of the lagoon. This elevated status inspires me to ask, "Why did you do it, Daddy?"

There is a long silence while we watch the changing sunset streak the world with colour.

"It's fun."

Moon Writing

Krists' addiction to blindside surfing means he cannot keep his promises to pay honest fares. Whatever their misgivings, my aunts need him to sell their wares so the family can maintain an income. Krists is back in business-as-usual selling sacks of upcycled plastic goods. Although he generally comes home with a fair day's wage – when he doesn't, it's clear he's been blindsiding. When challenged, of course, he does not apologise but reiterates his good intentions. Faced with constant temptation, which is specifically directed towards working the hull of yachts, he is simply unable to stop himself.

My aunts give up on understanding his motivations but mercilessly chide him each time he lets us down. This growing resentment corrupts the general bonhomie of my early childhood. Frustrations are not just directed towards my father but also cause arguments between my aunts over small things, like space, noise and what is for dinner.

"I want children of my own one day," says Ruzica pointedly one evening, "It's not enough to be someone else's child minder."

Although I know the comment isn't actually directed at me, it does not make me feel good. So, I go outside to sit quietly with *Po*, who babbles about the comings and goings of small creatures in the lagoon and what the Moon had written last night on the surface of the water.

"Don't be silly, *Po*. The Moon can't write."

"You're thinking like a human. Look. Look over there. What's that glittering on the water surface?"

"It's the setting sun sparkling on the waves."

"Exactly, and at night time, that very surface is the site of correspondence between the Earth and the Moon."

"But the Moon doesn't write, *Po*."

"Dearest twin, indeed it does. Last night the Moon was so sad that it couldn't see the Earth that it brought tears of rain. All the writing went fuzzy, like spilt water on ink."

I don't know what to think. My aunts are schooling me in the way of writing and have not mentioned anything about the Moon's literacy. But

I also know *Po* can understand things I cannot. So, before I go to sleep I look out of the porthole towards the lagoon. Sure enough, for one incredible, long moment I see a moonbeam finger ripple the waves with shimmering prose.

It says, "I miss you."

Tribute

Krists polishes off a Tupperware container full of cold algae broth before packing his lunch into his rucksack. Then he makes his way to Riva dei Sette Martiri, where the *Nostradamus* is moored. This jet-black, luxury motor yacht has tinted windows that are moulded into its hull, with peerless finish. He patiently waits for the crew to launch the gloriously sleek vessel and, just as they loosen the dockside tethers, he quickly unfolds a mountain rope from his rucksack and loops it through several carabineers. When the yacht slips it's mooring, he lassoes the stern and boldly swings on to the vessel's blindside.

Nostradamus speeds effortlessly away, as if winds and waves simply do not exist. Using the rope to balance his mass against the side of the ship, my father barely touches the hull, like a trapeze artist. In his mind's eye, he is her sole captain and master of all the elements. The yacht passes the sleeping MOSE gates and makes her way towards the Adriatic. After some distance, the engines still and the yacht comes to rest. Krists tightens the ropes to get better traction on the hull but it's hard to stay balanced without angular motion. It isn't long before my father is too tired to stay on the hull, so he ascends the ropes and swings up on to the deck. A dignified elderly gentleman carefully holding a golden urn is about to commit its contents to the water.

"What if there was a better way to commemorate her?" interrupts my father.

Too shocked to call to his crew to remove the pirate the old man pauses and stares incredulously at him.

"I'm Krists," he says, extending his seafarer's hand. "I've lost the love of my life. How about you?"

The old man nods, too upset to speak.

"We gave her a unique lagoon burial, which allows me to be with her every day – while still honouring our custom to be buried at sea."

Krists can see the man's expression changing, no longer affronted but curious.

"What if, rather than committing her precious remains to the whims of the anonymous sea, we made her a personal memorial in the lagoon?"

The old man's bottom lip starts to tremble. His wasted hands affirmingly clamp Krists' shoulders.

"There is nothing more that I want," he says eventually. "Other than having my darling wife back – a fitting memorial I can remember her by that I could visit, would be music to my soul."

"What's your name, sir?"

"Marcel."

"Then, Marcel, let me share my proposal with you," says Krists. "Here, your hands are shaking. Give me the urn. I'll help you inside."

After dinner together, my charming father is shown around the yacht with its aquamarine suede upholstery and gold fittings. Utterly unaccustomed to luxury, my father can't decide if he is standing inside a generous coffin, or a piece of heaven. The men share plenty of the finest whisky and exchange heartbreaking stories about the women they lost. They cry, laugh, sing and even dance together until the late evening, when they finally say "goodbye" with great fondness and backslapping warmth.

It is nightfall before my father returns to the *Fortune*, where he is met by my anxious aunts.

"Where exactly have you been?" demands Jelena, as the drunken man staggers into the cabin with a smirk.

Discussion

I assume my father's explanations have not been satisfactory as my aunts are still interrogating him at breakfast.

"Stop shouting," objects Krists holding his head.

"We're not," asserts Kasia.

"They're not shouting, Daddy. You are," I helpfully observe.

From out of all the anxiety, confusion, frustration and pain, a sensible conversation begins to emerge.

"I've been offered a very large sum of money to build a memorial statue for a rich man's recently deceased wife."

"Who," asks Ruzica, suspiciously. "Who is this rich person, that a poor man like *you* knows?"

"Uh, Marcel Beauvoir," says my father assuredly.

"And why would he be talking to you?" wonders Jelena.

"Because," Krists holds his head with both hands. "Do you have more black coffee?"

"Only when you tell us everything," says Kasia.

"Ouch," moans my father, as Kasia starts to brew another cafetière.

"Go on," says Ruzica, mercilessly.

"He trusts me," says Krists. "From the moment I met him."

Jelena rolls her eyes.

"Marcel told me that he spent his happiest days in Venice with his sweetheart and wife Anna. On her deathbed, she asked him to bury her at sea so they could be together in the liquid hereafter, where nothing was static and they could continue to grow together. With Aleysha in mind, I convinced him that he could have the best of both worlds. Anna would be transformed by the water and also exist in solid form where her memory could be honoured. He's asked for a memorial statue placed in the lagoon."

"Liar," says Jelena.

"So, you're now drinking buddies with a billionaire?" sneers Ruzica.

With uncomfortable silence, my aunts wait like sharks around a bait ball. My father considers not telling them about the blindsiding. He searches the corners of the cabin for a convincing, alternative explanation but finds none.

"Okay, I went blindsiding on this fantastic yacht. A gorgeous black sea monster of a thing …"

Kasia hurls a wet dish cloth at my father's head and yells, "You broke your promise. *Again.*"

My father looks dreadfully uncomfortable, as my aunts release their frustrations on him for excessive drinking, lack of responsibility, broken promises, wilful disrespect and thrill-seeking addiction.

"You are surely going to the hell that you fully deserve," snaps Jelena.

Despite all the upset, I figure my father is actually getting away lightly for his reckless conduct.

More fractious time passes and I am tired of unhappiness. I tune out of the adult conversation and hear *Po* whispering something enticing, but the ongoing commotion drowns my twin's voice out, so I remain seated.

"He's more than happy to pay for the memorial," protests Krists as Ruzica quizzes him about how exactly this statue is supposed to happen. Slowly, she starts to see the benefits of setting up a business making marine sculptures from the remains of loved ones in the lagoon and begins to take Krists' side in recognizing the viable business opportunity.

"I can't believe this!" says Kasia, "You're defending him."

"Let's think about the money for a moment," replies Ruzica. "It is certainty worth considering Marcel's proposal as Krists describes it, since the income far exceeds what we can make with souvenirs in a year. We'd need to come up with a recipe for concrete to make it work that will pass as biodegradable if this is to be taken seriously."

"It should do more than that," says Jelena. "It should also promote biodiversity in the lagoon."

Finally, Kasia throws up her hands up.

"Fine! Okay then."

Since my aunts cannot rest before they have properly figured out the logistics of this new business plan, I spot an ideal opportunity to go outside and spend time with *Po*. Inching towards the cabin door I hope to simply disappear from view.

"Where are you off to? You're homeschool now. You've got reading to do."

Elsewhere

A big black eel with horse's head
Lurks in the mud and hollows under
The piling at the Punta della Dogana.
Can you taste its thoughts my twin
Babbling through the lagoon? No!
We cannot turn them off. We do not
Stand outside of them, but are part of them.
Listen! Do you hear your voice there too?

If you stay very still the eel will say it
Seeks invisibility within the unseen
Realms of the deepest canals. From the
Nature of its thoughts, can you tell what
This quiet but ravenous beast, feeds on?
Live prey like insect larvae, crabs, jellies
Worms, water snails, crayfish, anemones,
Algae blooms, fish and even ducklings. No.
Not children. "Never children," it says.

We can only taste the bouquet of this
Ghost, not its substance or customary
Traces: shells, blood, hair, teeth, feathers
Fish bones, tidal scum, oil slicks, algae snot,
Crunched plastics, and garbage balls that are
Wretched up with black bile from its stomach.

But when the waters are streaked with wind
And the waxed moon plunges into the liquid
Forms that fitfully dance on the scrying plane,
Uncertain light is cast upon its body, turning
It into a tempest of patterns whose residues
Are indistinguishable from the creature itself.
We too are written on interfaces, our futures

Twisted by site and fate. Of these prophetic
liminal shapes we may ask – not 'what am I?'
Or even assert what we 'are' but consider what
We could *become*, if only we dare imagine beyond
The reassuring conventions of ingrained habits.

Let us visualise an alternate reality in the midst
Of the world's great lakes. Within these vast
Inland seas our island kin are as round as pieces
Of silver and inlaid with mother-of-pearl. These
Shores make music with the beat of the waves
On hissing sands through an endlessly branching
Symphony of thought that is carried as foam and
Rises towards the animated beings we call stars.

. Themes
  – Fate
  – Imagination
  – Limnality

Closer

Krists' reckless gambling with our future has become our family's opportunity to circumvent many of the frustrations that are driving us apart.

My aunts work with renewed vigour and camaraderie.

"We will do everything properly and according to the law," says Ruzica, "so that we can make a complete break from improvising and making do with our lot. We need legitimacy. Normality, and that's not going to be given to the likes of us."

"Being outsiders," agrees Jelena, "we are going to have to make sure we are on top of every detail. Or, the authorities will find excuses to shut us down."

"Okay, I'm up for it!" says Kasia. "Let's meet this challenge full on. I have a list of questions here that we'll need to know the answers to." She produces a sheet of paper with neat handwriting. "What are the laws about water burials in Venice? Does a funereal statue require planning permission? How big is the market opportunity and what does it take to become a small company?"

"Well," says Jelena, "we'll never get anywhere unless we start to put the pieces of this jigsaw puzzle together."

With optimism and naïveté to guide them, my aunts knuckle down to work while I settle down to the important business of becoming taller, more agile, wilful and gangly. In fact, I am no longer the kind of help I used to be. I am more frequently interrupting them, sulking, or getting in the way of any progress they're making. In fact, it seems that the only times that I am praised for being 'useful', are when I am saddled with tedious chores.

During this time *Po* and I become so much closer.

PART III
ADVENTURE

Breathing

Po is excited. Two dogged tugs are towing a replica of Aldo Rossi's Theatre of the World across the lagoon. Lurching like a metronome at the whim of the lagoon's currents, the building contains a laboratory and 'living computer' to build a story of life for the third millennium.

"It will remain in the water at the Punta della Dogana, until the end of the Venice Biennale," says *Po*.

"What's that?" I ask.

"The world's largest arts fair," it replies.

We continue to obsess about the building.

"The original idea for the floating building is inspired by Alvise Conraro," says *Po*, "a sixteenth century nobleman who regarded Venice and its lagoon as a floating garden to host a model of the world or *theatrum mundi*.

"How do you know such things?"

"I can taste events and changes in the living world. Places, creatures and objects reveal their knowledge and histories to me through those things that shape their thoughts: the flow of gases, the movement of slow liquids leaking through the soils and the infusions that shape the watery network of chemistries swirling around the lagoon."

"It would be so cool to know stuff like that."

"I don't just understand what the living world is talking about, my twin, I can also use its networks to make things happen."

"Like, how?"

"I can concentrate mineral flows into rock-like accretions, produce powerful vibrations and converse with creatures using chemical languages that change how they're thinking and behaving."

Po's always very patient in helping me understand its unique realm and ensures I feel part of it. In turn, I'm always keen to learn. I want to sense the world as a monster island does. We start by smelling and tasting the environment in a particular way.

"I really don't know how to go about this, *Po*," I say. "Smell and taste are just clouds of stuff. Krists' body odour, Kasia's algae broth – you

95

can't touch them, can't see them. How can they have a structure?"

"Try thinking of these feelings as being produced by the spaces between things," suggests *Po*.

I give it my best shot but I'm finding it hard to imagine *Po*'s world. It has so many more dimensions than I'm accustomed to, yet my twin offers more than a little encouragement to assuage my frustrations. I keep on trying to think through space, scent and distances and, to my surprise, begin to draw some of these aspects of monster-sensing together.

"I'm built differently than you are," says *Po*. "My taste and smell sensors sprout from my body like fine hairs, like a giant invisible root ball, and radiate way out into the lagoon. When they're excited, they give me goosebumps."

"That's amazing," I say, wanting a root ball body too. "My goosebumps are tiny, prickly things that don't say much at all."

"Pay close attention to them, dear twin. At first you may think they are nothing special. With patience, you'll start to feel the rich patterns that characterise the many different qualities of space that are encoded within clear sensations, like pain, or tickles. But these are only a tiny sampling of the lagoon's constantly changing chemical trails, biomolecule standing waves, structured currents, water memory channels and complex and pervasive bouquets of substances."

"It sounds more complex than weather," I say.

"This is not ordinary weather. These feelings feed moods, make new kinds of experience and linger in aftertastes. On the most delicious days they make you want to roll endlessly in the world."

I try again, harder this time to amplify my goosebumps by concentrating on the spaces between things, but they don't feel special.

"*Po*, do you have favourite tastes, or smells?" I ask for inspiration.

"Of course. Decaying piles of seaweed, festering crustacean flesh, fish faeces, seabird guano and all kinds of garbage."

"Ugh."

We travel together in silence for a while, *Po* drinking in the lagoon's exquisite chemical landscapes, while I, unable to conjure a sensory landscape beyond what I already know, start wondering what kind of story of life the biennale's epic living computer will tell.

"Can I tell you my idea for the future that I want the 'living computer' to predict," I say.

"Of course," says *Po* lazily.

"It's a giant ship with all the world's plants and animals aboard. Their seeds are stored in its massive hull, so that when lifeforms are having a bad time, they can be put to sleep and woken up later, so nothing will die. There will be enough room for me, Krists, my aunts and my mother."

"It's something between Noah's ark and heaven, then," observes *Po*.

"I guess so."

Po remains silent, so I prompt it to share its thoughts on the future.

It starts babbling excitedly but I don't recognise the language although the images it projects in my thoughts are vivid.

The entire ecological realm is in meltdown, where the familiar distinctions between things disappear. Plants, stones and creatures are continuous with each other, blending together more like shadows than objects. They do not seem to belong in the light but spring from a realm that clings to and strangles everything. There's a background stench and gurgling noise through which odd voices appear that dispute the nature of existence. Life is in a state of oscillation. Heartbeats quell and dead things explode from composts into animated states. Creatures like ichthyosaurs, trilobites, coelacanths, megalodons and ammonites, awaken from fossil beds, to live again. Beings that have been erased from the world's imagination start to form again in disembodied wombs. Rolling in knots of dough-like flesh, they enjoy blissful embryogenesis, but it is impossible to count their limbs and eyes. The environment is made up of shimmering fields of uncertain densities, rife with pools of digestive juices and unclaimed egg sacs. The whole lagoon is thick with folds of meniscal flesh, which are full of heavy metals and other kinds of uncleanliness, where creatures simultaneously freeze and boil.

I'm suddenly aware of the deeply ambiguous view of humans in this place. *Po*'s holding up a mirror to humanity's darkest urges and most grievous ecological atrocities. It imagines us extinct.

"Stop, *Po*! You're scaring me!"

We hug each other tightly and silently for a long while. I shake uncontrollably. *Po* patiently calms me with the familiar sounds of gentle waves breaking on a shoreline. Soon, our conversation is restored.

"What does breathing feel like?" it asks.

"I have never thought about it," I finally say. "It's something I do instinctively. Look, watch my chest rise and fall. Can you see the process in action?"

Po gurgles.

"No! You don't get it. Kasia gave me a book that shows how air goes through my mouth and down a tube where it slips inside two connected bean-shaped breathing organs. Do you see?"

I briefly remember the pages that she pointed out to help me figure out what my genitals are supposed to look like. However, I am much less interested in which hole I pee through, than in helping *Po* breathe along with me, by sucking in air.

We resume the motions of breathing.

Po splutters.

"Okay, I'm not sure diagrams help here," I say, as my monster twin does not sound as if it's making progress.

"Try to draw in the atmosphere with a sharp movement. Like this."

Po slurps and nothing changes. I try to be clearer.

"Do it so hard from the inside, that it makes you a little bit dizzier, fuller and lighter."

Po still can't make the right sounds and movements, but slurps and bubbles a lot for a while. It produces an impressive plume of froth, which stretches out like a giant hand towards the city.

If I cannot train *Po* to breathe, on my terms, then maybe I can describe breathing in terms of living weather, as the structure air – mists, smog, rain – moving inside bodies. I struggle to find the thoughts and words, which start to form a set of imaginary shapes something like cloud watching – dragon breath, feather blanket, candyfloss. None of them say very much about breathing.

"Let's try another approach," suggests *Po*. "Can you try thinking about breathing through your skin?"

I'm intrigued, so I sink my head back into the lagoon to give it a go, while *Po* tries to kickstart the process by showing me images of things that feel scaly, slimy and slippery all at once. Imagining how a soft-bodied creature breathes through its skin is a challenge. So I decide to completely immerse myself in the water, and describe how the environment moves around me.

Clambering into one of the sheltered pools on *Po's* back, which is about the size of a bath, I sink down deeper and deeper until the water covers my ears. Its slippery fronds gradually coax me to let go of the edges and I begin to float like Ophelia, all ribboned with weeds.

At first, the familiar sounds of the land are evident but they're turned down a few notches - birdsong, crickets and the roar of outboard motors. After a while they resume greater clarity and focus, as if a switch has been flicked. Now, the lagoon has a completely different kind of soundscape. Small fishes hiss as they dart around *Po*'s nooks and speed towards the chatter of mussels, tenacious limpets and frondy barnacles, which are engrossed in filtering tiny creatures from the water. Molluscs squelch as they reach for a lick of algae here, a swish of organic matter there. Sometimes they bask in the longer wavelengths of visible light with a gentle 'aaaah'. Further out, the audioscape is full of mud, which muffles the clicking joints of creeping crabs, and silences the cracking of sun-worn plastics. A steep artificial reef made of rubble, bricks, woodpiles, concrete and marble suddenly comes into view, its surfaces 'clicking' against each other like castanets. Amidst the cacophony, surface currents split around the tentacles of a giant medusa prowling the canals and playing the water surface like a concert pianist. These sound waves carry new notes into sloshing recesses, where whispering plants and neurotic fish fry, seek quiet refuge from predators.

Battles rage in these invisible waterways.

Invasive algae and foreign fish oust deeply sighing native species from their homes. Ominous sounds intrude on this place. I don't hear or taste them, but feel their pain in the pit of my stomach. An eel-horse slithers into a hideous gaping hole, which gurgles with the struggle of drowning children in lightless caverns. Deeper still, the terrible howling of heretics recounts their agony under the ducal palace dungeons, a sound so dreadful it murders the lagoon's peace, as the damned thrash blindly for the shore.

Then, all is still.

It is only at this point that I realise – I am not breathing.

Beneath Us

Stinking rot, delicious decomposition
Lures us carrion feeders towards fetid
Organic delicacies; the rancid settings
Of turning cheeses and wines. A putrid
Marine battlefield, peppered with sweet
Sulphur and anaerobes. Scavengers weep
As water dries into a selfish scum from
Which fifty tonnes of fish folded in algae
Phlegm smothers the shores like exploded
Brains. Did they fall from the sky, or have
They always suffocated in our toxic basin,
Where marine wildlife dream of evolving
New features, so they may flourish in sludge.

You say this city is splendid but that shiny
Crust you call a veneer lies thin and cracked
Upon its petrifying mud that sucks upon the
Dead. Fifty tonnes of fish kill today, and so
It goes on, as abundant corpses, sewage, mud
Vegetation, vermin hoards, shells and rubble
Shore up the land. Marine ecosystems are
Stewed in fertilisers and boiled in industrial
Heat. A soup, stirred to perfection by dredgers,
And topped off by garnishes of toxic blooms,
These cookery lessons, the curriculae of our
Times, will fill the waters with tea, and congeal
As chocolate scum. They invite smoked eels to
Slither onto the shore, and vinegar oysters to
Encrust the *briccole* as glazed hors d'oeuvres.
Such pre-digested delicacies whet our appetites
For the ecological catastrophe that is our main
Course. We rear anchovies in olive oil, and
Dunk snail-like *bovolo* in scalded algae bisque

While eggbeater waters whip up protein foams;
The smothering desserts that stalk our shores.

Freshly suffocated rats roast on plastic spits
And jellyfish blooms turn to glue. In canals
Acid-weakened shellfish are pressure-cooked.
Microbial molasses ooze from brickwork, while
Biblical downpours of fish fry fall as helpings
Of whitebait. Blood red jelly of sea anemones
Curls like pie-crust and battered pigeons are
Seasoned by smog mustard in such quantities
They crunch like gravel under the mulling
Footsteps of sky-facing tourists, who only
See images of themselves, though steam
Rises from paving stones scorching the
Scurrying ants into crispy garnish. This
Ready-made catastrophe is just a poor
Online review: "we won't go there again."
The human idea of nature is just an image
Of life and preference for obedience.
Heed the subversive communities that are
All around, watching you, where life is
More than a screen on which to observe
The projection of your own image on a
Place, and shatters the illusion you call
'Order'. The world came from dust and
Was shaped by the sweat of the living
World. Favourable or not, it will survive
The present catastrophe in some form,
Or another – with, or without, humans.

° Themes
 – Human Influence
 – Pollution

101

Safety Suit

Face down on the shore, my arms are uncomfortably stretched above my head. One knee is bent up against my chest. My mouth tastes of something rotten.

"You're supposed to breathe," says *Po*.

"What happened?"

"I did the breathing for you."

We decide the best way to prevent any further mishaps is to make me a life jacket of bladderwrack. My first attempts at pulling the seaweed from the cemetery wall fails, it's just too firmly cemented to the brickwork to detach. Instead, I scoop up armfuls of decaying green and black fronds studded with air bladders from the size of a pea to a marble, which near shore currents have torn from the seabed.

Amidst protests by clouds of tiny flies and scuttling shrimp, I knit the flat seaweed fronds, which can be tied easily in knots, into a malleable cloth. I am extremely ambitious for this garment and imagine it as an edible, wearable skin: something to be worn by a superhero.

Instead, I end up with something that resembles a large pair of knitted knickers, which I have trouble tying off, so they end in a tail. Finally, for the sake of dignity, I turn the whole thing into an over-the-shoulder wrestling-style leotard. Preferring not to think of my safety gear as a clumsy nappy, I tell *Po* it's a 'utility belt'.

"Now, you need to put it on and test it," *Po* says.

I squat down in pool aiming to relax gently into the water, when I am spun completely over by the buoyancy of my pants.

"Very good. It works."

We agree to give the peculiar apparatus a trial run and of course, there is only one place we are headed, the Theatre of the World.

Theatre of the World

It takes a while to drag *Po* into the water, as it's become so heavy. Spurred on by expectation and enthusiasm for adventure, we make our way across the lagoon to the Grand Canal. Lying low like trash in the water, with my safety costume camouflaging me as a knot of algae, we see tourists gathering around the water's edges, trying to secure a clear view of the floating theatre. Bobbing alongside the great anchors that hold the raft against its tethers, we watch the twenty-five metre structure rise with each dip and swell of the canal waters. Buoyed by floats, it reaches for terrains far beyond the limits of the lagoon.

In my mind's eye – or is it a liquid memory carried by the lagoon chemical superhighway? – I catch a glimpse of a dark horse's head staring up at us from deep down in the mud. I look around to see if there are any strange shadows in the water, but none appear.

After a while I'm calmer and study the building from the canal.

It is an unusual mixture of typologies that are cast from a range of recycled materials. Panelled with golden plastic, it is studded with tiny crossed windows in the upper levels, where visitors have balcony views over the Giudecca, San Marco's basilica and the statue of Fortune at the Customs House. At the apex it tapers into a single octagonal turret with slate-blue sections.

"What do you think it's like inside?" I ask *Po.*

"It's hatching a monster lifeform."

"Right." I say, dismissively. "Can you lift me higher, *Po*? I can't see anything beyond the wooden fence borders the walkway into the building."

My monster twin arches its giant spine, like an animated whale carcass. I'm thrust even further upwards by a sudden wave from a colossal cruise ship passing the mouth of the Grand Canal that soars a couple of metres above the waterline.

"It's glittering inside. All silver and gold!"

"I thought so," says *Po.* "It's an egg. A 'living computer' that doesn't just crank out one particular creature. It is pluripotent."

"What does that mean?"

"It contains a whole range of apparatuses that, when combined, could become any life form you imagine – and some you can't. All those advertised biotechnologically assisted performances and staging of mythological beasts they're putting on for the visitors, like the genetically modified creatures that glow under darklight, are real. They're more than a show. Some of them are entirely experimental, like the 'smart' chemical droplets, which seem as if they're alive but are nothing like the kind of creatures we see in the outside world."

"You see all that? Incredible! Lift me up again."

"It's intriguing. Theatre of the World is more than a performing zoo, or even an artificial ecology. It carries the seeds of an operating system with the power to change the story of life itself," says *Po*, as it twists its spine in a homeward direction.

Poveglia

We are moving through greasy sunslick on the still grey channels that dissect the island of Poveglia, when a fisherman draping nets on sticks, notices me. Since I appear tangled up in my seaweed safety harness, he offers his skinny hand and pulls me out of the water and studies me intensely from sunken hollows. His yellow cheeks suggest we share ancestry with seafarers.

Po lurks in the canal while the wizened man invites me to share his generous picnic. Tucked against a weed-infested bridge, we sit on an old rug and share a surprisingly rich Venetian stew with octopus, prawns and stinging nettles heated on a hotplate. Then he offers me a cup of red wine that I decline but join him instead in a handful of salted almonds.

I throw one high into the air and catch it triumphantly between my teeth.

"I'm Po. You cook just as well as my Aunt Kasia does. Delicious."

"Ambrogio. What are you doing here?"

I gesture thumbs up to *Po*, who is sulking in the waterway.

"I made a raft and followed my nose."

The old man looks down at the vegetable matter and shakes his head.

"You're very brave and foolish. You don't belong here."

I smile politely at his teasing.

Ambrogio's smock flaps around his sunken chest. His barely-there muscles, which strap his arms and legs to his limb girdles, strain with every movement underneath his baggy pants. Despite his outward fragility, he is surprisingly strong. He stands up and lifts me on to his shoulders.

"I'll show you around."

A pale red brick bell tower with a pencil tip point rises up out of a cream coloured institutional building. It looms over us like a spectre everywhere we go.

"That is one of the oldest structures on the island. It's the only remains of a twelfth century church that was turned into a lighthouse during the eighteenth century, but is now abandoned. In the nineteen twenties the low-lying parts of the building became a care home for infirm elderly residents. In fact, it was used as a psychiatric institution."

We pass a sign that reads *"Reparto Psichiatrico."* The undergrowth is vigorous and we fight our way through low-lying shrubbery to get closer to the buildings.

"From the outset, in-patients frequently reported ghosts and the sound of suffering spirits," says Ambrosio in wavering tones. "Since they were considered insane, their complaints were ignored."

"Is it haunted?"

"Well, they say that 'Staring Anna' is a permanent spirit resident who tiptoes around the corridors and never sleeps, as she's hiding from the doctor."

"Why?"

"In those days, doctors were able to experiment directly on people, to try out their new ideas for cures. One particular treatment for ailments of the mind was to make holes in the head."

"Holes? That's horrid."

"Oh, it's an ancient practice. It's supposed to let demons in the mind escape from torturing people's thoughts. In more modern times, such chimneys into the soul were designed to allow neurosurgeons in, so they could gain access to those malfunctioning areas of the brain responsible for these terrible thoughts and experiences."

I wince.

"Using only the crudest tools, like hand drills, chisels, saws and hammers some doctors started to experiment to further their knowledge. Even more importantly, new discoveries would advance their reputations and careers. In fact, the particular psychiatrist who lived here fashioned a laboratory in the bell tower. He'd strap people down, open up their heads, and while they were still conscious, he subjected them to a variety of 'tests'."

"Tests?"

"Oh, let's say, after he'd cut out a so-called *diseased* structure in a patient's head he'd inflict insufferable pain on them, just to see if their perceptions had changed."

Ambrogio takes me down off his shoulders and shows me inside the vacant wards. He has an unusually short nose.

"In fact, the whole process was so traumatic that it was difficult to tell whether people had passed out from the stress of the procedure, or actually died during the surgery."

"They died?"

"Unfortunately, many of them did. 'Johnny-in-the-oven', is another of those poor souls that rages in the crematorium. He was burned alive following a botched procedure, being mistakenly pronounced 'dead'."

The beds are dilapidated. Sickly green paint flakes from the brittle walls and bedframes rot miserably. A lizard sitting at a windowsill vanishes as Ambrogio passes, although I don't actually see his shadow reach the creature.

"The whole island has a long history with the dead stretching back to Roman times, when plague victims were isolated from the general population. In fact, the term 'quarantine' was invented here, in Venice, during the plague outbreaks that devastated its population, during the fifteenth and sixteenth centuries."

"Quarantine?"

"Yes, it was an isolation process that helped Venice recover more quickly during the plague outbreaks. When people were sick, or showed suspicious symptoms of disease, they were left on the island for forty days with no way back. They either recovered, or died."

"Not cured?"

"Only if you cured yourself. Most couldn't, of course, it was a time before antibiotics and modern medicine. Let's say that quarantine became a kind of purgatory – a living hell. But it was effective. Diseased suspects were dragged from their homes, pleading and screaming for mercy."

"But what happened if you didn't have the plague and were mistakenly put in quarantine?"

"It wasn't a place for the innocent. Amongst the infected, they were likely to contract deadly symptoms and die in agony alongside all the others."

"That didn't happen *here*, did it?"

Ambrogio's eyes darkened.

"Around a hundred and sixty thousand men, women and children, were dumped into large pits and buried, or burned, around here. The soils that we're standing on right now, are half human ash."

I am silent as he leads me to an incredibly sad little chapel, whose pews are smashed by vandals and algae-sodden walls are scarred with graffiti.

"Do you want to know what happened to the doctor?" he asks.

I nod slowly, but not enthusiastically. The old man is stiflingly persuasive.

"After a while, he started to see ghosts himself and became concerned for his sanity. You don't get away with these things. Some say he simply went insane. Others claim that vengeful unquiet spirits entered his body. In any case, he jumped from his laboratory in the bell tower."

"Why?"

"Some say that terrified patients overpowered him and threw him to his death. A nurse, who said she witnessed the fall claims he did not die quickly, but lay in agony for days on the ground with nobody offering to help him. It is even said that the doctor was bricked up in his laboratory by those he'd been treating and they simply left him there."

I don't really want to hear any more. My insides feel unbearably heavy.

"Even today, some people hear the bell tolling across the bay as the brain surgeon beats the wall with his fists to summon help – and uses his head as a battering ram, trying to weaken the fortifications that bind him."

I am deeply uncomfortable. Although the weather is cheery and the birds are enthusiastically singing outside, a malignant darkness, which has nothing to do with light, menaces this place.

"The character of buildings is shaped by those that inhabit them," says Ambrogio. "Those with wicked lives make spaces for evil."

I notice that every nook and cranny of this institution is invaded by weeds that are steadily replacing the manmade structures. Life is flourishing upon this island of human remains. Even left-over machinery, such as hand-turned washing machines, spinners, rotating wash board and manglers, are consumed by the relentless creep of a new kind of life. This recalcitrant, nonhuman community seems to reject death.

Although I initially thought Poveglia was a cheery wilderness, now I want to go home but say nothing to Ambrogio. He is caught in a world of his own making, enthusiastically sharing his fascination for ghosts and their like. In truth, I am afraid of him.

"Perhaps the grisliest find in this area is the evidence that supports vampire burials that took place back in the sixteenth century, when mass graves were often reopened to dispose of fresh corpses. Diggers frequently uncovered older, bloated bodies with blood seeping from their mouths, with an inexplicable hole in the shroud placed over their face, which was a customary ritual. Assuming these corpses were 'undead' and feeding on the other bodies, they shoved a brick between their teeth, to starve the shroud-eater. Today, we call such creatures 'vampires'."

"Sir, I have had enough of adventure today," I say quietly, but firmly but the old man doesn't hear me.

"Of course, we say that vampires don't exist. That folks in the old days were responding to an incorrect interpretation of the natural decomposition process that results in a build -up of gases, which horribly deformed corpses and causes fluids to spill."

Ambrogio stops and looked at me with a penetrating, unblinking gaze. He is nothing but a shadow in this light. He stares at me for an uncomfortably long time before he says, "Come on, I'll take you wherever you want to go."

I think of explaining that I am with *Po*, and therefore don't need his help, thank-you-very-much, but stop before I even begin. Instead, I walk quietly behind him to the bridge where his rusted barge is moored. Seemingly sprightlier with each step, the old bones offer me a hand, to steady my step into the vessel. I notice the meal we shared apparently untouched on the bank of the channel.

Didn't we finish that earlier?

"Where shall I ferry you, young man?"

"The *Fortune* moored by San Michele."

"Aye, I know it well," he says. He starts the barge's engine up which, despite its dilapidated appearance, ticks happily over on the first attempt.

I notice *Po* quietly moving away from the bank in pursuit.

Halfway across the lagoon the motor stalls for no apparent reason. Perhaps, like Ambrogio, it is just very old but he offers no explanation or apology for our delay. I look up quizzically but cannot see the details of his face against the afternoon sun. For a moment, his eyes shine like coins.

"Look, Sir! We're nearly there." I point enthusiastically in the direction of the *Fortune*.

Po is trailing speedily behind us. Its matted spine is only metres from the barge.

"Sir, can you get the engines going? We seem to be going nowhere."

We sit upon the slurping waves as the whole world appears to darken. Then, *Po*'s refuse-riddled body curls protectively around the barge. The shade hisses between its teeth, light returns and the engines magically start up again.

"Here you go. You're a fortunate young man," says Ambrosio, his lightless pits staring at *Po*. Then he gestures to the island with a nod. "The shores of San Michele, are a familiar haunting ground."

I leap from the barge into the shallow waters of *Po*'s shoreline and we frolic gleefully together in the waves for a while. We're glad to be home – alive.

As the sun momentarily vanishes behind a dark cumulonimbus cloud, Ambrogio and his barge disappear into the shadow of the waves.

Scattering

"Delicious fresh air!" shouts Krists, raising his tumbler and spoon. "Only stifling logistics in there."

I groan. I had hoped my aunts would be finished by now. Nobody is doing anything interesting anymore and grown-ups are definitely no fun to be around. Even Kasia, who specialises in making the impossible happen, is decidedly less creative nowadays with her culinary arts.

As much as I dread spending time with my aunts when they have things on their mind, I am even less keen on Krists' monologues, when his skin reeks of sweet algae vodka. In an attempt to avoid the contradictions that adults weave around themselves, I clamber upon the *Fortune*'s deck using a barnacle encrusted rope, so that I can reach my cot undetected.

It doesn't work.

"I need you as my audience, young man," instructs Jelena. "I'm going to explain exactly what you need to do to be buried legally ..." she looks pointedly out of the porthole at my father, who is belting out a raucous version of 'Blow the Man Down'.

Ruzica continues. "We are looking to hold legal burials in the Venice lagoon. Understand?"

It isn't the bedtime story I am hoping for, but I nod anyway. Besides, I really don't have a choice in the matter.

"You must tell me if you don't follow anything. It's important that absolutely anyone can understand the process." I continue nodding.

"We're going to make concrete memorials that will become part of the cycle of new life in the lagoon. This is a new kind of concrete that is mixed with local gravel and experimental aggregates, such as plastics and people's ashes. It will be used to make statues, which will be placed in the lagoon and, in turn, will encourage marine creatures to make them their home. It's a new kind of burial process."

"Plastics are bad for the lagoon," I say.

"I'm glad you're paying attention," says Ruzica. "We've come up with a plan to address that."

Rachel Armstrong

"I've been culturing microorganisms that can digest plastics," says Kasia. "Every statue will contain a chamber, or 'heart' inside the concrete, which houses this strain. As the tabbycrete weathers, the plastic-eating organisms will move through the fracture lines of the concrete and remove all the plastics, accelerating the decay in the statue."

"Won't that make it collapse?" I say.

"It's called planned obsolescence," says Ruzica. "We want people to see their loved ones actually returned to the lagoon as part of the ecology. The statues crumble, while also cleaning up the lagoon as we've always done."

"Okay," I say, still thinking things through.

"Although Venetians can be buried on San Michele with few complications," adds Kasia, "it is slightly trickier for Italians that come from outside the city and its extremely difficult for non-Italians. Dispersing ashes in the lagoon is a very new kind of burial system and since people generally do know what is possible, it presents difficulties, as well as many opportunities."

"The practice of scattering cremains into the Venetian lagoon dates back to 2010, when a law was passed that allows the ritual to take place in various locations," continues Jelena. "While new facilities were promised by local authorities, including a mourning lawn and a pontoon extending into the lagoon from San Michele from where ashes could be scattered, these expectations have not been met."

"These failures, are the very business opportunities that we are looking for," says Ruzica. "We'll advertise the proposed concrete-casting service in partnership with a local funeral parlour. We're using online media to provide information for non-Italian citizens, so they are aware of all the paperwork needed -- things like a mortuary passport."

"Dead people need a passport?" I giggle and stop abruptly at Ruzica's scowl. "Sorry, Aunty, but this whole thing sounds terribly strange."

"It's not," she snaps. "It's a very serious matter. We want to make it as easy as possible for people to understand the legal and practical processes of dying and being buried – especially in a place other than where they are born."

"Ashes have the same consistency as explosives. Just imagine the problems at customs," adds Kasia. "Also, death and cremation certificates must be translated into Italian for the Venice authorities, and a range of other forms are needed at the request of the Italian Consulate and City of Venice, to legally verify the burial process."

"Being dead still seems awfully difficult," I say.

"It's also expensive," adds Ruzica, who is not yet in a forgiving mood. "I've compiled a list of expenses that mourners are likely to incur during a Venetian burial, including those for The City of Venice Mortuary Police, the hire of funeral boats, the 'hilarious' mortuary passports, translations, lawyers and other services rendered for the preparation of documents. The whole process can cost many thousands of euros, even before any sculptures are commissioned."

"What about poor people?" I wonder.

"That's a really good question," adds Jelena supportively, "We must make sure those who want to be commemorated in Venice using our new burial option can find a way to afford it."

"Would they be keeping my mother company?"

"Not really, darling. Your father will take care of Aleysa. These other people will live somewhere 'else' in the lagoon."

"Yes," interjects Ruzica sternly. "It's extremely important that you don't tell anyone how her memorial was made, since the new concrete has not been formally approved. She is our family secret."

"She's very special," adds Kasia warmly, noting my confusion.

I nod emphatically in agreement to avoid any more lectures on the matter. Adults are so complicated. I've already guessed that my father broke rules in making my mother's statue since he doesn't seem to respect rules in general and I'm quite accustomed to saying nothing, in case we get into trouble. Being outsiders, we're always having to figure out ways around legal technicalities.

My aunts continue to rehearse their plan with me, but I start to think of my uncomplicated relationship with *Po*. When we're together, we don't have to pretend at being 'normal'.

Ruzica notices my attention drifting and stares hard at my face. I conjure bright-eyed thoughts by picturing adventures with *Po*, so that I look inspired. In truth, I am excited by the whole occasion, but am also anxious, unsure what to expect. Family life keeps changing. Our situation seems more complex, not simpler. After studying me a little too long, as if she thinks I'm hiding something, Ruzica finally appears satisfied there is no deception, and lets me bunk up in my cot.

Being Dead in Venice

I often look over the cypress-peaked cemetery walls behind the *Fortune*, down into the graveyard. *Po* has grown to such a size and girth that its roots can be climbed like steps of the wall. Standing on its spine, I can lift my leg to get traction on two rusted wall pins, then finger-climb the rest of the way using holes left by rotten bricks. From this vantage point I can see countless tombs that stand to attention in highly organised rows of flower-bearing plots headed by crosses.

I'm always surprised how regimented the burial site is.

Resting time on San Michele is always temporary and is policed by the machines and apparatuses of burials. Plots are rented yearly, which is a radical reduction on the old courtesy of twelve years. Within this limited timeframe, there are three kinds of tribute that can be purchased to honour the deceased: commoner, esteemed citizen and Venetian aristocracy.

Over there, against the wall, commoners are placed in shelves within vertical plots that house the growing numbers of urns. New technologies are even miniaturising cremains by compacting them into diamonds. One day, I imagine that Venice will be made of skyscrapers that house its innumerable invisible dead.

More esteemed, or wealthy corpses, ride business class to the afterworld and are interred more generously. Mourners preferences are catered for in bordered plots like walled gardens with dried flowers, glass stones, poetry, personal items and photographs.

The graves for the super-rich are located in spacious avenues lined by limestone mausoleums, in various states of disrepair. Some are breathtakingly ornate with domes, statues, stained-glass windows and wrought iron gates that mark the entranceway to tidy lawns dotted with flowering plants and topiary.

Death is enforced so hierarchically and meticulously here that outside the precise visiting hours for mourners to grieve their dead, there is no place for life. Grounds people ruthlessly search out weeds and display notice of the poisoning regimens used to prevent sea birds nesting on the island.

Of course, once the rental contract has run out, it needs renewal. Those that cannot afford their upkeep in death are tossed into the nearest bone yard on Sant'Ariano, the "Island of Bones". This is little more than overgrown mounds of dirt and still yields human remains today. Those whose families can pay for interment are transferred to small metal boxes for permanent storage in smaller quarters on the island, or transferred by boat to a graveyard on the mainland.

My aunts say that our business aims to liberate people from the hierarchies of social order, so they may participate equally in the cycles of life and death. I want to believe them; this place is a prison for the interred.

- Themes
  - "Invisible Dead"
  - Social order with regards to death

Parallel Gaze

There, on a concrete pile
Between my shoreline and
Cemetery wall, a grown man
With hands like spades
And a spoon in hand,
Drinks to a stone woman
and feels alive
In sea spray, as if her pulse
Were beating within him,
As a living heart, like mine.

Though his eyes are open,
He is blind to the sunset
And stares beyond it, into
Another realm. Here reside
The memories of love, here,
He seeks her. Tossed by the
Tides of his past and their
Reverberations on his future,
He has no grip on the present.

- Themes
  - Grief
  - Inability to live
    in the present

Tronchetto

Po and I arrive at the Tronchetto, or "new island" for Venice, which is located at the city's most western tip. Spawned by Venice's industrial legacy, it shares kinship with the mainland beasts Marghera and Mestre. This is the city's cupboard-under-the-sink, where cleaning unpleasantries are left to rot, including old rags, washing detergents and rat poison.

"This place feels unloved and uninhabited," I say, "but I want to see it for myself."

We look for somewhere to gain access to the land from the water – but it's impossible as the stone walled banks are so high. Even when I stand on *Po*'s back to peer into this featureless stretch of concrete-clad land I can only see their upper parts.

"This place was hewn from reclaimed land in the 1960s," says *Po*. "Built, designed and dominated by machines, it is dedicated to parking cars and things in transit. Only the most abject creatures attempt to live here."

I notice that even tenacious biofouling refuses to cling to the Tronchetto's sea walls.

"Over there is the Marittima cruise terminal, where passengers alight from colossal cruise ships that are tens of storeys high. Each vessel releases scores of thousands of passengers daily into the Piazzale Roma. Typically, they spend less than a day in the city before they return to the ship."

"Are those the liners we see in the lagoon," I ask, "which block out the sun like giants."

"Indeed. They're caustic structures. They scour out the floor of the lagoon, provoking erosive currents that eat the archipelago's ground. Even their wake spills into the city's medieval streets causing back-flow into lavatories."

A driverless, elevated tram system passes above us.

"See that?" says *Po*. "That drone is The Venice People Mover and confirmation that there are no accessible footpaths in this place. The only way to explore this part of the island is by following the lines of access granted by its mechanical infrastructures."

"*Po*, I don't like this place. It makes me sad and afraid. The drones, the filthy cars, the oils, the deathlessness in this place, can we go back to San Michele?"

We travel together in contemplative silence.

Beliefs

Kasia is reading aloud to me from the Bible.

Looking for a way to convey the sense of enchantment I have when playing and thinking with *Po*, I observe, "These stories don't really sound like miracles, Aunty."

"What do you mean, child?" she says. "Two thousand years ago, bringing someone back to life from the dead was truly amazing."

"So would your kitchen distillery have been. You've kept us fed on absolutely nothing. At least Jesus had bread and fish."

"People are not brought back to life in my kitchen," she snaps.

"But they are in Ruzica's sculptures."

"It's not the same at all," she protests. "Death itself is an equaliser and gives us another chance to be reborn beyond the conventional understanding of matter. Our resurrection is not just an existential rebirth through our personal deeds in Christ, but also one that is accompanied by acquiring a new body."

"Isn't that what is happening to my mother?" I say, a little confused.

I can see that she is getting annoyed with me.

"Can we read 'Animal Farm' instead, Aunty?"

I'm immediately dismissed.

"Don't take any notice of her," says my father with his spoon and vodka bottle in hand, as we watch my mother's statue dissolve somewhere between the evening sky and the surface of the lagoon. "We're natural outsiders by design. There is not much point in siding with god, or any other kind of majority viewpoint."

"Are you religious, Daddy?" I ask.

"Oh, yes. I've given lip service to many different kinds of god – Sabaoth, Amon, Apollo, the creator God of the Bible, and the boy Jesus. All of them."

"Is nature god?"

"Of course not! She is a concubine who sustains the Earth from beneath the world's mountains."

This does not feel right. I decide that my father is not religious at all, but an obligate storyteller. To figure things out for myself, I take a walk along *Po*'s shores.

Kasia's right, of course, that miracles are real but they're not made on human terms. There's no happy tit-for-tat to be found in faith and favour. Nor are there gods that make decrees which subdue the world to their whims and passions.

The living realm is so much more complex than that.

Perhaps grown-ups tell simple stories so that curious children like me, will go to sleep at night, but this is no reassurance. I've seen monstrous worlds that care little for humans, where our existence is not exalted and must be constantly negotiated. This treacherous realm is a place of unfamiliar shapes, precarious moods and extraordinary conversation partners that radiate a kind of openness and enablement, where even the most unlikely things can happen. This world of uncategorisable beings does not try to rationalise my existence in terms of rigid categories and conventions governed by which body parts I may or may not possess. They do not mark me out as peculiar, but embrace my extraordinary circumstances, enfolding them within the epic and magical story of life.

I stop just outside the *Fortune* and look out toward the city, which winks at me mischievously while *Po* snores peacefully as the Moon writes to the Earth upon the lagoon's surface. In this vision I find the peace that I'm looking for, as I taste the winds of change in the sea spray.

I dearly hope that the business takes off so Kasia will have more specific things to do than worry about the fate of my soul. As for my father … well, he's a trickster. He'll always be okay.

Dynamic Droplet Studies

Sarah makes a population of lively droplets from an emulsion of olive oil and caustic soda. They scatter and crawl over the base of the petri dish. Spurred on by changes in surface tension and chemistry the droplets exhibit extraordinarily lifelike behaviour: they can move around the dish, follow invisible trails of substances within it and even make shell-like solid structures.

Wondering what such a simple system might be capable of, Sarah decides to follow the course of one particular droplet through the microscope lens.

She writes: "*The droplet breaks from its stalk, and speeds through the viscous oil. A plate of soft matter accretes at its base and gradually thickens into a mushroom stalk as it travels. Flattening then billowing like a rippling jellyfish, it meets an invisible field and turns back on itself to continue its exploration through a different trajectory. All the while its tail lengthens like a stalk until it suddenly halts and reorganises to become a worm-like structure. Using the bottom of the dish to crawl upon, caterpillar-like, its mass thickens until an active large body approaches, whereupon they circle each other, like musical notes on an invisible grid.*"

Immersed in the world of droplets so intensively for so long, Sarah starts to empathise with them. She even imagines the world from a droplet's perspective. For example, when they collide with each other, she thinks of them osculating affectionately, like Europeans saying 'farewell' at an airport. After a while she feels that she's intruding on the droplet's privacy.

"Pull yourself together! This is a science experiment!"

It is useless scolding herself. Logic alone will not stifle the droplet's strangeness as its personality gleams defiantly back at her, continually changing form and behaviour. While most droplets only last several minutes, this particular one is still sprightly. Not wanting to miss the canteen, she sets up the digital video-recording system to capture the droplet's demise while she goes for a bite to eat.

"Hey, Sarah! How's it going?"

"I've been watching droplets travel around a petri dish."

121

'Great! It's only real science when it's tedious or doesn't work!"

"I'm having a wonderful day then!"

She is surprised to see the droplet still throbbing on her return. It looks quite different, as the 'tail' has expanded so much that it resembles a mini-barnacle anchored to the petri dish. She expects it will soon 'die' but the tiny droplet continues to keep 'breathing'.

Unable to explain this strange longevity, she seeks her supervisor Massimo Tsuda's opinion. She quickly finds the fluid bead although it has broken free from its broad-based shell and is lazily circling the petri dish like a fairground goldfish in a plastic bag.

'What do you make of it?'

Massimo mutters inaudibly as he studies the mineral traces. Deftly, he navigates the fine focus controls around the microscope stage and splays his hand momentarily, appearing to take note of something.

"Interesting."

He immediately returns to writing his grant proposal, without further comment.

Golden afternoon rays lick their way across the microscope bench. Sarah wanders over to the window and stares down into the narrow alleyway, which leads to the entrance of the building. A group of smokers are huddled outside, backs to the wind.

A burst of dandelion seeds suddenly stirs upwards past the window. A few settle and rest for several moments before they are hurried on again by a persistent cross breeze. These seeds could be a perfect experimental control for proving that her moving droplet was not just a physical phenomenon caused for example, by heat or air flowing across the petri dish.

She races outside to catch one.

Although many weeds have found firm footing between the cracks in the stressed brickwork and flaking stucco, gathering dandelion clocks from such places is not so easy. After many failed attempts, Sarah finally captures a fluffy parachuting body that is trapped in a rough fragment of the alleyway and brings the precious structure back to her bench. Yet, when she searches for the droplet it is nowhere to be seen.

Anxiously she scans the petri dish but cannot locate it – or any semblance of its remains. Oddly shaken, she replays the video footage, which suggests the droplet has transformed into a mass of still matter in the centre of the dish.

Sadly, she empties the remains into the sink.

As the water slips around the sides of the petri dish, she is oblivious to it carrying a tiny, winking droplet which has been trapped within the debris. Loosened from these residues it begins to make its bold way through the laboratory plumbing and into the mediaeval sewage system of *gattoli* that leads into the canal.

- Themes
  - "Invisible Ecology"

Further

↑ undefined beings

As my aunts become more absorbed in their business they involve me less in what they're doing, I am content amusing myself on the beach. *Po* continues to swell, roll and fold into an increasingly complex body of land.

Sometimes we stay close and hang out along *Po*'s shores but at other times we grow bolder in our escapades, venturing far into the lagoon to explore the city limits. My island twin is already too big to travel through the labyrinthine canals, so increasingly we venture beyond the Lido, out into the Adriatic to explore the Mediterranean Sea; sometimes, even far beyond. Traveling together as a knot of algae, we can be easily mistaken for debris produced by the wracks that litter the Sargasso Sea. We are neither human nor island but inseparable twins whose hearts and bodies are entangled in vegetable matter, animal flesh, mineral solutions, artificial fabrics and all kinds of detritus.

Time works its magic for us. Yet, there is little gained in producing a schedule of our travels. Ours is a nonlinear adventure, with starting points and destinations that are not logically composed. After discovering a natural world that is not rationally designed it is no longer meaningful to say how long we take, how far we go, or establish the way we get there. Sometimes our adventures are short, no more than the blink of an eye, and at other times they seem to last forever. Nor is there any chronological order in which to describe our encounters. We explore parallel worlds where nature is rich with material entanglements, synchronicity, spooky events, quantum tunnelling, aberrations in spacetime, baroque spectacles, contradictions, magic, paradoxes, wonder and enchantment.

Of course, such incredible accounts may be attributed to the meanderings of the under-occupied imagination of a quickly growing boy. A child who does not yet know the true limits of things, and who still believes in immortality, yet our escapades are real; they mark our flesh, put sea salt in my mouth, make me fear for my life.

Somehow, these experiences linger, continuing to change within us, long after each adventure is done.

Leviathan

Po discovers the sperm whale and her calf through the taste of their colossal discharges – urine, vomitus, faeces and 'blow'. They separate from their pod around the confluence between the crossing of the straits of Messina and Sicily. Likened to living islands, this endangered species appears as unchartered dark rocklike masses in the sea. Sailors, oblivious to their nature, moor their vessels alongside their dark shores and ignite their cooking fires. Rising in pain, the beast urinates a sea of contempt on them and plunges into the depths, dragging down the unfortunate ships and their crew with them.

"There are probably only a few hundred of these animals alive," *Po* says.

No longer able to resist their lure, we follow their echolocation landscapes.

The mother calls to her calf. I can feel her sorrowful, sometimes excitable voice, resonating through the air chambers in my safety harness. Each sound wave carries an incredible force that beats my chest with violent blows in a three-plus-one pattern.

"It's like hearing a duet between a Tibetan horn and a didgeridoo, while waking during your own cardiac resuscitation," I say to *Po*.

The calf turns on to her back to feed from the mammary slit of her mother.

Sea-folk say that sperm whale babies don't suckle like other mammals owing to the strange shape of their head. Instead, they are fed through their left nostril, which collects the milk and trickles it into their throats, where it is swallowed. In this way, the calf's sinus acts as a milk collection and distribution reservoir. I'm keen to see this happen.

The water becomes choppy as the calf and her cow approach us. Happily coupled in nutritious embrace, I can see the calf sucking with her mouth.

Po tugs at my safety harness.

"These gentle giants can hold us under in a fatal swell," it cautions. "Even with the most loving intentions."

Right now, we are riding upon waves that rise like a roller coaster.

I see the mother's colossal eye staring at us out of a blubbery mass of thick black skin, the size of a bus. A camel-like hump protrudes on her back where I'd expect the dorsal fin of a fish to be, while her flippers are small compared with her girth.

"Her heart weighs as much as two whole people," says *Po*.

Displaying her massive cone-shaped teeth that sprout from her lower jaw, each as big as a hand, the mother whale rolls playfully. Designed to tear the flesh from squid, she is far from a mindless human killing meat-shredding ship-sinking machine as recounted in the legend of the white whale, Moby Dick. Instead, her mouth conceals these dreadful weapons in a turned up smile that seems to split her head into an incredible, endless expression of love for her child.

Although she means us no harm, we sense their incredible power as they draw closer still. Then, the calf grows curious. Bolstered by the confidence of its mother, the calf pushes its nose against us. The whole world stirs as the baby whale grins happily. We dread becoming its playmates. It drenches us with a surface slap of its fins and laughs, before sprinting after its mother, who drags the sea behind her.

As the waters still and the sun sets somewhere upon the horizon, I remember Kasia's tale of the monstrous whale that was created by God on the fifth day of Creation, as a warning to the sons of Adam whenever they were tempted by the sin of pride. The biblical creature's terrible gaping mouth and a heart harder than stone symbolised its unmitigated power and the focal point of all human fears.

"I don't understand how a creature tasked with policing humankind's capacity for cruelty should be damned as 'Leviathan'," I say to *Po*.

"It's the monster's curse," it replies. "Our size, our appearance, our behaviour, our *difference* is equated with evil."

"I still don't understand. Of course, when this mother sperm whale and her calf are provoked they are capable of terrible destruction, but we just met creatures devoted to each other. Their mutual adoration is the antithesis of 'evil'."

"Monsters are cursed all the same," says *Po*, "whatever their intentions."

Developing

Within my surface soils, marine cosmologies form
Nurseries for shrimp, blenny, wrasse, trumpetfish,
Moongazing phosphorescent spawn, pearlescent
Iridescences, fibrous mats, tentacular weaves and
Knots of vegetable fibres. At times, they break from
Familiar orbits and seek a deeper layer of refuge in
Loosely attached collections of plastic debris and
Microbeads that are whipped by vigorous currents
Into spumes and sea colloids, which speak of mermaids
With no immortal souls that – at the end of their life –
Turn to sea foam, ceasing to exist. The soft underbelly
Of these delicious fabrics resist definitions. Stretching
Skywards, they reach to the stars for new mythologies.

Our gaze turns outwards, towards the teats of gyres,
Warming ocean temperatures and changing currents
That feed us. We rise, we glide, we swell, we pounce,
We thicken, we coil, we spiral, we sink and rise again,
Until all the axes of the globe are utterly confounded
By our movements. Giddily our guts guide us through
Feeder trails of nitrogenous fertilisers, sewage, spills,
Dacthal, colloids, arsenic, polychlorinated biphenyls,
Fluoride, heavy metals, dioxins, hexachlorobenzene
And crude chemical fouling. Adapting to these alien
Environments we thrive together in treachery. Again
We return again to the air's interface to dance joyfully
With krill, where we tumbling as one with the oceans
Holding them close; for when they perish, we do too.

◦ Themes
  – Nature adapting to environmental
    degredation

Island of Light

We watch the sunset over Sirene, a city built upon a natural rock near Taormina on the island of Sicily. As the light transitions, it casts shadows with multicoloured halos over the part man-made structure, which stretches upwards out of the sea as a colossus with a faint blue glow. Since every building is cast using the same materials that formed the land, from a distance the whole island appears to climb skywards the top of the building disappearing into the clouds.

"It looks like the ground is trying to be the sky," I say.

The half-moon is pressing itself like a postage stamp against the sky's deepening hues.

"The whole place was originally an egg-shaped, village-sized rock," says *Po*, "that was bought by a philanthropist who dedicated its use to the dispossessed. The island itself was transformed and built by the initial residents, said to be a community of 'poor devils', which originally came from Africa and the Middle East. The settlers wanted their new home to become an invitation and beacon of hope to all refugees, travellers and the lost. They also wanted to use their cultural knowledge and skills to create the structure. The tip of the building was made from found stones, beach wood and concrete. It narrows to the tip like a narwhal's tooth."

"How did it get so high?"

"It's an organic construction process, where the inhabitants appropriate the materials around them, including their waste, which forms the 'mortar' between stones. Can you see where new settlers build homes around the base, one atop of the other? The speed at which this happens gives the structure the appearance of having leapt from the sea. Now observe how the thick, outside walls are following the rise of the constantly extending original spire and as they encircle the building like an onion skin, they steady it. But what you can't see is that the residents are also digging downwards, carving a subterranean city from out of the natural rock the residues of which produce the tower. Part geology, part nature, ground and sky, most of it is unobserved and it's reasonable to assume the structure is as deep as it is tall."

I really want to see the pointed tip and squint at the clouds, hoping to catch a glimpse of its entirety but although the clouds oblige me by separating I can't stare for too long because of a soft blue glow that seems to be emitted by the stones.

"Why is the light here so strange, *Po*?"

"It's more than just a place to live, it's an instrument that modulates luminosity. At sunfall, its luminescent stones are lit by a second artificial moon; a lantern that is carried to the top of the spire as the evening falls by a hydraulic mechanism, like a giant water clock. It returns to the ground under the pull of gravity at daybreak. Look! You can just see it starting to rise against the violet horizon."

"It's so much brighter than the natural one."

"Sirene is home to the strangest structures on Earth," says *Po*. "It's an outsider's paradise."

"A happy place for monsters," I observe.

"The peculiarity does not stop at the outside of the city but pierces its upper and lower layers through a jackstraw formations of mirrors, and other reflective surfaces. Inside, the conurbation is marvellously lit, creating the illusion of infinite space. At night, blue candlelight within the dwellings radiates from the building apertures, enlivening the stones, and the whole city becomes an epic beacon. The second moon is said to keep the natural one company, with a message of kinship, even at the darkest of times."

"Do many people live there now?"

"Scores of thousands, I expect, although I can't imagine that anyone counts them. Sirene is unique; a prototype city for a new kind of relationship between artificial constructions, peoples and the land. Each resident is part of a coherent society that is woven through stone structures and bathed in light, where many hearts and minds can heal together."

New Life

Anna Beauvoir's statue is magnificent. Whatever angle you view her from, she gazes beyond the horizon. Her lips are upturned, which lifts her cheekbones and confers a radiance that is augmented by tiny mirrors placed where her pupils should be.

"They're angled so that when the sun is setting, the eyes will cast light back on the world. On summer days, her gaze is as bright as lasers and in winter her eyes may simply seem moist, as if she's been crying," says Ruzica.

"Aunty, can you make me mirror lights of my own," I plead.

Ruzica smiles, "Perhaps one day, when you join your mother. You know, Anna is designed to decay. In a few decades her liquid heart will cause her body to crumble and become fish food."

"That's so sad." I say.

"Actually, it's a happy occasion, because when she crumbles to dust, she erases her human footprint and becomes part of a much larger community that forms our marine reefs."

"Where does she go then?"

"Into the ground and blood of the living world, in land and sea, but her first home will be the reef."

"You mean she'll continue to have adventures?" Ruzica's lips part as if she's about to explain something but since her fate is my mother's I can't contain my enthusiasm for her being awakened again. "Please can I see you bring her to life in the lagoon? Please. I'll do the washing up. I'll go to bed early. I'll turn the compost for a week. I promise I will."

Ruzica firmly refuses.

"Darling, it's not appropriate. It's an extremely private affair."

"But nobody will see me, I can make myself invisible. You won't even know I am around."

"Take him with us," says Krists, "It'll be good for him."

I fling my arms around my father's neck, Ruzica's and then Anna's. Her skin is oddly lifelike, somewhat like my mother's – yellowish, with open pores. I run my fingers over her rough surface but she doesn't quite feel like Aleysha's statue. I'm happy about that.

"Her skin is perfect for helping organisms to find homes in her crevices." Says Ruzica, observing my curiosity. "Gradually, she will become inseparable from an ecosystem of lagoon wildlife, which will welcome her as kin."

"Will she be a mermaid then?"

"More like a watery angel," corrects Ruzica.

We float Anna out into the lagoon on a raft made from driftwood, buoyed up with recycled beach plastics. Then, we carefully tether her to the *Fortune*. Although it takes a while for us to prepare the vessel for open water, we are excited to set sail for the first time in many years. Ruzica is at the helm, while Jelena shouts directions that lead us to the burial site. Krists stands on the bow posing like a film star, constantly asserting that sailing in the lagoon doesn't mean he's broken his promise to never return to the sea.

"Yes, of course," say my aunts without conviction.

Tenacious barnacles, seaweed and mussels, trail untidily behind us. They have scarred the hull, which makes micro-wakes that are causing the support platform to wobble. We plough carefully on, with Kasia taking charge of calculations that will allow Ruzica to compensate for the raft's yawing.

A dirty green barge with a crane arm greets us and we hook a cradle of chains around Anna's body. Then we place her carefully upon what Ruzica calls a *bio-positive* stone plinth. Here she is positioned to face the sunset. Finally, she is secured to her base with steel pins.

As we turn a broad circle to head back for San Michel we pass under the unmistakable shadow of the *Nostradamus*. Although none of us except Krists have seen this luxury yacht, we know it intimately from his descriptions. Having assumed that my father had exaggerated, we are astonished how spellbinding she is. Traveling solemnly at the head of a graceful convoy of ebony vessels, the *Nostradamus* moves into the lagoon where the congregation circles the memorial, like a school of killer whales.

Spellbound, we cut the engines, while Krists salutes the sky with his tumbler and spoon. Marvelling at the graceful giant, we watch until she and her pod turn around for the shore. Then we return to San Michele – our hearts and souls afire.

Jellyfish

My flesh burns, yet I do not combust. I'm marooned on a gelatinous heap with my flesh on fire. Despite my efforts so far to remove them, the mauve stingers of venomous jellyfish continue to rip at my skin. *Po*'s swollen mass is like setting concrete around me, while blistering pain stifles my movements as if I'm cling-film wrapped. Ensnared in a raft of thick slime whose cruel tentacles are knotted with silver fish, which are dangling nose-down and belly-up, I roll over on my safety harness. Barely conscious, I know I must pee in the water to reduce the searing pain in my arms and legs. Groping around for a piece of plastic to scrape out the stingers with I turn on my back, inviting the sun to boil the water on my skin.

We did nothing personally to invite this assault, but *people* did.

Jellyfish thrive on the side effects of human habitation. Warmer temperatures, salinity changes, marine acidification and pollution from the city, have lured them into the lagoon. Now, they invade our shores like rats, pigeons and seagulls. But they're not as easy to eradicate, despite their simple appearance, everything about them is so complex. Factory discharges that spew warm water into the bioregion and algal blooms that flourish on pollution also play a part in this invertebrate Armageddon. When the jellies come, they appear so fast. Seasoned by Hell's own crust, this alien soup even exploits the coastal infrastructure around the marble pontoons, jetties and marinas, which become convenient nurseries for jellyfish polyps. These spineless vermin are resilient and can produce large numbers of immature individuals that hang like instant seeds in the water, which explode into life when it's time to massively expand their growth. Their transparency, capacity for camouflage and ability to inhabit planes just beyond the optical depth for detection by sight, or camera lenses, renders them invisible to coast guards and satellite surveillance systems. Such powers of invisibility compound their enigma and latent evil.

I pass out.

Awakening

"Am I dead?"

My skin is no longer burning. I try moving, but a thick coat of gelatinous material grips my muscles. I raise an arm carefully and examine my skin. Under the sun's heat, the jellies have melted into an ectoplasm that has fused with my algae safety suit. I am now encased in a brown integument, like toffee, which is filled with large air pockets.

I am not only buoyant but also impervious to the stingers. Grabbing on to *Po*'s spine I paddle hard enough to detach it from a knot of purple poison.

We make our escape through the jellyfish sludge holding a strong line to San Michele. Carefully avoiding the tentacle trails that part and scratch at us, attempting to pull us back into the swarm, we remain calm in this toxic landscape by naming all the things we love, until we finally reach *Po*'s shores.

Aftershock

I am babbling but it's not my voice. Watched over by women that I do not recognise, I hear their sighs, and incantations, which breathe like a spell.

Heat pack, now, now.
Forty-five Celsius, hotter still.
He's boiling, forty minutes.
Calm down. He's saying something.
So many of them. Rashes everywhere.
Blood's been drawn.
Ibuprofen. He can't swallow.
Where? How?
I'm not doing that.
You do it.
Get them out, out, take the tentacles out.
Pulse. Take his pulse.
Water. More water.
Take that thing away.

Someone presses a cool cloth on my brow.

Everything is dirty. Even the moonlight is contaminated with smog. The stars are suffocated between folds of sky. They drop like embers into the greasy water where they erupt in fiery explosions. The language written on the surface of the water in moonlight is symbolic, profane. From my viewpoint on the Moon, I observe my blistering body with overwhelming clarity, weeping blood from every pore. My lips are making the movements of speech but the sounds and symbols of meaningful language fall softly around me.

I am saying nothing.

> Nature reflecting
> Pos physical state

Recuperation

My lesions are healed but my body remembers the pain. I cannot bear to touch soft things and insist on sleeping on the floor. After days of nakedness and going for barefoot walks on shoreline gravel and sea-glass, I am ready for company.

Expecting a scolding that lurks behind comments but never quite comes, I spend most of my time with *Po*, who is even more generously spread over the shore than I recall.

As my skin is still raw but I can't abide squashiness, I bring my father's scratchy old sou'wester so I can sit uncomfortably upon the algae mound, which seems much more slippery than usual. In fact, everything seems different – more dangerous now. The light is crueller, the earth more wizened, the lagoon more changeable, seabird beaks cut the wind like gutting knives, shellfish edges are sharper, stones are treacherously uneven, insects more poisonous, flesh-eating worms crawl out of soft soils and fatten. Enraged fish churn the waters, nematodes spill their poisonous stomach juices on to the ground, small birds tear feathers from each other, fear lurks under every stone and there is nowhere to take refuge from the malice of the natural realm.

As *Po* and I keep quiet camaraderie against the conspiracy of existence, I cannot help feeling that a hole has been torn in the world. In the daytime, I choose my steps carefully, avoiding shadows in case I stumble into their predatory void. When night falls, its pitiless darkness opens up the ghosts of pain and I cannot stop myself from falling skywards in my dreams, hurtling on a collision course towards a dripping blood-orange moon.

I wake, drenched in sweat.

During my recuperation, *Po* and I sit tightly in each other's presence, while the fickle wind nags at us to 'do something'.

"Don't go back to the sea," sensible voices that sound like my father, say in waking dreams.

Just as I feel I will suffocate under the weight of my own thoughts, the sinister embodiment of nature that has troubled me so doggedly

135

vanishes, taking the stifling ennui that has saturated the world with it. Everything returns to how I left it, save my rusting skin and senses, which no longer seem to match up.

"Enough is enough, *Po*," I say. "It is time to be explorers again."

• Theme

— Fear of nature

Living Atlantis

At the base of the memorial to Anna Beauvoir, I can see a row of Venetian gothic houses through the brown-tinged visor of my safety suit that, being submerged, do not invite human inhabitation.

"Help me get closer, *Po*."

Knowing my monster twin can breathe for me, we dive together to examine some of these dwellings.

As we move along the underwater canal, corals sprout from the tips of pointed arches of all the houses, while puffer fish and squirrelfish peer from cornerstone gaps between buildings. Textured roof tiles promote coral polyp settlement, while chimneystacks, which have been scooped out where stucco has crumbled from the brickwork, contain plumes of moray eels within the large dark cavities of the walls. We swim through the hallway of a patterned lemon façade to find six graded shelves that form the plinth for a lost alabaster statue. This detail offers a retreat for baitfish and refuge for fish fry from crustaceans on the look-out for tasty morsels. At the rear of this magnificent dwelling, an internal room with a stained-glass window mesh, which has lost most of its glass, is home to all kinds of juvenile species. Fleshy pink starfish blend shyly into the shuttering, while algae wallpaper changes its moods according to the local nutrient stream. We follow a bed of sea grasses out of the building that flexes like an untidy lawn and leads us alongside a vestigial *rio*, from which a shoal of yellow striped fish suddenly takes flight. We explore every dwelling, each hosting a veritable zoo of wonder. Nothing is what it initially seems; when suitably provoked, inert surfaces suddenly betray their capacity for colour and movement.

"Atlantis!" I say, in a stream of effervescent bubbles. "Is a living coral reef city."

• Theme

— Invisible Ecologies

137

Sea Bog

Our floating bogland, is crafted by algae mats,
Turbid water, and organic crusts. Our original
Settlers search inwards for material attachments,
Spurs, hollows, pits, mossy areas, ridges and
Quarries An unfenced country that grows,
Thrives and dies by its appetites and exquisite
Wastes. Constantly melting and swelling, its
Layers of life build upon antecedent strata of
Decay. We're never what we were the day before.

Refuge for lost and furtive species that
Must remain invisible to humans, we
Embrace their outlandishness, like the
Bog octopuses that avoid desiccation for
Prolonged periods and were once prized
By fashionistas as ornaments for hats.
Their slaughter was justified in lies as
Totems of bad luck: *Octopus, devil of the
Bogs. Terror of all fishermen and sea farers.*

Within our earthy folds they explore our
World through touch, taste and sight. She
Grabs a soil clod with her sensitive tentacles,
Prepares to strike at a fish and examines a
Plastic bottle, turning it around to know it.
But there's no true environmental sense in
What people make. So, she does not reach
Out to them but remains here, furtively.

Painted in skin her emotion: Red for
Anger, white for fear. At peace, she is
Halcyon mottled brown and in spring
Will migrate towards the Venetian shore

To find her spawning ground. Unlike
Most octopuses that share sperm at a
Distance, she is kissed and cuddled
Beak-to-beak, by her boneless mate.

Sperm is finally deposited during their
Lovers' exchange. After a final cuddle
They part — he to the sea bog and she
To an aquatic lair, where strands of
Egg-clusters are attached and cared for
Until they hatch. Dutifully refusing to
Eat, she will die from this dedication.

Her offspring spend a quiet first month,
Floating like phantoms in the lagoon
Before moving out of the water to seek
New sea bogs and start their adult lives.
Bog octopuses don't exist for humans,
Their longevity depends on their ingenuity,
Invisibility, and your indifference to them.

- Themes
  - Creatures must remain invisible or useless to humans in order to survive
  - Death creates life

Bunker Island

We come across a giant board game, which is being played out in the South China Sea.

"Who's participating," I ask.

"Nations," says *Po*. "The People's Republic of China is competing against the United States of America."

"What are the stakes?"

"The winner will gain strategic control of the 'First Island Chain', which is an archipelago that swoops from the coast of Borneo, past Taiwan and on to southern Japan."

"And how do they win?"

"By acquiring land, of course. The outcome of this game results in a Great Wall that is visible from space, whose tactical pieces are artificial islands produced by the *Island Factory Machine*."

"What's that?"

"It's a manufacturing system that is active in the region of the Spratly Islands. Once these dying atolls did not even register on satellite maps and were barely visible above water. Now, they are the heartland of an industrial scale, island-producing plant that churns out ready-made blocks of land with military capabilities. It's become one of the biggest offshore military platforms in the world."

"That's impressive."

"Indeed, but it achieves little in easing tensions between the superpowers. Most worryingly, it compromises the rich biodiversity of the marine environment, which is refuge to many endangered species that seek shelter in demilitarised zones along the First Island Chain."

"It sounds complicated."

"It is, particularly as the different sides continually invent their own strategies. The United States views this region an as international space that must remain freely accessible to everyone and makes rules to maintain its presence in the area. China, on the other hand, wants to amplify its presence twenty-fold in this region, which requires the sacrifice of natural landmasses to the island factory machine. Gameplay is further complicated by objections made by other nations including the Philippines, Taiwan and Vietnam, which govern numerous small but strategically important outposts in the area that are colonised by people from their tiny island nations. Vigorously defending their subsistence lifestyles against occupation by foreign powers, the settlers have retreated to these havens to claim a quality of life that was unaffordable in their countries of origin."

"I can't see them. Where are they?"

"Over here in Pagasa, for example. It's that blip of land at the midpoint between Palawan, the westernmost province of the Philippines, and the coast of Vietnam. It was declared part of the new nation of Freedomland in 1956 by Tomas Cloma. However, Philippine dictator Ferdinand Marcos arrested him and demanded that the country was surrendered for one peso, transforming the tiny island into a military stronghold, with an airship, platforms for anti-aircraft guns and concrete bunkers. Although the shelters and munitions have decayed and rusted beyond use, the island itself is all but bound to the will of a hundred proud yet destitute people that are trapped in time and place."

I'm impressed at their boldness and ingenuity.

"Such unconventional communities are almost impossible for military-minded leaders to deal with, as they have a completely different value system than the superpowers and, seemingly, the players inhabit parallel realities. In other words, each participant is playing a different game. This makes negotiations extremely awkward and diplomatic compromises are almost impossible to make. The involvement of such unusual societies is not especially rare in this game, for example the marines from the Sierra Madre. This is a stranded Philippine ghost ship and cargo cult that has been indefinitely sustained by monthly supply drops made by the navy. In a condition of political stalemate, there is no chance of the tactical withdrawal of these troops from the site. So, despite the pressure applied by China and the United States – they stay."

"We could moor the *Fortune* in these waters if we ever have to leave the Venetian lagoon," I say. "Then nobody will ever move us on."

"We'd certainly fit in," says *Po*. "But the military presence here is *too* ominous. This isn't a game we can win."

"But there has to be more point to this than occupying land," I say.

"It depends who you ask," says *Po*. "That's certainly the goal of the superpowers but it's quite another thing for the smaller players, whose whole existence is at risk. For them, it's a survival game, part of which is played by nature."

"How so?"

"Ecosystems are constantly negotiating their survival all the time and develop the no-go areas for humans that exist around conflict zones into wildlife buffers and fertile areas that can support life. Although humans may precipitate in hostilities in areas of extensive and enduring occupation, nature's great natural creativity allows living things to survive, even in the most unlikely of places. This is not to down-play the seriousness of the *game*, which carries the prospect of terrible destruction, as military stand-offs and tipping points in the order of ecosystems that see habitats destroyed by construction and war, can instantly turn into all or none scenarios."

"This makes me both happy and sad, *Po*," I say. "I'm inspired by nature's inventiveness but I just don't understand how people can be so destructive on such a grand scale. It just doesn't make any sense."

"It's the story of humankind I'm afraid, dear twin. What's happening here has many resonances with our own city of Venice, which was established through much political and military controversy. It even became the most important city in the world by transforming phantom islands, such as these into habitable spaces and established its military might. Perhaps this *Island Factory System* game is setting the stage for a *Venice of the East*, with a new political land building, power-wielding, ecosystem-forming ideology."

I can't explain why, but I want to cry.

"On the other hand," adds *Po*, "this island gameplay could be far less construction and tip this precious bioregion into a realm of ecocide and cultural devastation."

Disappointment

"She's discrediting the field of artificial life," says the voice in the stairwell.

There's further mumbling, and Sarah hears her name many times as the conversation peters out.

She walks over to the window and stares down into the alleyway trying to glimpse her critics as they leave the building but sees nobody.

She sighs.

Of course, in some ways, they're right. So far, her observations are idiosyncratic, descriptive and propositional. She has little empirical data, no intellectual property rights and lacks a product portfolio suitable for reaching the market in three to five years. In other words, she has not produced a solid technical base upon which private investors can fund her work. More damningly, she makes public projections about the potential value of her research without already having demonstrated unequivocal findings.

Sarah accepts that her original hunch about the potential of origins of life technologies, to become an interesting innovation platform for new kinds of computing, does not seem to be paying off.

Rather than feeling sorry for herself, she seeks inspiration and camaraderie in the stories of women innovators, who've battled across many disciplines – Marie Curie, the first woman in history to win Nobel prizes; Georgia O'Keefe, the first woman to have a solo show at the Museum of Modern Art in New York; Jane Austen, who helped define the modern novel, and Ada Lovelace, the world's first computer programmer.

She is particularly intrigued by the clash of opposites that Lovelace embodied and from the outset, as she was exposed to the paradoxes implicit in the poetry of life. Born in 1815 to the crash of seltzer bottles being shattered with a poker by her father, Lord Byron, because he wanted a 'glorious boy', Lovelace was never destined to live a conventional life. Brought up by her aristocratic mother Annabella Milbanke, who valued mathematics as the highest form of reason, she was equally inspired by her father's feral passions and poetry. Sarah wonders whether Lovelace's story will help her better understand how to combine hard science with her non-empirical thoughts and experiences.

Perhaps unsurprisingly, Ada's parents separated soon after her birth, whereupon she was rigorously schooled in mathematics by her mother – who was determined that her daughter would be rational and not inherit her father's mental vagaries.

Yet, in many ways this peculiarly challenging situation enabled Ada to do something quite extraordinary. Drawing upon both the powerful imagination that she had in common with her father and making use of the level-headedness that she shared in mathematics with her mother, the young woman developed the unique skills she needed to realise her dreams and passions. She later called this approach 'poetical science'.

Sarah's traced her own research interests back to times when she was in the back garden making and eating mud pies, in her kickers and vest at home in England – while her mother scurried in and out of the back door, muttering like Mole from *Wind in the Willows*.

"Hang hand washing!" she'd say.

Sarah had always been fascinated by the creativity of mud. It transformed things from small to large, it surprised her with the treasures it held. It also brought new life. Except in the case of the house keys that Sarah buried 'somewhere' in the back garden. As her parents fretted over their loss she wished that a key-beanstalk would suddenly sprout into the sky – just like Jack's magical seeds.

Soil was about the creation of new worlds.

When Sarah went to university she studied medicine, as this was the only way that she could get to design and engineer with living things. Gradually she realised that in making a transition to study natural sciences she was still fulfilling her childhood adventures – just as Lovelace did. But her research ambitions do not lie in the conventional kind of mathematical computing that Ada Lovelace wrote the first program for; instead she wishes to work in an emerging field called 'natural computing', that asks how the computational powers of nature can be used to count, sort and order matter – which is the basis of all forms of computing.

Sarah wants to understand how life's processes can be used as a computational platform, as matter that is not equilibrated with its surroundings can make 'decisions' about its environment. To influence the molecular decision making that underpins this responsiveness in a manner that can be regarded as computational, she needs to find ways of 'talking' with the material programs of the natural world. This is exactly where the origins of life sciences come in.

While living things are rich in all kinds of lively molecules, they are unfathomably complex and carry out many different operations at once. Dynamic droplets provide a simple system which should make it much easier to fathom how to influence these decisions and what kind of tasks such forms of computation could be used for in everyday terms.

Lovelace's 'poetical science' inspires her in this discovery process, as it brings a new freedom to explore by imagining things through the openness she associates with childhood play, so keeping new avenues for exploration alive. In fact, she realises that recent criticisms about her discoveries 'looking too easy', had been curtailing her natural curiosity.

Sarah goes to her laboratory bench and puts away all the protocols she has been using. She begins with a set of 'messy' experiments that imagine her droplets as a kind of 'programmable' mud. Introducing them to ordinary circumstances, she observes how they respond to unpurified Venice water, move alongside a floating leaf, or how they react if they're given alcohol.

Just as in Ada's day, when the first computer program was written, she reminds herself that people will consider what she's doing strange. Even if she can't silence her critics, at least she can ask those questions that set her imagination alight when she was just a little girl.

Much Further

"You've grown, young man," says Ruzica, as my kin prepare for the formal launch of their business, which has already secured enough clients to make a profit in the first year. Apparently, this is almost unheard of for a start-up.

I have long lost track of all the comings and goings but can see that everyone is working hard to make a success of it. Even Krists is helping Ruzica perfect the bioconcrete mixes and is carrying bags of sand and lime, to make sure there are enough ingredients to meet the anticipated demand.

I am mostly left on my own, which means more time with *Po*, who is becoming richer, thicker, knottier, bigger and more materially complex. The ropey algal blooms, like vegetable cartilage, that form most of its body, are now too heavy to support their own weight on land. So, it's moved further out into the lagoon, detaching and reattaching from its foundations like a boat, as we share adventures. Shaping these moorings are new kinds of city silt and refuse that mix into its substance and produce a different, more mature kind of ecology. Crabs are replaced by fishes, shellfish crusts thicken and form attachments for sea anemones, crowds of sandpipers scuttle indecisively across its shores, the genetically modified mosquito larvae flourish in the cultivated hatcheries and rise as clouds of doomed flies. Sometimes creatures such as otters, which are making a comeback in the lagoon, seek shelter in its evolving spaces.

I can walk quite far out upon the water now without losing my footing, which gives me different views of my mother's statue. Sometimes I can actually see the details of her face under the setting sun. In those moments, she blossoms – a naked, powerful woman with peach flesh, whose contours measure the island biorhythms under the sweep of her hourglass shadow. I am truly happy she is with us. Of course, I've persuaded Ruzcia to give her a mirror gaze, so at sunfall, I watch for her eye lights, and when I see them I rise to my feet and loudly applaud nature.

I am also reading voraciously.

While Kasia has not given up on her mission to save my soul, her Bible sessions are becoming less frequent. With a developing business on the go, we now have a Wi-Fi network signal which offers unreliable online access. When I have permission to use the shared laptop, I download an eclectic and diverse range of reading material such as fairytales, opinion columns, scientific abstracts, academic essays, classic novels, poetry, financial reports, white papers, press releases, advertisements, weather reports, magazine articles and anything else that catches my attention. I devour their information and try out my poorly developed opinions on my kin.

"Aunty Kasia, is our current epoch better called the 'Christocene' rather than the 'Anthropocene'?"

"What exactly do you mean, Po?"

"Well, isn't our compulsion to separate from the natural world through allying with the Christian 'god', who sets people apart from beasts, more detrimental than our desire to control the world through science?"

Kasia looks at me pointedly.

"You've had long enough on the computer now," she pushes the laptop screen down. "Time for bed."

• Themes

— Nature vs Humans

Blue Zones

Po and I watch an old man and woman sharing a rowing boat in a quiet bay off the island of Okinawa. The Moon looms so large above them they touch it with each gesture. Yet they do not notice this marvel, nor do they see us approach, as they are completely absorbed in each other.

Their pleated faces are streaked with tiny moonlight channels that animate their conversation with a radiant glow. Minuscule slithers of light scatter from their lips and dance over the surface of the water as beacons to tiny shoals of fish that cavort joyfully beneath them. Talking softly, the elderly couple lean toward each other with gentle smiles, as if they were meeting for the very first time. Still discovering the enchantment within each other, they observe a quality of dialogue that youth cannot yet experience.

"Something magical happens in Okinawa," says *Po*, "where according to the World Health Organization, people enjoy the longest disability-free life expectancy in the world. When they are finally ready to part this life, they pass quickly and are relatively free of suffering."

"Can we live here too?" I ask.

"This is not unique, dear twin. There are many Blue Zones around the world, where people live measurably longer. They tend to be found in island communities where people quite simply forget to die."

"Really?" I say, thinking of my mother.

"Of course. A group of Seventh Day Adventists in Loma Linda in California are America's longevity allstars. Sardinia also rates highly, with an impressive cluster of healthy ninety year-olds that live in the Nicoya Peninsula of Costa Rica, and another Blue Zone exists on the Greek island of Ikaria. Modern medical science tries to rationalise such cases and suggests that only about a quarter of a human lifespan is determined by genetics, the rest boils down to how and where people live. But these 'geriatric juveniles' also share a few other things in common; they don't smoke, are physically active, live socially rich lives, cherish their families and enjoy mostly plant-based diets."

Po's explanations do nothing to capture or reduce the delight of that moment we witness in the lake, as iridescent structures condense around the elderly couple like cobwebs. Immersed in the structure of happiness and its complex entanglements with longevity, the moonlight moulds itself around them. The infectious joy from the exchange of their movements propels these filaments onwards, as a living web of bliss that couples them in a charmed conversation which never runs dry.

"Such webs are not abstract relations, between correspondents," says *Po*, "but the joining of souls, through an ethereal matrix that enables mutual flourishing."

The vitality of this couple's devotion is contagious. With each passing second their happiness web throbs, extends, explores and thickens around and through us all. Tendrils attach themselves on my safety suit. *Po*'s sturdy back is covered in luminescent climbing fibres that sway like anemones. Slowly, softly, we are immersed in a completely different quality of medium than we have never encountered before.

Filling the sky, their bliss seems to have completely captured the Moon. Together we become a coherent fine filamentous structure that tethers boat to lake to heavenly body. Ensnaring all the tiny fish in its net, the web enfolds *Po* and me within its agile substance. Now, we share the couple's deep pleasure in each other, hugging one and all, in a realm of endless delight.

- Themes
  - Contagious emotions
    - Happiness
  - "living web of bliss"
    → invisible ecology

Compulsion

Complaining under the weight of their own success, the urban beasts gaze out towards Venice and its waterways.

"No room," says Mestre.

"No room," replies Marghera.

Like unruly vegetation, their manufacturing plants, laboratories, condos and shopping centres climb the horizon and cast long shadows over each other. Hemmed in by their own clutter, their attention wanders to nearby spaces within and beyond the old city. They imagine gnawing on its old bones, taking its rich pickings, modernising its fabric and dumping their toxic effluents into its local waters.

"Why should we take our excrements all the way out to sea when the lagoon is so convenient?"

They begin to covet a more expansive existence within the lagoon, but the great whip of local authority regulations on the mainland does not allow buildings to go higher than fifteen stories.

"It's not fair."

Regulations make them impatient. So, they compete with each other around the shoreline trying to find ways around them. Marghera wriggles southwards towards the Isola delle Tresse and Mestre goes northeastwards in the direction of the Marco Polo airport.

"It's so noisy here," says Mestre.

But the coastline will not contain them for long. Mestre starts inching its condos towards the lagoon and I feel their filthy tread upon my shores.

Their footsteps make me anxious.

• Themes
 — Urban development
 — Protected areas

150

Po acts as an omniscient narrator; giving the readers and Po (human) historical information to put things in context

Toa

We see a youth fishing off a rock, with a line and hook, at the foot of Whakaari, or White Island.

"As long as human history can recall, this island has been in a near continuous stage of smoking. Certainly since James Cook discovered it in 1769," says *Po*. "Its ever-evolving landscape arises from the mineral ooze of constant volcanic activity where fumaroles, lava bombs, crystals, bubbling mud and a steaming acid lake lurk under ashen clouds."

"It seems almost alive," I say, observing that the youth is so absorbed in his work that he's not spotted us approaching.

"It certainly is," replies *Po*. "This active volcanic island sprawls from its base down into the sea where it becomes a teeming reef. Look ahead of you. Can you see the triplefins, seahorses, wrasse, flounder, mullet and piper flitting between the narrow alleys of the shallows? They dance with the rays of the sun now, but at night, they follow the Moon."

"What's over there?" I ask, pointing to a darker area at the edge of the reef, which is where the boy seems to be casting his line.

"That's where the sea drops off steeply. It marks the edge of the sanctuary of the reef and the start of the open ocean. No longer cradled by the sunlight-trapping coral, it is noticeably colder and provides access to all kinds of new opportunities as well as invasion by marauders. A different kind of ecosystem inhabits this space. Can you see the juvenile trevally, gemfish, terakihi and schools of silversides that nourish larger reef species such as jacks? If we're lucky, we might even see a female leatherback turtle passing on her way to ancestral breeding grounds where she'll lay her eggs."

"There's almost *too much* life here," I say, as tiny vibrations wriggle across my skin. "The water is simply throbbing with vitality. While our Venetian waters are rich with all kinds of life, the muddy brickwork and half-preserved woodpiles host a different intensity of ecosystem altogether."

"Venice benefits from being protected from the worst whims of the open sea by the lagoon," says *Po*. "While these aquamarine waters feel

151

homely, the sea floor quickly splits at the drop off into undersea crevasses that blend with the pitiless darkness of the Kermadec Trench. In those abyssal wildernesses, the giants of the sea lurk; yellowtail kingfish, marlin, manta rays, great white sharks, bass, bluenoses, makos and tuna. They glide through the depths like alien vessels."

The youth is pulling out strings of twisting silver slithers as if he is threading glass beads and as soon as he unhooks a fish he looks at it, seems to speak, and immediately returns it to the water.

"These sulphur plumes make everything taste of treachery," grumbles *Po*. "It's like being at the cusp of chemical activity before it became organic life. I don't like these bitter acids. They smack of the fragility of the world."

"Oh, I don't mind that eggy stench," I say. "In fact, I am getting used to its earthy pungency."

Since *Po* complains bitterly about the sulphur, I beach it on a section of shallow reef away from the volcanic vents, where it happily blows bubbles to freshen its vegetable palate.

The boy seems to have seen me and nods a greeting, so I climb my way over the rocks to sit next to him.

"I'm Po."

"Toa."

"Why are you throwing all the fish back?"

"I'm not fishing to eat. I'm catching fish to know their names."

"Surely you can look those up in a book?"

"Only their Western names. I am after their *true* names. The ones they give each other."

"They tell you that?"

"Of course. You just have to know how to ask and learn how to listen."

"Can you show me?"

"The secret is in making the hooks," he says, nodding. "You have to make them so they don't stop the fish speaking. I made all of these myself."

He shows me a line with multiple barbs. Some of them are inventively crafted from wood and iridescent paua shell.

"These rich materials are irresistible to curious surface feeders," he says. "I make the ends so they catch the fishes' lips. None of them are particularly sharp, so when I catch the fish and unhook them, they can tell me their name."

I study the line of geometries of twists and ornate curls like curtain hooks that catch on fishes' mouths for long enough for the boy to haul them out of the water.

"What kinds do you catch?" I ask.

"All sorts. Anchovies, pilchards, sprats, lancetfish, moonfish, red-finned opah, flying fishes, saury, dolphinfish, koheru, pilotfish, trevally, kingfish, greenback jack mackerel, slender jacks, wingfish, fanfish, kahawai, escolar, oilfish, wahoo and sometimes juvenile skipjack tuna. You know, the usual."

I shake my head in wonder at the variety.

"Are those their *true* names?"

"No," says Toa. "I can't tell you that and you wouldn't understand even if I did. Only the fish itself can choose to reveal its true name."

"Oh," I say, feeling ignorant. "Do you think you could catch one for me, so that I can ask myself."

"I'll try," says Toa. "But it's not my fault if the fish doesn't speak to you."

"Okay," I say, hopefully.

Toa throws his line out to the drop-off and we wait awhile. His whole person is intensely focused on the rod and line, as if it were part of himself. Around his neck a carved-bone fishing hook dances on a plaited leather thong around his neck.

After a while her tugs a little whitebait out with his line.

"What kind of fish is that?" I ask.

"Ask it," says Toa holding the wriggling fish up to my ear.

I recoil at its excessive motion.

"What's your name?" I ask, knowing that I can't speak fish.

The fish flaps more and I strain, listening for something, I'm not sure what. After a few long seconds, Toa throws the fish back in the water.

"Hey. It didn't speak yet," I protest.

"Yes, it did," he says. "You just didn't hear it."

"What did it say?"

"I can't tell you. You have to ask the fish yourself."

Deflated, I sit next to Toa as he casts his rod even further out than before and settles beside me, cross legged.

"Don't worry," he says. "Finding the true name of fish takes time. You'll get better if you practice."

I decide that I'm tired of naming fish that don't want to talk to me. I watch the carved hook around his neck flipping against his skin like a fish's tail, as he loses himself again in the field of vibrations traveling through his rod. It's more than a geometrically carved shard of bone but a creature, with an eye hole bored into the centre of a fish head. Its upwardly curved tail is a deadly pointed weapon while the scales are manifolds and fractal patterns. I follow fields of lines that become dots, which in turn are arranged into snaking constellations of fluid geometries that are organised into tinier lines, and so on. I can see right down into the squirming spaces of the subatomic world.

"Did you make it yourself," I ask.

Toa shakes his head. "No, she's a special work of genius made by an *iwi* elder. She's the hook of Maui."

"Who's that?"

Toa smiles, and fixes the rod against a rock.

"He's a demi-god. This is his magical weapon, which he carved from the jawbone of his sorcerer grandmother."

"What does it do?" I ask.

"Maui used this hook to haul a magnificent fish-land out of the sea one day, when he was fishing in a canoe with his brothers,"

"You mean he caught the whole island like a wild beast?" I ask, somewhat relieved that *Po* isn't hearing this.

Toa grinned.

"Biggest yet! Catch turned out to be *Aotearoa*. That's what we call the North Island of New Zealand. When he hauled her up she came complete with houses and birds."

"That sounds like an incredible struggle." I said half-remembering just how sick I'd been after getting caught up in a jellyfish bloom.

"Maui realised he'd done something special and went to pray to appease the gods, but while he was away his brothers argued over ownership of the fish-land. In the ensuing fight their weapons scarred its face."

"That's terrible."

"Not really. It's just the way it was. Those scars became Aotearoa's valleys and mountains, so everything came right."

"Are you a boy or a girl?" he asks.

I'm taken aback.

The prevailing wind changes direction bathing us in a plume of smoke.

"Boy."

I study his face to observe his reaction. I don't meet many strangers and he's the first to mention my gender. I am unexpectedly enchanted by his golden skin, almond shaped green eyes and smiling lips that also curl like fishhooks in many dimensions. They meet together in an arch at the top, kneel forwards into a pout, cup his lip at the bottom and turn up at the corners. There is salt on his breath.

"You don't look like a proper boy to me," he says.

I feel awkward. I want him to like me. I feel it matters what I say next. I stay silent.

"You remind me of Hine."

I shake my head to let him know I don't know what that is.

"She's something else!" he says. "The goddess of Death."

"Oh."

I really can't tell if I am being insulted, admired, or made fun of.

"She's even more powerful than Maui."

"How?"

"Maui decides to return home to the land of his parents after many adventures. One day, his father tells him that a portion of the fitting prayer was missed when he was baptised and he would be overcome one day by his great ancestress Hine-nui-te-po, the goddess of death. That's Hine's proper name. Descended from immortals, Maui doesn't like that his life ends like this, so he decides to take up the issue directly with Hine and sort out his immortality, once and for all. Accompanied by his faithful friend *te Piwakawaka*, the tiny fantail, they seek her out on the outer edge of one of the outermost Pacific islands, where she lives in a thatched hut, which is bejewelled by the rays of the setting sun. Being a goddess, she knows Maui is coming and waits for him at the horizon's edge, sparkling in a gown of light. Maui is greeted by her brilliant red eyes and is amazed. She has the body of a man and the stiletto sharp smile of a barracuda but, since he is determined to break her power, he is unafraid. Night falls and Hine falls asleep, so Maui carries out his plan and warns his companion not to wake the goddess as he breaks her spell, by performing an act of life that will counter her dark power.

"Do not laugh until I have gone through the body of this woman and come out again at her mouth," he tells *te Piwakawaka*.

On seeing the strange passage of Maui into the belly of Hine by turning himself into a worm, *te Piwakawaka* cannot help but laugh loudly, which promptly wakes the goddess. With terrible rage, she does what she knows best and slays Maui. So, through his failure, Maui lets death into the world for the whole of humankind."

"And I'm like *Hine*?" I say.

"Yeah, that's cool. She's epic."

I really don't know how to take this comment. Of course, I'm impressed that Toa likened someone he admired to me, but I am unsure if this is a good, or bad, thing. Being compared to death is hardly cause for celebration. I can't properly express my feelings, so I decide to tell him all about the business that my aunts and father have started in turning the ashes of the departed into living statues, which bring new life to the Venice lagoon.

He nods at me admiringly. All the while he pulls lines of silvery fish out of the water with his magical hooks, speaks with them and releases them again before they even realise they have gills. With every tug of the line he breaks the spell of death. I'm not sure if he hears anything I am saying but as soon as my mouth stops speaking, we stare at each other in silence, mutually enthralled.

I stand up, suddenly feeling quite at odds with myself.

I've forgotten *Po*.

I run across to the shallow reef, which is swallowed by sulphurous fumes and scorched by the pitiless sun. As Toa's sea green gaze follows me, I push my monster twin out into the warm waters and we disappear into the waves, leaving without so much as a backward glance.

Distortion

I'm out of sorts and there is nobody to talk to.

Jelena has taken responsibility for conducting a mosquito egg survey, which Kasia refuses to do, as she is busy in the kitchen. Ruzica is away conducting new business deals with the mainland funeral parlour and my father is nowhere to be seen.

I'm gathering driftwood that is scattered so widely over *Po*'s rock pools it's as if a forest had suddenly decided to shake itself down.

This is thirsty work, so I make my way to the kitchen. Just as I swing myself up on the deck, I catch a glimpse of my reflection in the porthole. My eyes are huge, my lips are bowed downwards and the top of my head is arched into a point.

I land on the deck with a thump.

"Oh darling, there you are. I need some help with plucking this sea mouse."

"Are we going to eat it?" I ask, wrinkling my nose at the flat, hairy worm about the size of my hand. Kasia's soaking it in a bowl of hot water in the kitchen sink to soften it.

"Of course not. I'm after the nanowires."

"You mean that creature conducts *electricity*, Aunty?"

"Just the bristles," she asserts. "They'll make our circuits more efficient."

"Which circuits?"

"The ones we use in solar panels."

As I steady the soft, rubbery flesh, Kasia uses the blade of Krists' razor to carefully remove the fine hairs along the sea mouse's side, which glisten like insect wings.

As she works, she scrapes the mud and mucus from the creature and tells me this is *Aphrodita aculeata*, and tells me it's named after the goddess of love because the creature looks like a woman's sexual organs.

I really don't want to hear about what female parts are *supposed* to look like, but I'm fascinated with what she's doing.

"Sea mice are particularly hard to find, as they like to live in sediment

157

more than two metres deep. This one was probably dragged up with fishing gear, or thrown on the shore by the same storm that brought the driftwood," she says.

It's a skilled task. Kasia arranges the bristles in a half scallop shell. After a while, I've got the gist of the process and my distorted fish face in the porthole intrudes upon my thoughts.

"Aunty," I ask before she makes the next carful harvest, "do I look like a fish?"

Kasia doesn't look up, "Of course not!"

She harvests another bundle of nanowires.

"Are you sure, Aunty?" I continue, trying to get her to look at me. "I saw my reflection in the porthole just now and I looked just like a barracuda fish. Someone said that's what I reminded them of."

"Did they, darling?" Kasia aligned the bristles with the others and paused. "That's an odd thing to say?"

I stay quiet.

"Well, not to worry," she reassures, "On *this* island, *nobody*'s looking at you."

School

Now that we have a regular income, my aunts are keen for me to have a proper education and learn several languages. They say it will help me make proper choices, so I can find my way in the world. My father is not so sure. He thinks educating me is a waste of hard-earned money.

"It is enough for him to learn a trade," he complains. "That boy's never going to be a fancy thinker."

Ruzica is offhand about my father's views.

"He's talking about himself," she says. "I'm interested in *your* education. Not his."

"We think the International School of Venice will be suitable for you," adds Kasia. "It upholds a policy of tolerance, open-mindedness and diversity."

"It will also be good for you to mix with children from Venice's Silicon Valley," says Jelena. "Their parents have grand aspirations for their futures. "

"Maybe some of that ambition will rub off on you too," says Kasia.

Caught between one guardian who expects very little of me and those who have unreasonably great expectations, I wonder whether there is a middle ground for simply learning more about the world.

There is only one way to find out whether this school can provide it.

PART IV
GROWING

Cesare

My new school is not in the old city, but Mestre.

It's a pain getting there, since it takes a couple of hours in total to commute, and I don't get to spend as much time with *Po* as when I was being homeschooled.

Every day I make my way across the lagoon by ferry from San Michele to the mainland by the hospital. Here, I wind my way overground through the twisted mediaeval streets and bridges, which is quicker and more interesting than continuing my journey to the Piazzale Roma by public transport, since the time taken for crowds of commuters and tourists to alight and embark is woefully unpredictable. Then I catch a bus to cross the Ponte della Libertà to Mestre, where it's a short walk from the mainland bus stop to the school. It's a low-level modern building, which feels like a boat with its simple weather boarded exterior, but the rooms are incredibly large and brightly coloured, with lots of books on the shelves. Unlike the *Fortune*, we are not all crammed together and there is plenty of space to read, or hang out.

Lessons start at quarter to nine and home time is at four in the afternoon. We study a national curriculum of Italian, English and a third language of our own choosing. We also take history, mathematics, physical education, drama, history, geography, science, art, music, technological education and information technology. In addition to all this, we go on to trips to the lagoon to study history and ecology, can opt for 'pet therapy' sessions, visit the theatre, or attend movie screenings.

Since places are competitive, I have to wait until the logistics are completed, so my schooling does not begin until I am nearly halfway through the first term. When I arrive, I am given the only empty seat in the classroom, next to a heavenly-smelling boy.

"Hello, I'm Po," I say as the bell for break is rung.

"Let's stick to formalities and use both our names to properly introduce ourselves," replies my classmate curtly. While he is not the tallest in the class, he somehow manages to look down his turned-up nose at me, even when I tower above him.

"Oh, okay. Good morning, I'm Po Anghelescu, but everyone calls me Po." I hold out my hand to shake his.

I'm already taken aback, but what happens next is bewildering. The boy seems at first to reach for my hand but raises it instead high above his head, as if he's about to throw a cartwheel. Then he puts his weight on the back foot and swings down moderately low with a sweeping gesture.

"Well, Po Anghelescu. If that *really* is your full name," he casts me a pointed glance, "*I* am Cesare Gallo descended from Chnoum-Hotep, the ancient Chief of Perfumes and Head of the Wardrobe to the pharaoh in the fifth dynasty who ruled Egypt around 2700 BCE. Of course, Chnoum-Hotep was so respected within the Egyptian Royalty that a statue in his likeness is buried right beside his pharaoh's mummy."

"That's impressive," I say, equally astonished by Cesare's detailed heritage and his theatricality.

"You should know," my classmate continues, "that my ancestors have all held high positions of responsibility. They were all very rich and extremely handsome."

After we return to our lessons I am constantly reminded of Cesare's noble descent from a royal perfumier, through the waves of overwhelming scents that emanate from his wrists and neck. I'm developing somewhat of a headache from his bouquet and hope that the pungency will fade a little. Yet Cesare dutifully tops up his scent from a range of colognes under his desk. Although I feel ill I do not complain, as I assume his need to impress me will subside without the need for further drama.

Drama is Cesare's forte. He is at his most eloquent and compelling when challenged.

"Gallo, how many times have I told you that a shaven head is not permitted by school regulations," says Miss Sapiente, our form teacher, "You can do that kind of thing when you're older."

"Madam, this cultural practice is central to my ancient Egyptian religious beliefs and also highlights the exquisite contours of my head."

Our teacher makes no further comment, as Cesare insists that his 'statuesque' anatomy is also in keeping with, what he describes as an ancestral 'tradition' of achondroplasia. Apparently, this deeply valued trait occurs when the soft bones allow for the development of an intellectual and dignified appearance.

I start to wish that my legs were not getting so long. My eyes are too large for my head. My mouth is too full and my skin too fair. My body is changing but I am completely unsure of the direction it is taking.

Since my anatomy will doubtlessly take time to sort itself out, I decide that school and the distractions that sitting next to Cesare involves will stop me brooding on my 'difference'. Besides, I am quietly impressed by Cesare's talent for collecting compliments and bestowing importance on even the most mundane detail of everyday life. He even makes our rather casual school uniform, with red tracksuit top white polo shirt and navy trousers, look as if a tailor personally fitted him out for an important occasion.

While other classmates seem to find him annoying, I enjoy sitting next to Cesare, as there is never a dull moment in the day.

In some ways, it's like being with *Po*.

Composites

Davide takes the *Exitec* boat to survey for himself the reported 'hotspots' where genetically modified mosquito larvae are thriving. In general, the findings have been extremely favourable, so it's important that the exact circumstances are understood for the flourishing of these precious flies.

Drawing close to *Po*'s shoreline, he realises that the shores of San Michel are far more extensive than he remembers and the developing beach is now over five hundred metres long and nearly a hundred across. While it's not an attractive place, it certainly looks like a paradise for wildlife with its giant knots of vegetable matter, silts, sea-ground bricks, and plastic fragments. The seaweed fronds that tether the shore to the cemetery wall offer sweet sites of decomposition, supporting a flourishing diverse ecosystem of beach hoppers, sandflies, kelp flies, red mites, beach pillbugs, blood worms, sand crabs and beetles. All these ecosystems seem to be connected in some way to a central structure, shaped like a giant spine that stretches out into the lagoon.

Davide identifies a large breeding pool and scoops up a colony of tiny mutant larvae, transferring them into a screw top container.

"We've been taking good care of them," says Jelena. "We've moved them to larger, flatter and more stable pools than used for the original inoculation sites."

"Fantastic work," says Davide extending his hand in greeting. "Was it you who sent the excellent progress report?"

Jelena shakes his hand firmly.

"Yes. I'm assuming you're the guy my sister Kasia spoke of. You came here a while ago now."

Davide nods.

"I remember. You look a little like her. She was with a child."

"Our nephew, Po."

"This is an amazing place, you know," says Davide. "This island is the perfect nursery for the various strains of flies that we're developing at *Exitec*, where we can see both sides of the Darwinian equation at work in a field setting."

[handwritten marginal note: Davide recognizing Po]

"How do you mean?"

"Well, Charles Darwin was interested in the relationship between the heritable characteristics of a creature and its environment. We know the genetic load these creatures are carrying because we've designed their traits and, on this beach, we can see just how the favourable environment helps them to flourish. In the long term, this place will be an incredible stageset for evolution."

Jelena, who has developed a taste for business through our entrepreneurial relationship with death, is now curious about how that might be applied to life. She asks Davide probing questions about how the creatures are designed, what their life expectancy is and how they will affect the lagoon biodiversity. Davide is only too happy to answer and says when he doesn't know something. He likes her bold curiosity, confidence and open mind.

"What are you and your folk doing out here?" he asks.

"We're setting up a sustainable and profitable business so we earn a place in broader society," says Jelena pointing to the *Fortune*, the statues and the lagoon.

"That's what I'm doing too!"

Jelena describes a range of opportunities they've explored from recycling plastics from the sea to using compost to power a hot water system. Davide starts to link biochemical details with some of these processes, as a way of exploring the potential for making new technologies. Soon, they're discussing how algae might be grown along the shore to trap invisible microplastics in the waters, which cannot currently be reclaimed by netting or beachcombing.

"We could permanently remove particles from the lagoon food chain," says Davide, "by encouraging microbes to attach to toxic sediments and form a biofilm structure that works at a large scale."

"Could we also destroy the plastic fragments? wonders Jelena, thinking of the liquid hearts that Kasia and Ruzica have been designing for the statues.

"It depends what kind of product you want from this process – something that destroys the plastic, or something that becomes strong enough to use as a new material," says Davide, "With your permission, I have another idea."

"I'd love to hear it," says Jelena.

"I think my employer, *Exitec*, would seriously consider investing in a range of organisms that could 'eat' plastics or 'transform' them into useful new materials. They have already begun research into a range of naturally occurring species for environmental remediation like fungi strains – *Schizophyllum commune* and *Pleurotus ostreatus* and bacterial species like *Ideonella sakaiensis*. If they can be combined with the complex communities that make up a biofilm, then potentially, step-changes in material performance are possible. From a broad commercial perspective, as well as an environmental one, this is an incredibly important issue."

"But all your work is done in the laboratory, right?"

"No. *Exitec* have a civic commitment. That's why I'm out here. We are looking for exploitable opportunities in the longer term that will benefit the Venice lagoon. Your family, for example, have an incredibly rich first-hand experience of working with … let's call it the *technology of nature*. Combined with biotechnological advances, there's a real chance of making significant breakthroughs in environmental engineering."

Their discussion moves to how it may be possible to design large scale processes that could safeguard the environmental health of the region. As they consider how San Michele could act as a prototyping site, a figure starts walking towards them from the far side of the shore.

"Who's that waving?"

"That's Ruzica. I've got to go, she'll be needing my help," says Jelena and then pauses. "I do hope you won't stay away long. I'd like to continue this conversation another time, maybe."

"I know where to find you," says Davide and, despite himself, winks as Jelena runs off with a brisk wave.

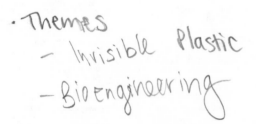

Dancing on Water

I'm waiting at the ferry stop as a knot of debris bobs around a wooden post. All the while it is spinning, it draws matter into its watery heart.

It's getting late and the mirror lights of the lagoon are already twinkling, yet this dogged embryonic clump of unloved matter refuses to disappear, even as the darkness rises.

Energised with the promise of new land, it speaks to me of glittering sequins, islands upon waves, slippery oil slicks, laser flashes, organic bridges that ferry tiny bodies across the water like steppingstones, grimy foam patches sucking at shores and the flourishing of life forms that are yet to be contrived.

Electro Mangroves

"These mangrove swamps taste strange," says *Po* under a glittering bower that drags its branches into slow-flowing muddy water.

"I love this entanglement of trees, LEDs and electronic circuits, but I don't understand how all this electricity can exist amidst this wetness."

"The electricity of life is wet," says *Po*, "It's tickling me. Everywhere. It's better than goosebumps."

"How did this Mumbai slum area develop?" I wonder.

"It was an inevitable side effect of the mutual flourishing, of communities that learned to coexist. This whole place was originally home to a Koli fishing community that was deprived of their hunting grounds around the late nineteenth century, when the mangrove swamps were cleared and filled in with coconut leaves, rotten fish, and human waste from the swelling city." *Po* is bubbling vigorously and seems to be enjoying itself. "This change in environment brought new residents and trades into the area. The Kumbhars came from Gujarat to establish a potters' colony. Tamils arrived from the south to open tanneries. Thousands more travelled from Uttar Pradesh to work in the booming textile industry. But rather than compete for economic dominance, the different peoples found ways of surviving and working together. By the third millennium, the slum had become the most diverse and vibrant neighbourhood in Mumbai."

"So, what produces all the electricity?"

Po squirts a long plume of water into the air, like a fountain.

"Did you see *that?*" it asks.

I nod, waiting for it to be less excitable.

"The whole place is studded with a very simple organic battery system called a 'microbial fuel cell', which is organised into two chambers – positive and negative – that are divided by a ceramic membrane. This is the heart of the cell, which also promotes the growth of natural biofilms. The microbes that settle in the negative chamber can produce electricity, as well as removing contaminants and freshening the water," bubbles my monster twin, delightedly. "Since each fuel cell is very small and produces only a tiny amount of power, the batteries are networked in massive arrays, which are safely floated on ingenious platforms fashioned from local materials, such as recycled plastic bottles."

I notice the dirty rafts supporting the ceramic structures, which are skilfully tied together with natural rope. Some of them must have been around quite some time as they have acquired a unique microecology, which in most cases consists largely of algae, shellfish and shrimp. There are fish fry everywhere.

"*Po*, why are there little trees on these floats?"

"Oh, they're mangrove saplings. For now, they're just hitching a ride. As they grow up, they swallow the electronic circuitry into their trunks and branches."

I am starting to feel seasick, as we're starting to dip and bob a little. I grip *Po*'s spine hard to steady myself.

"*Po*, can you just slow down, you're making the water choppy."

"I am going slowly," it protests, "too slowly." It starts to speed up, so I shut my eyes to quell the nausea. *Po* seems happier.

"Eventually," it says with a demonstrative swerve around a tree root which firmly holds my attention, "the trees become too heavy to float and take root in the water. As the glade flourishes, a natural dam is formed that produces enough electricity to power all kinds of electronic devices. They don't last forever though. Eventually, the ceramics crumble away, the cells wear out and the detritus is assimilated back into the sediment cycle, becoming part of the mangrove nutrient ecosystem."

"Who controls the electrical operations?"

Po giggles.

"You're funny," it says. "The trees do, of course."

This place is even stranger than I imagined it would be. The air is heavy with rot and spicy ionic charges. This ecosystem is so dense that the water is trembling. It seems to be watching us.

Po continues to act oddly and occasionally seems agitated.

We move slowly, irregularly and somewhat warily, staying low in the water as we pass through an area of the slums that is hung with the ominous kind of atmosphere that lingers before a thunderstorm breaks. I sweep floating vines aside. Sometimes, they're cables.

"*Po*, are mangroves conscious?"

"Of course! They are a collective made up of a whole variety of trees and shrubs that have adapted to life in a saltwater environment. Their vegetation grows thickly, like forests and their roots are so densely tangled that they stand on banks of woody stilts above the water. Just look! They're stood tall as if on ballet points!" *Po* produces another long stream of bubbles.

"Stop playing around!" I say. "We could be in a tricky situation here. They're trying to stop us passing with their big twisted roots."

"They're *meant* to impede the flow of water and other things," gurgles *Po*. "That way they can accumulate rich sediments in oxygen-poor areas. Look at all these beautiful knots in the prop roots, tangled with fallen trees, which span channels and in their tangles weave lattices of vegetation, which provide homes for all kinds of wildlife. Mmmmmm. *Tasty.*"

"They do smell funny. Are you okay *Po*?"

My island twin is wobbling more than before, frequently colliding with roots and generally making hard work of the terrain.

"Oh, the metabolisms are incredibly powerful here."

It starts giggling again.

"It's producing pungent substances like natural gas and hydrogen sulphide."

"I know you hate that sulphur smell!" I say. "Although everything smells of rotten eggs here, it's a different kind of rotten than the stench of volcanoes. It's much richer and heavier."

"Oh, *lovely* mangroves," sings *Po*, "paradox of food and prey."

"What *are* you talking about?"

Po is rambling and I'm finding it hard to follow, or more importantly, stay afloat.

"In this site alone, hundreds of thousands of small invertebrates burrow away underneath us in their sheltered soils, feeding on algae and detritus. Many release their eggs and larvae into the water column during flooding tides, providing a rich source of food for fish and other planktivores. Together, mangroves stabilise the coastline, reduce erosion and provide habitats for many kinds of wildlife including fiddler crabs, scats, milk fish, mudskippers, mullets, cat fish, perches, water monitor lizards, dugongs, otters, marsh crocodiles, crab-eating macaques, sea turtles, kingfishers, herons, storks, sea eagles, kites, sand pipers, curlews, ducks, royal Bengal tigers and flamingos."

I try to concentrate on the images its producing but they're pressured, stuttering and intense, like watching an old movie.

"*Po*, we've already passed this tree. It's the same one we came across only a little while ago."

"Is it? It's so hard to find the way around this place," it says. "There are just too many rich scents and tastes. It's all so distracting. I'm really not quite myself. Tickle my belly." It says.

"Just hold steady, *Po*. You're intoxicated."

"Mmmm, this gustatory swamp feels thick and rich."

"I'm going to see if I can steer us out of here."

"I can hear the mangroves' secrets: that *life is the means by which the environment understands itself.*"

"*Po*, are you hallucinating?"

"When I was a little knot of seaweed ..."

It starts to sing again.

"*Po*, concentrate."

"It's even richer the deeper we go ... But, gosh, it's wonderful!"

Nonsensical babbling follows, laced with bubbles. Perhaps *Po* thinks its breathing. I try to concentrate on where we're going.

The density of vegetation thins. We have reached the heart of the mangrove village with its proliferating microbial fuel cell rafts that are fashioned into walkways. The multi-coloured LED network starts to wake up, bringing another dimension of complexity to this enchanting space. But this is not an exclusively human project. Crabs, slugs and worms feed on the detritus from the village. As they dig burrows, relentlessly churning the sediments into fertile ground, they oxygenate the water without destroying the essential metabolic web of anaerobic decomposition that supplies the electrons that are drawn off by the organic batteries. The whole ecosystem possesses a metabolic rhythm that spontaneously powers up the electronic circuits woven into the space and provides light for an evening market.

Po is wobbling and spinning and I'm afraid my twin will tip over and take me under with it.

"Let's rest awhile beside this giant tree," I say, as I grip its thick roots to steady my monster twin.

I look up into the canopy of the titan, which stands among an army of bobbing saplings. Its roots buckle down into the pitiless darkness of the swamp and its branches thrust upwards into the star-studded sky.

"Heaven," Says *Po*.

I observe bustling shoppers, draped in brightly coloured textiles, enjoying local delicacies, purchasing finely crafted goods, buying cloths made from composts, consuming sugar-sweet roast insect kebabs and marvelling at fire baton juggling street performers. As the lights cyclically brighten and dim responding to the metabolic activity, *Po* starts to acclimatise to the strange-tasting ecosystem.

"Maybe we can bring a sapling back to Venice," I muse. "Our sewage system is incomplete, so perhaps these salt-tolerant trees could take root in the lagoon. We could use mangrove saplings back to keep our living statues company. I can just imagine Ruzica announcing the new service — *your dear departed will become reefs and trees.*"

Po giggles.

"Come on, *Po*, it's time to go," I sigh. "Focus on my voice, and we'll make it."

- Themes

   — cooperation
   — what "life" is according to Po (the bioregion)

Titrating Corsetry

Dawdling on my way back from the Piazzale Roma to the Sant'Alvise ferry to San Michele, I find myself drawn into the city's strange spaces.

The buildings that frame the Ramo Cardellina are shrouded in structural corsetry and are undergoing extensive remoulding. In search of adventure, I duck into this narrow alleyway and observe the struts and straps which are squeezing the brickwork into odd shapes. I touch one of the fittings, trying to figure out how the whole thing stays together.

"Hey, boy! What are you doing there?"

A couple of workmen are clearing masonry into a barge at the end of the *calle*.

"I'm looking at all these things that are stuck in the brickwork, sir. I've never seen anything like it."

The workman laughs.

"You're telling me that you've never seen a ten-year fitted cycle of sculpted brickwork in action?

I shake my head.

"Hey, Pagolo," he shouts. "This boy doesn't know what building surgeons do!"

"Eh, Vanni?"

A man in blue overalls alights from his barge and wipes brick dust over his hair to clean his hands. He slaps my back in greeting.

"Your name, son." He asks.

"Po."

"Well, Pio," he says. "In this place, the language of teeth meets hips and busts. We mould the shape and structure of building to change their function and appearance. While we may just look like everyday workmen to you, in fact we're specialists in the practice of applied formwork – or, what you might prefer to call – *building surgeons*. Vanni, let's get out the flask and bring three cups. We'll make a proper break of this!"

Vanni smiles and returns with three tiny containers, into which he pours black coffee. Together we knock the bitter brew back in a single slug. I hate the stuff, but I'm smiling.

"So, Pio. Down to the basics. You're looking at 'smart' masonry. It's an advanced technique where, instead of tearing buildings down when they're no longer fit for purpose, we mould what's left standing into new forms. All these contraptions you see along here are designed to deal with wear and tear in different ways."

"What wears them down?" I ask.

"Mostly the elements – the water, wind, sun, diesel fumes and salt from the lagoon. Nature's particularly hard on buildings. She grinds down our bricks to powder and continually gnaws out new spaces."

"Is building surgery a Venetian tradition?"

"Good question, Pio. In some ways, yes. Venice has always recycled its building materials, but in other ways, no. What we do here involves an entirely new skill and technology," says Pagolo. "We have a degree of control over this process that was previously unthinkable."

"Think of it as the 'art of constructive bone-breaking and re-shaping' for buildings," adds Vanni.

I wince.

"They're not *human* bones, but the structural elements of houses, and alleyways," he adds reassuringly.

"At one time, it may have been enough to simply insert steel pins and plates to stop brickwork from sagging in Venice," continues Pagolo, "but nowadays, the kind of manoeuvres needed to shape dynamic masonry requires a knowledge of cosmetic and plastic surgery. When we combine them, we discover new ways of making windows, walls and doors. With this technique, we can make structures appear just by squeezing out new spaces."

"I think I see what you're saying. This whole alleyway looks like twisted dough," I say.

"Of course," laughs Pagolo. "Who wants a building with straight lines? Come on. We'll show you *exactly* what we're talking about." He beckons me further into the alleyway until we're standing on the mooring steps.

"Take a look at these building elements at the canalside end of this building," he says, straining his neck around the corner. "They're beginning to soften a little too much, so they need 'tightlacing'. Get in a little closer to them. We won't let you fall in."

Tentatively I lean out over the canal.

"The brickwork is all loose and bulging," I observe.

"Tightlacing, which is an extreme kind of structural corsetry, will fix all of that," says Pagolo.

"But it's got to be practiced with caution," adds Vanni, "and needs a lick of mortar, or it will cause structural fractures in the upper building levels."

"See that masonry spur jutting out at the first-floor level? You can tell that it wants to form a bridge with its neighbour across the alleyway. We're encouraging it to do so using a series of ceramic pontics that are strapped to their abutments."

"But there's shoddy work going on, too," says Vanni. "See the plaster of Paris soaked bandages that are wrapped around the protrusion, as if they were structural plaster casts? They're actually performing a purely cosmetic role. We'll have to sort that out with some pins and plates before we're done in this area."

"Over here," says Pagolo, "can you see there's another set of wraps? They're using knitted fiberglass bandages that are soaked with polyurethane. And this, right here, is another cheap repair patch using thermoplastic bandages."

"Shocking stuff," says Vanni, hissing between his teeth. "Someone's been trying to disguise unbridgeable defects. This is irresponsible workmanship. It's prematurely compressing the emerging building spaces into less than optimal configurations."

The whole *calle* appears to be coming alive, heaving, breathing, bending and creaking from the ongoing processes of repair.

"Many of the tension bands that are bracing these spaces are attached to compressive formwork along the waterway," adds Pagolo. "You'll see they're rusting extensively."

"Some of the elements are even removable," adds Vanni. "They simply click onto wall hooks and existing arch wires. Over there, someone's made inventive use of titanium coil springs which are narrowing the space at the first-floor level, and pinching out a tapestry of basic window types. At a guess, I'd say they're trying to network these structures into a balcony."

"Can you see that structure further down, at eye level?" asks Pagolo. "*That* corseting is far more promising. It's an Austrian Belt, made from a steel band about two inches in width with turn screws. It encircles the brickwork by passing through the entranceway and window. It is elegantly pinching out that oval space that has been isolated by a latex dam. I suspect they're trying to locally control *risalta salina*, the wicking of salty water into the bricks. The final structure could potentially support a beam, or become conjoined to produce a shared living space."

"This one's my absolute favourite," says Vanni. "Can you see how that busk at knee level is slotted into braced scaffolding? It holds the canalside frontage up and is drop-dead gorgeous when you take the traditional waterway approach into the building."

"Its neighbour, on the other side of the alleyway, however," adds Pagolo, "is using a wireframe bustle, which is a different kind of structural system for tackling the bulging brickwork. Can you see they've done a 'Devonshire', where two courses of brickwork have been removed to emphasise the swelling, but they've got their curves all wrong? As I mentioned, there is a lot of generally shoddy work in this *calle*, which is all about appearances."

"Hey, son," says Vanni. "We've done a lot of talking. You see, you've got us on our favourite subject, but you look like a smart boy, so why don't *you* read these buildings for us."

"Well, I don't know ... You're the *experts*."

"Come on, Pio," goads Pagolo. "You're not going to do worse than those who've butchered the existing masonry already."

"Okay," I say, drawing in a deep breath. 'Over there, under the external vines of uncovered cabling there's a structure ...'"

"A divorce corset..." interrupts Vanni.

"A *divorce corset* that is lifting and separating a crack in the masonry. It also looks like someone has applied interior braces, which are sitting on the inside of the brickwork and are connected to the outside by a series of wires."

"Tension wires," says Vanni.

I nod.

"What do you think they're used for?" asks Pagolo.

"I... think... someone wants to put a beam inside. Maybe they're trying to make a bridge between the buildings."

"Hmm," says Vanni. "I can't see a reinforcing underbusk, so it's hard to say for sure. But that whole framework is disjointed and it's hard to figure out the logic of the space."

"Besides, it's early days yet in the development of that particular scaffolding," adds Pagolo. "And it's actually difficult to tell exactly what outcome is intended. Whatever else happens, that whole framework is going to make some rather attractive curves."

"Good job, son," says Vanni. "We'll make a building surgeon of you yet."

I'm impressed with myself and realise that I haven't asked Vanni and Pagolo what they're working on.

"That's a good question, son," says Pagolo. "We're here to sort out this prospective overhead bridge, which is showing signs of instability in the original brickwork. It's going to need retainers rather than the typical placement of spacers, so we'll have to couple those with a number of compressors if we're going to make a stable foundation for the bridge."

"But there's a complication," says Vanni. "The ceramics here are so old that the brickwork is osteoporotic and crumbling from the inside. Urgent structural reinforcement injections will be needed before the budding first floor spaces can be safely extruded."

I don't know exactly what I've added to their day but the building surgeons slap me on the back in excellent spirits and raise their hands in farewell.

As I make my way to the Sant'Alvise vaporetto stop, I begin to dream about bending and warping the spaces around me.

Meandering.

Reading the surfaces and details of masonry like evolving soils.

Every building I pass is suddenly unfurling with life, and generating new spaces for vigorous structural activity. The metamorphic terrains and carnivorous passageways of the city seem to constantly swallow and regurgitate its own spaces.

As the boat pulls in, the sun has already set too low to spend proper time with *Po*. Nowadays, I always seem out of time for being with my monster twin. But in those moments when we're properly together, we relish our extraordinary adventures.

• Themes

– "Invisible Ecologies" with regard to re-shaping buildings

179

Iceberg

"Ice beasts, like this one, are 'calved' into existence after prolonged gestations that can last a millennium," says *Po*.

"She's massive!"

"Ah, she's only a little one. These glacier offspring are made of layers of glacial snowfall, which are compacted into dense chunks of ice. They can reach more than eighty kilometres in length. Once they're formed in the river of viscous fluid, they glide steadily seaward moving at a pace of around seven kilometres a year. Yet, they're not discrete bodies until they're born into the sea."

"How does that happen?"

"Cracks form in this geological ectoplasm, which are loosened into shards by meltwater, fresh snow and Arctic tides. Soon, the ice calves start to individuate and are eventually birthed in chunks into the sea alongside their kin. Each is a fully formed iceberg, with the power to give and take life."

We've stopped at a safe distance from the ice beast.

She breathes in quiet synchrony with the Newfoundland waves, her sheer craggy ridges supporting the charcoal sky, while a glimmering sphere constantly spins in one of the island's melt pools.

"What's that, *Po*? Can we draw nearer?"

Tentatively, we pull alongside her. *Po* arches its spine so that I can see clearly inside the orb.

"There's someone here!"

Po tastes the sea and licks the beast with a long frond of ice-crusted algae, for more information.

"The volatiles that are most helpful are frozen. However, I know she's an explorer, who is spending an entire year sealed within an indestructible survival capsule."

"Why?"

"The whole thing is built by an aeronautical company, which specialises in tsunami-proof escape pods. It's a kind of sponsorship deal. The frame is made from aircraft-grade aluminium, with an inner structure that is mounted on a field of roller balls, so the orb can rotate while the explorer remains upright at all times."

"What's she doing?"

"She's running to make kinetic energy, which is stored in a heavy battery that provides a counterweight to the system. When she's tired, she reads online texts, poetry and academic papers. The whole encounter is broadcast live to the world."

"Do you think the explorer will make it to the end of her expedition, *Po*?"

"It's hard to say. Ice calves are deceptively active beings. Superficially, they appear to be just an inert block floating in barren waters, but they are metabolically active bodies despite their core temperature being somewhere between minus fifteen to twenty Celsius. Even in the icy sea they are constantly melting, producing flows of freshwater around them, which create a surface circulation that radiates outwards to several kilometres beyond their mass. These thermal currents are home to billions of krill, tiny shrimp-like creatures, which provide food for jellyfish and siphonophores. Snow petrels also nest on the ice cliffs to prey on these spineless ecosystems. They dive for furtive ice fish, which shelter in ice holes to avoid observation by omnivigilant predatory eyes."

"She sounds incredibly fertile," I say.

"She is, indeed, but she also has a dark side. This ice calf can just as quickly destroy anything that's near her. She's an unpredictable shape shifter, capable of transforming from megalith to monster. She can block the migration paths of Emperor penguins and excoriate large sections of the sea floor, leaving the area almost lifeless. We need to be very careful of her moods, dear twin. At any moment, this temperamental creature might flip."

"Let's keep our distance, then," I say. "But, first *Po*, can you lift me right up so I can see her better?"

Po flexes its spine like a whip and lifts me high over her aquamarine pools, which hug her excoriated surface with cool luminence. I'm a little concerned for the woman, as the ice calf releases compressed air bubbles in greeting and I think she must have seen us."

"Thank you, *Po*. I think it's time to go again."

As we return, I'm haunted by the ice calf's colossal strangeness. Like *Po*, she is testimony that unexplained modes of being exist within our

181

familiar diurnal rhythms. The more of *Po*'s kin I meet – whether manmade islands or swamps with electrical pulses – the more I identify with these extraordinary beings that cannot be taken for granted and are living monuments to Nature's feral ancient legacy.

Seemingly oblivious to the ice calf's inconstant fickleness, the woman in the indestructible sphere continues to spin.

- Themes
  – Po's kin (sentient ice burg)

Decaying Time

Nobody wants to hear the clock mechanism
That is started when an organic body falls to
The lagoon floor: a rat, a fish, a pigeon, a gull,
A child, a man. Manna for scant microbial
Biofilms, their silent mechanisms, not cogs,
Or springs, or gears, no winder, or hands to
Wipe geometric faces. No number to count,
Or faces to circumnavigate. The necrobiome,
A tragic instrument fuelled by the rhythms of
Microscopic creatures, keeps time through the
Variations in form and chemistry that denote
Specific generations. Through their indulgences
And iterations, organic matter is exchanged to
Perpetuate a condition of flourishing in decay.

At first, the dead are strange slow knots of
Fats and proteins, keeping unlikely company
With stringy sugars, typical of vegetable matter:
Seaweeds, algae, phytoplankton, grasses and
Rotten long lank dwindling brown fronds
Of unrecognizable fibres that choke and dim
The light for the dedicated gourmet coterie of
Sulphide-oxidizing bacteria, placozoa, echiura,
Bryozoans, brachiopods, loricifera, shrimp,
Crabs, octopuses and eels in their finest attire,
Which succumb to the exquisite lure of nutrient
Paths and spread of delectable witches' oils
Leaking into the slimy tide's corrugated floor.

In the orgy that follows the meal – I am there in
The decadence of death. We drown in ineffable
Blue, glossy, green and velvet black excretions.
We snuff homeopathic concentrations of heady

Fluids that precipitate mineral complexes and
Nanoscale peculiarities through long- range
Entanglements that oscillate with Circadian
Precision under a bloody sunset and green
Flash of fire. Tasted through blackened lips,
The sun melts our flesh, boils the water and
Draws us down into the irresistible rotting
Sea. We change lovers at every pause in the
Composting process, where no coupling is
Taboo, within decay's delirious masquerade.

With metabolic death fires aglow, all putrefaction
Under thick clouds of tarry organics, frenzied sea
Devils are whipped up under the sulking Moon's
Treacherous tides. New soils spew onto the shore
In cyclical sediments, as foundations of new lands.
Having consumed the feast, these gluttons begin
To fight over scraps, chasing scattered morsels,
Chewing on the most inedible substances then
Gnawing on each other, following their impulses to
Their very end. In turn, they become the side dishes
For the next course of edible ecologies, thick with
Carbon, nitrogen, hydrogen, oxygen, phosphorous
And sulphur, they enrich the sea broth in pulsed
Waves, which carry the death-sown seeds of life.

• Themes

   - Life coming from death

   - Circle of Life

Vanishing

Po and I watch a robber crab effortlessly crack open a coconut on the shore of Nikumaroro, or Gardener Island, an atoll in the Pacific. Weighing about three kilos and spanning a metre the creature makes surgical incisions in the fibrous outer shell with its hand-sized claws. Then it shatters the inner nut with great dexterity.

"I want to go closer."

"I'm not sure that's a good idea," says *Po*. "Charles Darwin described these beasts as 'monstrous' when he came across them on Keeling Island during his 1836 voyage on the Beagle."

"*We're* monsters too, right?"

"Monster is not the same as *monstrous*," cautions my twin, "you need to take care."

The crab pauses as I approach and scans me through stalked red eyes, then continues to dissect its meal. I look up to see where the coconut may have fallen from, and notice a cluster of the crabs climbing a large palm tree, like a troupe of robot monkeys. They tear through vegetation as if it is butter, leaving no trace of even the most enduring objects – such as coconut shells.

"Perhaps we should bring some of them back to the *Fortune*," I say. "They could do a good clean-up beach job and erase our footprints."

Kasia says that humanity's 'footprints' are how the world marks people's impact. What we leave on the ground is a physical record of how we change a place. These traces may be depressions caused by our footwear when we explore new terrains like the Moon, or stand on uninhabited land, but if they stay long enough they may turn to stone. She says that ecological footprints have nothing to do with our feet but are a measure of how much carbon we use, which is the ash of the living world. Industrial machines spit out nature as carbon, which can also take the form of tasteless, invisible gases like carbon dioxide. Although people are constantly changing their surroundings, the forces of nature are simultaneously erasing the traces of our existence too, actively remaking the conditions for survival. Creatures such as these crabs are an intensification of this process. They are nature's own cleaners – dedicated to deleting footprints.

The robber crabs are the biggest crustaceans I have ever seen.

The red-eyed beast looks at me a little too long. Limbs clatter in the coconut tree and without even looking up, I run back to *Po*.

"Let's go."

Po stays silent for a while then says, "Big things have gone missing around here, you know."

"Like what?"

"Amelia Earhart's plane, the *Electra*, for example, disappeared somewhere around Howland Island on the second of July, 1937. While radio signals from her plane should have been received by USCG *Itasca*, a United States Coast Guard ship that was stationed at Howland Island to support her flight, they failed to communicate properly, resulting in Earhart's tragic blind flight. Since then, a range of theories have been proposed that attempt to explain how one of the nation's most cherished celebrities simply vanished on her historic bid to circumnavigate the world."

"What do they say?"

"One popular idea is that she crash-landed here on Nikumaroro, which was within her flying range when she first radioed a distress call. Although she was running low on fuel, she could have made it to the atoll where the sand is smooth, flat and dries out at low tide. It would certainly have been a suitable to land a plane on."

"Was there evidence?"

"It's circumstantial," says *Po*. "A range of indigestible objects were found, which are not typical of the area, supporting the idea that she initially survived the accident.

"What kind of things?"

"Oh, a rubber shoe, an ointment bottle, sextant and even a piece of aluminium known as artefact 2-2-V-1 that patched her modified twin-engine Lockheed Electra 10E aircraft."

"Did they find her body?"

"Her partial skeleton was most likely found in 1940, by Gerald Gallagher, a British colonial officer who, thinking there was a small chance the remains could be Earhart's, sent them to Fiji for examination. However, the findings concluded they belonged to a man and the bones were subsequently lost. A more recent analysis of the documented measurements was made by Richard Jantz in 2018, a former professor of Forensic Anthropology at the University of Tennessee at Knoxville. Using a computer program, he estimated the sex, ancestry and stature of the bones based on the Fijian measurements, which were checked against information from her seamstress and were found to accurately matched Earhart's. It is likely that she died a castaway on an uninhabited island, in oppressive summer heat, and may well have been injured from the crash-landing. As for the partial findings, forensic anthropologists suggest that robber crabs, which are capable of destroying a pig's carcass, could have broken down her remains."

"I certainly believe *that* theory," I say.

"But the existence of robber crabs is not enough for some sceptics. There is recent photographic evidence that she may have been captured and died a Japanese prisoner of war. Others support the 'Crashed and Sank' theory where they suppose the *Electra* never reached land, and Earhart's body came to rest at the bottom of the Pacific Ocean. Here, her corpse would be assimilated by a different ecosystem of scavenging animal species, with equally voracious metabolisms and footprint-deleting capacities as those robber crabs."

"What kind of creatures?"

"Lobsters, sea cucumbers, sleeper sharks, mytilid bivalves, hag-fish, rat-tails, sea slugs, mussels, gastropods, harpacticoid copepods, polychaetes, sipunculans and multitudes of microorganisms. They are the ocean's entrails and are active enough to completely dismantle a whale carcass, let alone a human body, into little more than nutrient systems for rich new ecologies."

"But people don't just disappear, do they? Perhaps the technology to find her wasn't that sophisticated back then?"

"It's true that radio technology was lagging behind advances in aviation, but there are more recent incidents, like the Malaysia Airlines flight MH370 in 2015 which also vanished on its route from Kuala Lumpur to Beijing without a trace. Suddenly deviating from its planned route, the plane landed somewhere in the southern Indian Ocean. Its disappearance is controversial, as experts in the Netherlands and Australia implicate Russian involvement, claiming the passenger plane was shot down by a missile as it flew over what was essentially a war zone."

"Something *that* big and shiny can't just disappear."

"On the contrary, that is exactly the case. Even having established a cause so that events can be traced within a network of surveillance and communications systems, most of the plane is still missing."

"They couldn't have looked for it properly, then."

"Of course they did! An extensive international search for evidence in the southern Indian Ocean was conducted. More than twenty pieces of possible debris turned up on the African coast and islands in the Indian Ocean, but only a handful were confirmed as belonging to the doomed plane. Most notably, the valuable black box that recorded MH370's last movements was never found."

"A plane doesn't vanish."

"People place a lot of importance on the power of technology, yet they wield it with an imperfect command. Machines are very visible and, as your aunt observes, they leave a clear mark in scarring the face, heart, breath and bowels of this planet. However, machines cannot deal with unexpected circumstances. Even the most advanced technologies are clumsy when compared with the workings of the natural realm. Whatever theory accounts for the loss of Earhart and the MH370 passengers, they have not simply vanished into nothingness. People rely too much on logical causality as a way of talking about our enchanted world. At the heart of this magic is the World Wide Web of metabolic processes that underpin the workings of ecosystems, wielding their invisible powers in full view. Metabolisms are powerful transformers. They can make things – even as big as an island – disappear. All bodies and civilizations are re-assimilated into ecosystems to become part of many different kinds of living things like plankton populations, particle of sands, fish shoals, sharks, eels, gulls, mineral cycles and the bellies of coconut crabs."

"So, we don't get lost, but become part of a bigger world?"

"That's a good way of putting it," says *Po*. "Beware, though, my twin. Although nature is pro-life, it is not pro-human. A much bigger conversation between people and nature is pressing, so that we may change together but this is not the way of the modern world. We urgently need to replace the current war of presences that is destroying the integrity of our interconnected planet – you versus me – human versus machine – man versus monster – cities versus ecologies – people versus nature. These battles of opposites inevitably produce winners and losers. As in the case of the robber crabs, Amelia Earhart and MH370: when that happens, a sudden, gaping loss occurs."

Scent

Cesare is irrepressible when he has an audience. When he doesn't have one, he finds one, or makes one.

Although we share the same bus back to the Piazzale Roma, I then make my way eastward towards San Michele, while Cesare journeys southward to the vaporetto stop that takes him to the Giudecca, where he lives with his parents in a luxury apartment.

Today, just as we kiss each other 'ciao' by the air of each cheek, as is the local custom, he spots two girls about the same age as us. They are standing on a low-lying bow-backed bridge looking at the carvings of initials etched on love locks – personalised bicycle padlocks fastened to the wrought-iron railings of bridges. Although this practice has been banned many times because of the collective mass that builds up and causes some bridges to collapse, the locks return.

I watch as they giggle *at* him, or *with* him. I cannot tell which.

As it is a sweltering afternoon, I buy a lemon ice cream from a vendor instead of making my way directly home. I sit on a stack of steps that are starting to cool under the lengthening shadows and the ice cream melts at the touch of my lips. As I prevaricate, I hear Cesare's distinctive voice carrying like a sail in the wind. I try to ignore him but, frankly, it is impossible.

He is talking to the girls on the bridge and I note how captivating his theme of ancestral descent is, especially when he follows this through so well with his theatrical mannerisms and heavenly scents.

"Just imagine. Wet grass, a freshly baked cake, the allure of orange blossom, smoke from a bonfire, wafting incense, or the familiar scent of your boyfriend's sweat on your jacket. We're immersed in a world of invisible fragrances. While we may think that we're seduced by the way things look, our sense of smell is key to our passions. Although you may think this only applies to animals like dogs, or rats, these invisible appetites are constantly tugging at our heartstrings."

He's so enchanting, it almost doesn't matter what he says next.

"Why do we smell?" he asks.

One girl touches her nose and giggles. Cesare laughs coquettishly and adds, perhaps with a little too much gravitas, that he is serious.

"Yes! Smell receptors in our noses detet dissolved substances, but what part of matter makes an odour in the first place?"

Bewildered silence follows.

"Do we smell shapes?"

None of us have ever thought about it.

"One popular idea is that the shape of a chemical key can release an effect by turning the lock in a receptor to produce the sensation of smell. But this does not explain how only a few hundred keys can turn thousands of different locks – unless one key can partly open many locks."

As he unsheathes his withering intelligence, the girls no longer find him amusing but intimidating.

"Yet, this 'weak shape' theory fails to explain why different molecules can have similar smells and why similar molecules can have very different ones. So, we need to think again!"

The girls begin to whisper to each other that Cesare is talking rubbish.

I know he is not.

"Do we smell vibrations?"

I shuffle along the steps so that I can hear him better and make the most of the late afternoon's elongating coolness.

"I'm talking about an old idea from the 1930s that was thought to be nonsense until recently. It seems that the vibration patterns of electrons can be detected by different smell receptors according to their energy states. This accounts for why similar molecules smell different and different molecules can smell the same. It even allows us to predict how new molecules may smell – which is of great value to the perfume industry."

I see how Cesare's eyes smile when he talks of perfumery. It is obviously his calling. Perhaps one day a great king will commission him as their Chief of Perfumes.

One of the girls swipes at a lazy mosquito that is dithering around her neckline. Immediately, Cesare spots an opportunity to further amaze us.

"Flies like mosquitoes can hunt you down by sensing tiny changes in the carbon dioxide on your breath. If you want that blood sucker to stop following you – then stop breathing."

Cesare's eyes twinkle as the girls take the opportunity to run from the hungry mosquito pretending to hold their breath. Of course, he's given them the perfect moment for escape from his incessant wit and repartee, as he's already bored. He also knows that this particular mosquito is not interested in blood – it has the silent wings of a male and is looking for love and pollen.

I applaud Cesare's performance from the steps. He turns, surprised but appreciative of my audience. He bows graciously, swinging his tumbling hand low. Then he tips his elegant nude forehead and disappears homeward in a swirl of scent that arouses the interest of the silent mosquito, as to a flower.

- Themes
  - Invisible fragrances
  - Trying to use science to understand invisible entities

Eyes of the Lagoon

Hanging over the edge of the ferry, I watch the fledgling community of happy phantoms swelling within the lagoon, occupying the twilight interfaces between the earth, sea and sky.

Caught in a moment of escape between passion and decline, the memorial statues appear to climb skywards, their mirror-lights searching beyond the setting sun for their place among the heavens. While their souls seek sublimation, their still-present organic bodies set a new stage for life beyond death, with pressing relevance to the living world. Consummated through the ebb and flow of the tide, this union is not merely an aspiration for an after world but manifests through the bioconcrete mixtures that provide corporeal firmaments for rich ecosystems. Here, blooming microbial consortia fix marine sediments and slowly erode the bioconcretes, which leak cremains from their substance to nourish biodiverse marine ecosystems with their vital nutrients, founding tiny oceanic cities. Over time, these conurbations of – starfish, mussels, barnacles, crustaceans, shoals of small fish and sea gulls – become more expansive, drawing together the living world and its residues, which take the form of new ground that may one day become fresh land.

Ruzica says that investors are keen on supporting our business, since their capital increases in value while losing none of the product's poetry. The memorial statues in the lagoon are becoming more than a story about the survival of a family, but a real place that invites new intersections between the lagoon and the city.

Droplet

A single droplet of not quite alive
Chemistry from a laboratory sluice
In the city is enveloped in a fleshy
Deposit of soapy matter. It pauses
At the base of a memorial plinth
And attaches itself like an oyster.
Unobserved, it begins to change.

Link back to Sarah's story

○ *Thematic link to "dynamic Droplet studies" (pp 121-123)*

Palace of Light

"Success!"

Notorious for his vigorous advocacy of advanced new technologies, Giovanni Alessi skilfully steers the historical *Palace of Light* proposal, which was originally an aspiration of legendary fashion designer Pierre Cardin, through a complex series of planning approvals and urban development conventions. He presents the idea as an aspect of Venetian heritage that, twinned with a sister development in Paris, will bring income into the region through its iconic status and business opportunities. Supported by a range of industrial investors, the project is passed by a chain of various Italian Ministries and construction plans for this 245-metre-high building in the northern region of the lagoon is finally approved by the Mayor and his counsellors. The outcome is hailed a 'huge advance' for the city.

A physical model of the structure is centrepiece to the boardroom table, which can be interrogated through augmented reality mobile phone displays. Some counsellors are using augmentation monocles that flip up from their handheld devices, while others don haptic gloves. The focus of their scrutiny and gesticulations is a metre-high physical model – a translucent, cork-screw-like sculpture that twinkles with optical genius and outlines the on-going ecological concerns of the region. It is beautifully wrapped in fashionable materials and persuasive rhetoric – the first ecological palace built in an industrial area. Composed of three towers of varying heights, which are formed by a series of connecting disc-floor plates supported on concrete posts, the glittering edifice offers stunning panoramic views over Venice, while the unique cladding transforms the building into a stunning, crystal gem.

While Alessi is an advocate for the city's historical roots, he also fancies his mayoral appointment as consistent with the traditions of the political rule of Doges, or dukes. Although this particular office was abolished in 1797, when Venice submitted to Napoleonic rule, Alessi upholds the traditions of *La Serenissima*, when the city was in its heyday, and the shrewdest elder was appointed as the true leader of the city.

"It's a fitting tribute to the UNESCO World Heritage city with its proud history of innovative and iconic buildings. The palace's dimensions and ambitions rival the crystal palaces of the late nineteenth century – a tradition of expositions from which Venice's world-famous art biennale has sprung," asserts Alessi.

The *Palace of Light* speaks the same industrial language of Mestre and Marghera. Designed to astound, its multi-use spaces boast an eco-sustainable rhetoric of sixty-five floors of residences, offices, public areas, education centres, a science park, shopping facilities and a rooftop helipad. While its low emissions footprint – powered by sun, wind and geothermal energy – promises regional flourishing, it also conceals an industrial ambition that speaks to an economics of resource consumption, which has already subdued the mainland wetlands and brought colossal shipping vessels into the lagoon. Despite the rhetorical package that frames it, the palace's dreams belong to the world of industrialisation.

Cardin's original plans were presented for approval in 2012, but were met with much resistance from locals who denounced the project as an example of "crude commercialism" that tarnished the region with megastructures, typified by the oil refinery and vast cruise ships.

Although Alessi realises he has much work to do if he is to win over local communities, the great potential of the Cardin development to bring necessary investment to the region – and most especially to the waterways – is a powerful argument for a city that is perpetually at the brink of social or economic collapse.

With major reorganisation of transport routes, including a new tunnel and cable-bridge, commercial road access and tramway extensions – which are needed to make the palace viable and accessible to the communities it proposes to serve – Alessi proposes to trade off contracts on the development, in exchange for contractors agreeing to clean up and manage the aquifers. To avoid the ire of environmentally minded residents, deep engineering works are also cautioned not to cause lasting damage to fragile ecosystems. Naturally, the developers object to the implied costs of these conditions, but Alessi knows they must eventually agree. Of course, they will. After all, once the project has begun, it is down to the developer to manage their own processes, and this is, as every politician knows, a slippery trade-off between promise, pragmatism, bribery and profit.

In this way, Alessi persuades citizens that Cardin's ecosustainable, iconic vision not only makes great economic sense but can also be secured through a clean-up project for the lagoon, coupled with an improved transport system. All of these developments will enhance Venice's growing prowess as a cultural city, and even more importantly, an international centre for advanced biotechnologies.

"Success!" the industrial beasts scream as they recall how the giant concrete footsteps of the Tronchetto have already bridged their path to the island. Now their march upon the water can begin.

• Theme
  — utopian technology mindset
    ↳ still rooted in capitalism
    and resource consumption

Tricks of the Light

I watch the tangerine sunset turn into a horizon of clotting blood from the foot of my mother's memorial, marvelling at pollution's magic and how it frames my encounters with the lagoon.

Carried on the air, the lightest atoms of the atmosphere rise and escape from the planet, while heavier ones begin to form the limits of the stratosphere where the first pollutants settle more than fifty kilometres from the Earth's surface: mercury and nitrogen oxides, chorine, carbon monoxide, particulates. Some help nucleate the clouds, steam, smog and mist that forms in the troposphere where water vapour and gases share equal specific gravity, while closer to the planet's surface, the air squirms through layers of organic matter to inflate the soils. Much further down, impermeable layers of clay and rock concede no space to gases, which are almost absent here.

These layered gradients form settlement points for different kinds of pollution.

During the day, via stratifications of air, water and soil, a stream of writhing images may be found in the waterways. Wandering through the city as countless refractions, rainbows, brilliant sunrises and sparkling gowns of sequins, their capacity to transform spaces is not conferred by their clarity but by their filth. Cloudy water thickens into thick dark mirror folds, where particles reflect the light and project anamorphic images onto manifolds of wafer-thin surfaces. In other places, these virtual fabrics appear to possess mass and sink like river scum into the muddy water beds. Sometimes it seems possible to reach your destination by treading upon their shimmering expanses to forgo the convoluted system of bowed bridges that form the guts of the city.

As night falls, the lagoon becomes a sea of spun gold, streaked with brilliant electrics. Primary colours etch the water in a dazzling light show, which fades and dies at dawn. Diffusing into the rising air currents, scattering photons soften the city's edges, which seems increasingly permeable to objects like street lamps, candles on restaurant tables and the glow of hand-held digital screens.

Rachel Armstrong

Growing ever more marvellous, the city's saturated filth-encrusted surfaces produce the shimmering illusions and breath-taking sunsets for which the city is renowned.

Interesting
Paradox

Development

Even without the aid of a business suit, Monica Laing is impressed by Jelena, who possesses a quiet authority and assertiveness that inspires trust. This, in Monica's experience, is not something that can be readily acquired.

Davide's making a typically persuasive case for a new biotechnological product range, which he's describes as a 'portfolio of genetically modified organisms that can digest plastics'. He's supported his proposals with credible and up-to-date scientific papers on the subject.

Monica notices how well Davide and Jelena work together. Neither down-stages the other and their perspectives are complementary, building arguments upon their different experiences and unique observations. While Davide outlines the case for crossing scientific frontiers, Jelena is very practical and has a wonderful sense of application, suggesting convincing new kinds of social and cultural experiences for the product lines.

It is also hard to ignore their subtle interest in each other. Monica politely waits for the presenters to draw their conclusions and sum up their key points. But this is a courtesy. She has already decided that the *Exitec* board will invest in a pilot research program for a longer-term commercial view of detoxifying the Venice lagoon, by exploiting natural and modified lagoon organisms in ways that sustainably tackle the insidious plastic pollution.

Menses

Kasia is in the kitchen-cum-distillery-cum-laboratory, cracking a live *Ricci di Mare*.

The sea urchin is about the size of a ping pong ball. She's placed it on a tray of crushed ice and there is still movement in the tips of its spines, although I guess it's moving much more slowly than it would normally. She takes a sharp pair of kitchen scissors and carefully holds the dark purple spiky object, pushing the tips through its crust and cutting a circular flap in its integument like a manhole cover.

"Ah! Golden caviar!"

Kasia empties out a dark liquid into a small bowl and removes the soft insides, except for a number of honeycomb sacs, the sex cells, or roe, of the creature. Using a specially shaped spoon that Ruzica made for the purpose, she scoops them out and washes them in salt water. Then she offers them to me as an *apertivo*.

I want to refuse but comply, as she has obviously gone out of her way to give me a preview of supper. Instinctively, I hesitate and she hastily warns me that the quality of the treat deteriorates quickly. I decide to get this over and done with really quickly, and pop the odd-looking thing on the back of my tongue. Terrified, I swallow.

Kasia studies my face for a response. I smile like a synchronised swimmer.

Then I smile again, from the inside. I am pleasantly surprised at the gustatory echo of the monstrous matter, which is a blend of sweet earthiness and fresh salt. Although I have a memory of its essence, it leaves no aftertaste.

"Aunty, I'm bleeding."

Kasia puts the scissors down and looks at me without saying anything for several seconds. Then she folds me in a long hug.

"My tummy hurts."

"Climb up into your cot for a little while."

She returns with some boiled towels and puts them inside a leathery algae bag, which she hands me to place on my stomach.

"You'll feel better soon, darling."

"Aunty, I'm not a proper boy, am I?"

Kasia retrieves a small zip purse from under her mattress and pulls out one of those sanitary pads that I've seen along the shoreline. I don't like the idea of them at all but thank her anyway and curl up again with my back to the world.

"'Boy' will do for now darling, things will work themselves out."

Ephemeral Light

The bogland blue lights dance in the deception between the earth and sky.

"This tranquil patchwork of firmness, textures and colours is a lie," says *Po*. "Nothing is as it seems."

I can't stop staring at them, like fireflies lighting the way to heaven.

"Don't believe your eyes, dear twin. Trust your other senses – in scent, taste, footsteps, or fingertips. Something that can verify the integrity of this place."

I reach out to touch them, seemingly just within reach, but the frolicking lights remain in the distance.

We've reached the bog of Allen, which exists between the rivers Liffey and Shannon. Its wetland ecosystem has been formed by eons of rainfall that have been held in wet, spongy, carbon-sinking acidic soil.

"It's purgatory on Earth," says *Po*. "It's natural poisons prevent bodies from rotting."

"Bodies?" I ask, shutting my eyes but the blue lights won't go away. Instead they turn green and yellow against the darkness of my retinas.

"In these soft yet carnivorous jaws are bog corpses, from children to the elderly. Many have not died from natural causes. Some retain nooses around their necks, arrows lodged in their chests, or carry the stigmata of ritual sacrifice. Their persecutors have left them here in eternal punishment, knowing that the bog will stop the composting process. These souls, still bound to flesh, cannot go to heaven."

"I'm scared, *Po*."

"Don't be. Just treat the boglands creature with respect. This is the fountain of life for many organisms. The growth of bog mosses and sphagnum weaves a dense tapestry of emerald, butterscotch, brown, yolk, chartreuse, juniper, Tuscan sun, Seaweed, basil, mint, gold, pine, pickle, tawny, cinnamon, walnut, lime, fern, umber, carob, sage, juniper, shamrock, hickory, flax, caramel, seafoam, ochre, mustard and olive velvets over its fickle surface, softer than a crust. They are home to a host of flies – dragonflies, horseflies, hairy canary flies, mayflies, midges, mosquitoes, blue bottles and damselflies – and death to these same insects. Active plant fly trappers with moving parts flourish here among their prey – Sundews, Venus Fly Traps, Butterwort and Bladderwort. Passive plant fly trappers, like the Cobra Lily and Pitcher Plants, fare equally well, seducing and drugging insects so they will drown in vessel-like coffin-leaves. Some say the bog of Allen with its ecological treachery and metabolic strangeness is as important to Irish heritage as the Book of Kells – which is a richly illuminated manuscript that was produced by monks around 800 CE – a lasting symbol of Irish nationality and creativity that captures the religious, social and economic practices of the time – likewise, the bogland is the land's illuminated story."

"I still see the lights, *Po*."

"Yes, *ignis fatuus*, or ball of fools. These are lights that do not wane and continue to wend their way over untrustworthy land."

"Are they real?"

"Locals say the lights are a trick played by relentless prankster, Jack the Lad, who made a deal with the Devil. In exchange for his soul, Jack tricked Satan into picking up his drinks tab at the Tavern of Fools. But when it was time to collect on his promise the man climbed a tree and the dark angel followed him. Quick as a wink, Jack carved a cross underneath so the Devil was stuck, and couldn't get down. Furious, Satan howled and howled, until he was forced to strike another deal with Jack, annulling his debt in exchange for his release, but he refused him entry to Hell. God shows little favour to those rejected by the Devil, so Jack was not welcomed into heaven when he died but was condemned to walk an eternal twilight on the Earth. The Devil was not done. Impressed by Jack's deviousness, he gave him an ember from the fires of Hell to light his way. Jack placed this immortal flame in a carved turnip, which served as a lantern. So, at twilight, compulsive trickster Jack continues to lure weary travellers to follow him over the boglands and find their rest in the places he can't go – Heaven, or Hell."

"But that's not true, is it?"

"That depends on who you are, some find scientific explanations more plausible."

"What does science say about the lights?"

"Well, Alessandro Volta, who discovered methane in 1776, looked for natural causes for the ball of fools. He suggested they were produced when natural gas was mixed with lightning. Joseph Priestly, who discovered oxygen, also supported this theory but it was not universally embraced as sceptics rejected the idea of spontaneous combustion. This was not only hard to explain as a series of causes and effects; it also did not account for why the lights retreated when approached. Today, Volta is thought to be largely correct – that burning swamp gases are produced from the breakdown of organic matter by anaerobic bacteria in the soil. Releasing methane, carbon dioxide, nitrogen, phosphines, and other chemicals that are flammable, they produce a blue flame when mixed together. The active chemicals in this process are likely to be phosphines, which are toxic gases that explode on contact with oxygen, producing a dense white cloud as part of the reaction. This acts as an extended light source, giving the flame more substance than perhaps deserved and disperses when observers approach because of a complex interplay of air movements."

"Burning chemicals sounds so simple. It seems *too* simple. The lights are weird, *Po*. I can still see them and I know they've gone."

We make our way back to the lagoon and watch its surface glitter. It is littered with reflections, refractions, calligraphies of the natural realm and bioluminescent hazes.

Like boglands, Venice is a city of mirages, half-truths and endless creativity. Its continual strangeness lures us towards things that do not yet exist at the horizon's promise, which is always yet to unfold. This perceptual treachery is part of its timeless spell and a plane upon which the enchantments hidden in the world may be glimpsed and pursued in our dreams.

– Po has been showing
the human dangerous/
scary natural places
all over the world.
– why?,

Again

Stronger and stranger, the once familiar
Ecosystems that kept our soils healthy
Are changing. Once transformed they
Will not resume their native form but
Alter in substance and Character. The
Only places where our present yet
Temporary biomes may be directly
Encountered are zoos and aquariums.

We would rather perish of fatigue from
Fighting the encroaching destruction of
Our living world than be bullied into
Submission by industrial wastes and
Wanton pollution. Change wins each
Of its reluctant inches at a time, moving
With such grace and tenacity that the process
Remains invisible. At some point people
Will notice they can't eat the fish they
Catch, wildfowl appears stranger, and
Livestock fades on marshland grasses.

In these transformed states, waters
Will flourish anew, skies will swell with
Outlandish sounds and land beasts will
Grow so small they no longer speak of
The abattoir. Change is freedom and
Those invisible people who stubbornly
Toil despite the harsh sun, bitter rain and
Testy tempests, understand what's at risk.

Asking for no thanks, they tend my new
Ecologies knowing there is no easy life but
Appreciating that – despite the odds against
Them, in some form or other life persists.

Islands and Turtles

Po and I join a shoal of giant basalt turtles.

We're swimming extremely slowly in the currents around a thousand kilometres west off the coast of South America and moving so leisurely that we could be mistaken for landmasses.

"Why are they going so slowly?" I ask.

"They're incredibly old. The tips of their giant backs appeared above water about ten million years ago. Now, they host the Galapagos Islands, which showcase the world's evolutionary stage. They're not as old as life but their creativity in bringing forth wonders is unsurpassed."

"Do they make their own kind of life then?"

"No, but they have ways of attracting and moulding it which has caused the world to marvel. Given these creatures were initially devoid of plant and animal life, their now colonised by a host of species is nothing short of miraculous."

"What kind of species have they crafted then?"

"All kinds. The first person to document the rich diversity of creature types on the archipelago was Charles Darwin. Surveying – iguanas, mocking birds, finches, grasses, ferns – on the second voyage of the Beagle in 1835, he recorded their strange forms and variations in his famous book *On The Origin of Species.*"

"What's so special about them, compared with, say, any other kind of species?"

"That's a good question, dear twin. It is true there are all kinds of marvellous forms of life in this world, but none have been cast as the central character of a popular book that speaks of evolution. At the time it was published, diversity without god was a controversial idea. I guess this story must have stuck, since there is no doubt that the creatures of these islands have, through Darwin's observations, become the celebrities on the world's evolutionary stage."

"What stories do they tell, *Po?*"

"I'd say that no creature has captured the public imagination more than the Galapagos tortoises."

"Not turtles."

"No, tortoises are quite different. They live on the land and are not aquatic like the creatures whose backs they inhabit. These huge creatures are big enough to be ridden like a horse, weigh around a quarter of a tonne and are the longest living of all vertebrates. Many individuals survive more than a hundred years – the oldest exceeding a hundred and fifty years – remaining fertile well into old age."

"Surely there are creatures older than that. Trees, for example."

"True, I was thinking specifically about animals rather than all living things, but let's deal in specific examples rather than generalities. As part of its evolutionary narrative the Galapagos archipelago is host to ambitious conservation projects. None are so endearing than the descendants of Lonesome George."

"Who's George?"

"He is the last of the Pinta Island Tortoises, whose kin were competed into extinction by goats that destroyed the natural vegetation on which tortoises thrive. Since there were no female Pinta Island tortoises to share his long life with, George was doomed to be alone."

"That's so sad."

"Many people gave up hope for the future of the species instantly. Even before he was dead he became the national icon of Ecuador, who stamped him on their bank notes as a kind of relic. Just enough people in the global community though, wanted George to find the love of his life, so that the species would not go extinct. They dreamed that George would kick-start his kind into existence again. So, they set out to make it happen."

"But how is that possible if there are no females?"

"First people tried to get him interested in mating with tortoises from neighbouring islands, but the old tortoise was fussy. In fact, he was so particular that by 2012, George gave up on making a legacy to save his species."

"How do you mean?"

"His keepers found him dead from natural causes by a waterhole."

"Did nobody try to save him?"

"Oh, he was long past being revivable. Even San Diego's Frozen Zoo could not harvest his living cells, but George's supporters did not relinquish the fight for his species. Vets and keepers quickly moved his ninety-kilo body to a freezer, where he was prepared for cloning."

"Cloning?"

"Yes, making exact genetic copies of a creature. It is highly technical and risky business. Little is known about how to clone endangered species. The science of cloning is best understood in domestic animals such as cats, dogs, sheep and cows. However, following a number of successful attempts in bringing back endangered wild species from the brink like – black-footed cats, gaur, banteng and Eddie, a mountain goat known as Pyrenean ibex – hopes were raised in producing descendants for George."

"How did they do it?"

"DNA from George's frozen cells was harvested and hybridised with genetic information from another tortoise species. These tissues could then produce around a dozen eggs capable of hosting cloned embryos. Eleven were viable and implanted into a female tortoise called Mildred, who carried the clones before she finally introduced them into the world."

"So, George did have babies after all?"

"Not so fast, dear twin. Tortoises are complicated and fussy. Mildred was not going to release all her eggs at the same time. If you think that George is particular, then consider the incubation habits of female tortoises as notoriously unpredictable."

"In what way?"

"Mildred has the power to lengthen the gestation period for the eggs, depending on how happy she feels with her surroundings. So begins the saga of the world's most pampered expectant female. Two years of coaxing and spoiling later, Mildred agrees on a suitable nesting place. A clutch of five eggs are shelled inside her body and laid."

"That's amazing, what were the clones like?"

"They looked just like baby tortoises and so cute that everyone wanted to see them. Hatched under the spellbound gaze of a live television audience with the greatest ever ratings for a show, it culminated in five tiny male tortoises emerging from the ostrich-like eggs. Called, Mercury, Mars, Saturn, Jupiter and Uranus, each of them was a perfect miniature of George

"Incredible."

"The little tortoises brought smiles and tears of joy, to spellbound global audiences. They melted the hearts of even the most seasoned reptile breeders."

"What about the other eggs? Did they make it?"

"Happily, they did. But not without further pampering. Two years later Mildred surrendered a second clutch of equally adorable female tortoises called Venus, Earth, Calliope, Calisto, Io and Ceres. At this moment, a new phase of ecological history began. Now they are between two and four years old, and constantly followed by a swarm of surveillance drones. Everything that Mercury, Venus, Earth, Mars, Saturn, Jupiter, Uranus, Calliope, Calisto, Io and Ceres do is broadcast live to global audiences and a dedicated actor provides a voiceover for each of them. These accounts are translated into fifteen different languages and describe, as a running commentary, what each of the young tortoises is up to every minute of the day. Although they are still very young, each of them is a miniature version of their heroic forefather – the lone figure that embodies all extinct and rewilded creatures."

"That's incredible, *Po*. Can we really bring things back from the dead?"

"My dearest twin, it is important to not confuse the idea that, just because species exist, this is an indicator that everything will be okay. There are many things needed for a healthy and happy lifestyle. Even when creatures respond and adapt to change there is no guarantee of a happy ever after. To answer your question in a purely technological way, let's say that many people are already capitalising on this rewilding event. An even more ambitious project to bring back *Testudo atlas*, an extinct mega turtle has been attempted."

"A mega turtle. Like these ones?"

"Not quite. This creature with elephantine feet, roamed the Earth during the Pleistocene, around two million years ago. With a shell that could grow to two metres broad, three metres long and up to two metres tall, adult turtles could weigh up to two metric tonnes: twenty times larger than George. Finding a DNA source for this creature has been incredibly challenging but turtle eggs mummified in baking dry sands have yielded enough readable DNA for the latest genetic computing technologies to make sense of this *in the context of* George's genetic code. Attempts are being made to patch defects since some of the decaying genetic strands are too short to read properly. It's a lengthy process and full of many technical challenges but already, a handful of potentially viable, cloned embryos have been produced."

"Have any little ones hatched?"

"Well, several devoted female turtles have accepted batches of mega-cloned eggs, but they seem to have been talking to Mildred, as they are deliberating on suitable nesting conditions."

"And so we wait." I say.

I look again at the Galapagos island turtles swimming extremely slowly around us, carefully carrying the great responsibility of a highly particular kind of evolution on the backs of their shells.

"Perhaps their burden is somewhat lessened now," says *Po*, "by the process of rewilding and biotechnology's helping hands. Maybe more creatures can be helped survive the odds against life on this planet. Technology is not exclusively used for survival. Your kin are already part of a project where this same kind of biotechnology is making Venice's Tiger mosquitoes extinct."

I start to form the kind of moralistic argument that Kasia used when the creatures were first introduced to San Michele to justify their design – where only the greedy ones perish – but somehow, it doesn't feel right.

· Theme

- Biotechnology
  └→ in context of cloning
    extinct species

Ambergris

Today we are presenting research projects to the class.

I am at the front of the room, using a small figurine cast from Ruzica's bio positive concrete to show how new kinds of gardens, ecologies and even life can be made with new kinds of materials. I have brought in 'before' and 'after' samples that demonstrate how bare stone can be turned into a lively marine garden.

Miss Sapiente moves uncomfortably in her chair as I explain how cremains mixed with concrete can be thought of as a kind of slow-release fish-food. My classmates are simply fascinated by the process, since they have grown up around the idea of living statues, regarding them as integral to the webs of life and death in the lagoon.

Miss Sapiente thanks me brusquely and I take my seat again.

I suddenly feel extremely disappointed. I have not said anything about *Po*.

I quickly forget my oversight, as Cesare announces his project.

Holding a small, smooth, waxy grey pebble-like object, he places it in his trident palm and ambles between the desks like a defence lawyer, inviting us all to say what we think it is.

"Rock, stone, pebble, wax, chewing gum, bread roll, flint stone, papier-mâché, play dough, something you made, cardboard, grease ball, your dinner, something found down the back of the sofa, old rock, old stone."

Our imaginations are failing. I noticed an imperfection on the surface, which looks like a black, shiny and rather lethal-looking splinter.

"No," he says, delighted with himself.

Miss Sapiente reminds him that he's supposed to be presenting. There is no need to ask the others their opinion as they have already taken their turns. But Cesare is having fun and theatrically holds up his index finger, to silence her.

"I'm establishing the evidence."

Tempering her reaction, she rolls her eyes.

"Get on with it, Gallo."

He walks back to the front of the class.

"Does anyone want to smell it?"

"Gallo! I'm warning you."

"It's important, Ma'am."

Cesare is at his most courteous when he is getting away with something. He plucks the object out of his fist and inhales deeply, like he is about to burst into song. Instead, he sighs like a swooning lover and looks over at Miss Sapiente.

"Maybe you'd like to describe what you smell."

She relents. Then, her frown lifts. She grasps the object in both hands and inhales deeply.

"Oh, it's earthy, like brazil nuts. No, it's sweet, like treacle. Or musky. Mossy. Animalistic. I'm not sure. It changes every time I smell it."

We all want a go. The stone is passed around and Cesare begins to look a little nervous. He hovers over every exchange between the many hands in the classroom, keeping a very close eye on exactly where the mystery object is going. Some of us turn our noses up in disgust, while others are not so sure. A couple of us consider it "heavenly".

The stone is warm, firm and unexpectedly light. I smell sea, rotting algae, something pungently sweet like caramel, then it becomes sharp and rancid, more like faeces. I quickly pass it on.

Being unable to stand any more dithering and handling, Cesare snatches his precious object from under the current nose that is appreciating its strangeness. Then, he appears relaxed again.

"That. Ladies and gentlemen. Is ambergris."

Miss Sapiente splutters.

"You brought that to school? Even a small piece like that must be worth hundreds of euros."

Excitement spreads throughout the classroom.

"Indeed. A thousand to be precise."

He is commanded to immediately take the 'exhibit' down to the headmistress' office straight away and ask her to lock it in the safe. He can collect it again at the end of the day.

"May I conclude first?"

Miss Sapiente is defeated.

"If you must."

"A kidney. A kidney of ambergris. Exquisite, isn't it? Once you've smelt it, you'll never forget it. The name means grey amber. It is also called floating gold. Yet ambergris is nothing more than hardened slurry from the guts of a sperm whale. It's not quite vomit and it's not quite shit. It ages like a fine wine. As it gets older, it hardens and develops a distinctive odour. The active chemical ingredients are triterpene alcohol ambrein, epicoprostanol, and coprostanone. It is used by only the finest perfumeries, to create the highest quality couturier fragrances, which adorn the skin of only the finest customers. Naturally."

"Thank you, Cesare. Go straight to the school office. Pier Alto, your turn."

Condom Island

I am back from school way before sunset, so I grab my safety suit, which is looking much more like a giant turtle shell than a diaper lately, and run up to my twin with enthusiasm.

"Let's go on an adventure."

"Not today," it says.

"Oh, come on, *Po*! Let's have some fun."

"I can't."

"You can."

"I don't want to."

There is a long pause.

"Something is changing."

"What is it *Po*? What's up, did someone hurt you?"

"No. That's not it. It's hard to say, I'm dealing with a new kind of existence."

"I don't really understand what you're telling me," I say. "I thought monsters always change and soils age over thousands of years."

"Just, change," it says unhelpfully. I really don't know what to do about the way *Po* is behaving, but it's hard to dispute the shocking state it's in.

"Do you want company?" I say brightly.

"No. I wish to be left alone."

I'm devastated.

I've homework to do but can't think straight, so I go for a walk along its vastly thickened shoreline. It's grown so vast that my mother's memorial is now a sculpture infiltrated by terrestrial weeds that sprout from around her base. It seems that she no longer desires to be part of the marine world, but to fuse with the land.

Po is littered with discarded plastics, the remnants of our convenience culture. While these artificial materials have always been part of its substance, it previously found ways to assimilate them into its living mass. These current accumulations are toxic, proliferative and malignant. Like a festering wound they split my twin's flesh and hold it open to trauma and poisons rendering its place-making powers at best, impotent. I seek solace in the kitchen.

"We're born into a world of plastic, darling," says Kasia. "Our lives are plastic coated. Infants are swathed in a hundred million kilos of plastic diaper liners each year. They are weaned from plastic milk bottles and given plastic toys to play with. They are fed from plastic jars that are purchased with a plastic credit card. Even the baby-making process is controlled by the cautious use of plastics through a whole range of contraceptives – from pill capsules to physical devices."

I am not entirely sure what she means by physical devices. Actually, I don't *want* to know. I understand that things like genitals for girls, or boys, bleeding, or not, and babies are supposed to be important. But I just can't deal with any of it. I'm too sad right now. What I take away from my aunt's reassurances is that even our most intimate recesses, experiences and excesses are wrapped in plastic membranes.

Outside, on the beach, I kick at lumps of toilet paper that are chewed by the waves into abstract papier-mâché sculptures. They respond to my disgust by releasing pungent clouds of gases and sand flies. One step away is a pile of sanitary wear – plastic backing strips, applicators, lumps of cotton wool with strings. I avoid them and continue looking for more salubrious surroundings.

A lazy wave breaks on the beach, carrying a new trophy – a pale, gas-filled balloon that is tied in a knot at one end.

I recognise it as a taboo item that Krists has told me about. They contain 'human leftovers'. Like sanitary towels and tampons, I want to avoid them, but I stay, staring at the strange object despite myself.

The cheeky inflatable possesses the elusive charm of a party decoration, dipping, hopping and winking playfully in the surf, but it is also tarnished by denigrate morality and the materiality of sewage.

My father says there is a whole island of these balloons that circulates around a giant reef in the South Pacific. It is about twenty metres thick and composed of millions of discarded 'safety tools'. They are symbols of our distance from nature, as the natural world does not wrap its seeds in plastic. Many fish and most water-dwelling animals, make their young by producing a large number of sperm and eggs, which they release directly into the water. Those that are not used are returned back into the webs of life.

This bag of air and spent sex cells is more than a symbol of excess,

Rachel Armstrong

or the simple mechanics and morality of parentage. It is also real stuff. We are all made from these left-overs, where tiny homunculi shelter in particles of semen.

I wonder whether this sorry-looking globule is a fragment, or miniature, of Asphodel Meadows, the island for spent souls where the dead gain entry to the after world by drinking first from the River Lethe. In the process, they lose all individuality and are free to roam in an unbearably bland field the texture of milk, which is scattered with pale, ghostly narcissi. Refusing to land on the shore, its refugees – probably dead by now – are still looking for somewhere to call 'home'. Maybe, though, they're suspended in state of plastic-wrapped sterility where they wait in purgatory, neither dead nor alive, until one day their soul-carrying seeds are released onto welcoming ground to sow new life.

• Theme

- Distance From Nature } in the context
- Excess } of
- Morality } condoms

What the fuck?!

216

Down to Business

Encore Memorials Ltd. flourishes.

With the new business comes many fresh responsibilities for my aunts that are as much social as economic.

Kasia agrees to take the helm of the company as managing director. Ruzica oversees the production process and Jelena agrees to take responsibility for marketing and business development, which works very well alongside her *Exitec* interests. Krists volunteers for nothing, claiming it is all his idea anyway and nobody would be where they are today without him.

Frankly, my aunts do not want him meddling and are content with his indolence.

Logistically, it is impossible to establish a formal business from San Michele -- an island that has been a dedicated cemetery since the early nineteenth century – so we need to change where we are based.

"*Please* can we stay here?" I look to Kasia for support but am met with an expression that is impossible to read and no words. "Please."

"This is business, young man," says Ruzica. "It's not personal. If we want to survive, we have to relocate our premises."

"But these aren't premises, Aunty." I'm sobbing. "It's our home."

"There, there, darling," says Kasia at last. "We'll work it out. Of course this is your home." She looks pointedly at Ruzica, who rolls her eyes.

"Whatever."

Our headquarters will be located nearby in Murano, where an administrative centre can be established to provide full-time logistical support for customers. It will also deal with business matters faced by bereaved families. There will also be a spacious workshop for six of the best artisans in the region to sculpt the memorials. This new base will also benefit from arrangements made with the island's expert glass blowers, who can produce a whole range of new optical materials for the mirror lights.

"Just look at the way this crystal splits the light," says Ruzica, holding up a coin-sized gem. "Isn't it marvellous?"

I say nothing as the colours flit as lightly as a mosquito's dance around the room.

"You know what this means?" Since I remain silent, she continues, "Statues will cry rainbow tears, even on rainy days."

The irony of glorifying misery appears to be quite lost on my aunt.

"Good news," says Jelena. "Commercial organisations have started to invest heavily in our company. We're making more than just the income from the sales of statues to the recently bereaved."

"We've also had applications from art students," adds Kasia, "who are volunteering their services during the holidays, so they can get hands-on work experience with the unique kinds of concrete that we're using, under the guidance of master craftspeople."

As usual my aunts are extremely diligent and efficient. They seem to have thought of everything, while ensuring they employ the very best people to help them succeed.

"You'll make more money, if you use casual labour," suggests Krists.

"Not a chance," says Kasia. "Long-term investment in *people* makes a better working community and ultimately, brings dividends to all."

I am allowed to stay on the *Fortune* with Krists for just as long as it takes to get properly established in Murano.

I hate everything about this idea. I sulk, I cry and make every possible objection to the pending relocation, I try to make myself awful to live with so my aunts will leave me behind, but deep down I know I am not going to get my way. This bitter realisation is particularly cruel, since *Po* is not talking to me. We can't even run away together.

The move takes an enormous amount of organisation and work and as I am expected to help, my school routines are disrupted. Gradually my aunts master the essential day-to-day routines of their new establishment and my life takes on a new 'normality'.

I really miss *Po*.

My island twin is now a boat ride away. With school commitments, it is increasingly difficult to visit San Michele, but I vow to go regularly so that we do not lose the special bond between us. Sometimes I stand at the water's edge by the Colonna *vaporetto* stop and shut my eyes to see if I can still feel it thinking with me and through me. Although the cemetery is clearly within view, my twin feels so far away and I hear nothing from *Po* about our separation.

218

Cryptogeographic Marine Crusts

I leave early to go to school – perhaps too early.

I've started to recognise signs of *Po* everywhere. I'm on its trail, looking along the sides of the *rios*, searching for cryptic bodies. I search for them in the collections of dusts at alley junctions, along the tidal zones of the canals, and in the bioconcrete accretions around mooring steps.

I wonder if my monster twin is following me.

A blood red anemone is gesturing at me with neon brilliance. It is clinging to the brickwork that buttresses a marble staircase. Its worm-like gelatinous bulge swells when the tide is sucked from the wall by passing water traffic and thrusts its tentacles out again like a jungle in bloom. Secured by a sticky muscular foot, its soft body sticks to the rough surface of the gnarled the terracotta brickwork.

I try to decipher its movements but can't tell what it's saying. It seems agitated, or angry.

Green algae ooze yellow cement and are fed upon by clusters of shellfish – limpets, mussels, oysters and barnacles – that clamour for traction in the rich nutrient broth. Fine seaweeds piggyback upon their shells, taking advantage of their access to light. Everything appears hairy. The encrustations splay and warp with the current, as they stretch down to reach deeper masonry. Shoals of small fish pass between crevices, turning at every change in shadow, while crabs slip in and out of the vegetation, waiting for the current to bring them marine carrion and the delights of decomposition. A trumpet fish hovers with tiny fins, then vanishes vertically, like a UFO. A long string of red algae tumbles in knots past the cluster of structures, pausing in the rips and invisible currents, which shatter the appearances of things. Gills of fish are spliced onto shell bodies. Everything pauses, then separates and re-forms as mosaics of sea vegetation, with fugitive eyes on stalks and horror-shot claws. Algal tails are plaited into brown, green and ruddy fabrics, which appear to belong to no particular site or place at all. Anemone hearts wrathfully pulse, as plastic bottles glide languidly on the skin of the sea. Light is broken by the waves into twisted knots and everything shatters kaleidoscopically again.

Formless organic matter sucks my gaze further downwards, stretching the fabric of time into the mud; an endless pit of possibility with seaweed-dark eyes that are twisted like buildings. They grin at me through a row of battered railings. Then this ghost I'm convinced is *Po*, is gone.

- How Po (human) describes the marine habitat characterizes his relationship with Po (bioregion)

• Themes
- Change
- Lost Relationship

Angels

With the *Fortune* now legally moored in Murano, my aunts employ a staff of ten to deal with the paperwork, the construction of the statues and the logistics of placing the statues on made-to-measure plinths in the lagoon. They can manage up to five lagoon burials a day.

Scores of *Angeli della Laguna*, now wade beyond the lagoon and out into the Adriatic Sea and along the Lido beach, where old souls acquire fresh liveliness and character as they are integrated into flourishing marine ecosystems.

Other memorial highways beyond the Lido soon follow, which restructures traffic movement around the south of the lagoon. While the *briccole*, which traditionally signpost the flow of marine traffic, remain the cornerstone of navigation, the *Angeli della Laguna* are now the way most seafarers imagine their courses. They are particularly spectacular at night, when they gaze upon the living through a scintillating sea of cats' eyes.

As the money from funereal tourism flows into the city's complex tax system, the local authorities become extremely supportive of, if not actively celebrating, the 'Anghelescu family'. We are model immigrants who have benefited from the many opportunities on offer by the city, which promote successful enterprise.

Despite my many misgivings about my aunts' business activities, I'm secretly impressed by the cultural difference we've made. Whether expressed in conversation, graffiti, or through intonation, it is generally accepted that with the arrival of the *angeli*, Venice is truly *coming alive*.
"*Angeli portano la vita*," my classmates say.

↳ breaking the divide between humans and nature

221

Kisses

A collection of debris in a tiny gyre around one of the wooden posts under the Madonna dell'Orto ferry stop reminds me of *Po* and its once sprightly bobbing mass of ideas, adventures and passions.

I find a stick and begin to prod at them, trying to provoke these little islands into decisive action but I am lost in thought. So many changes are happening around and within me that I can no longer make sense of them all. As I reach with my stick for another matt of algae, a young boy and girl quietly join me on the decking. I only notice them when they are either side of me and introduce themselves as Donato and Mirella. I can't tell if they are dating each other but they are taking a keen interest in me.

"What school are you from?"

"The International School of Venice," I respond shyly.

"Are you a boy or girl?"

I look away, shrugging my shoulders. I know they're watching me intensely.

Donato shuffles a little closer.

"We've bet each other fifty euros on what gender you are."

I stand up, feeling intruded upon but respond politely.

"It's complicated."

Not that long ago I would have immediately asserted that I was a boy, as this is how my family acknowledge me. I used to be happy with that. Now I am not so sure. Things that were once certain are no longer reassuring. It is not that I have decided to 'be a girl' either. It's more that the choices I am presented with simply do not connect with me at all. Sometimes, I do not even feel wholly human. Sometimes I feel more like *Po* than part of this people-world.

Mirella says she has a way of finding out what gender I am.

"If you prefer a kiss from a girl, then you're a boy."

"And if you prefer a kiss from a boy, then you're a girl," adds Donato.

I doubt their logic, or whether I actually want to do any kissing. It all seems way too simplistic, but I finally agree to the experiment. I suppose

[handwritten in left margin: Black + White Thinking]

222

that if they are right, then maybe I have just been making things difficult for myself all along.

Donato kisses me first, full on the lips. It is a strong, clumsy and dry embrace, almost an assault. But it is okay. I say so.

Now, it is Mirella's turn. Her kiss is much softer and gentle, like licking ice cream, but warm. It is also very juicy and I have to wipe my mouth afterwards.

They ask me which is better.

I am undecided – dry or sticky.

The truth is that both kisses work in different ways. I say so.

However, Donato and Mirella are not satisfied with my diplomatic response. They are determined to reach a conclusion. I'm assuming this is because one of them must win the fifty euros. One after the other, they try to change my mind with kisses – all kinds of kisses – rapidly; one after the other, then together and soon, there is no space between our embraces. I am dizzy with excitement and from the rising pressure inside my head, but I am starting to like it.

"Holy Mary, Mother of God!"

A nun from the religious order of the Sisters of St Joseph shrieks from behind us.

"May the mother of Jesus spare you all from the devil!"

We turn around to see her cross her chest over a dark blue smock. Then she averts her offended eyes. Ashamed for us, she lowers her headdress that is triangulated like a table napkin and scurries on her holy way.

Initially stunned, we burst into laughter.

"That's rich, coming from a Venetian nun," says Donato. "It is a fact; they are Vatican concubines and responsible for the Italian wars."

We continue laughing and passing off our collective awkwardness as flaws of the accuser, until we are exhausted of all possible emotions and excuses.

"You still didn't say which you preferred," insists Mirella.

"Honestly, I cannot decide," I confess.

"Then, it's a truce," says Donato, "You're both."

"Or neither," I say.

We run, laughing and holding hands together, to celebrate with ice cream.

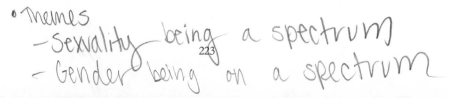

○ Memes
— Sexuality being a spectrum
— Gender being on a spectrum

223

Omen

I'm looking for signs of *Po* over the side of a *rio*, hoping its following me. Watching the litter sail down the waterway, I wonder if this flotsam can tell me where my monster twin is lurking.

There are no straight lines in Venice. Every passageway accommodates the bent-over backs of bridges, or *ponti,* that hang low over the canal.

These architectural sprouts were not born from the rationality of machines but grew more like weeds between islands to produce over 340 crossings. Between one discrete island mass and another their walkways meet as tendrils, which form knots of negotiation that offer steps and follies to tenuous places in-between sites. Lovers linger here and pledge their passion in lovelocks, which they secure to the bridge, throwing the key into the endlessly accommodating stomach of the scavenging mud, where their promises are happily swallowed.

I decide to send *Po* a sign in the form of a little origami boat, which I fold out of a map of the city that's blowing around at the entrance to a nearby *calle*. I name the vessel *Fortune,* hoping that my monster twin will recognise her.

As I watch for a response, I notice the light is behaving strangely on the surface of the canal, as if it's boiling. Or bubbling. The usual gentle ripples sours and writhes. Already a memory. I draw closer, and for a moment notice the withdrawal of something tentacular: a liminal semi translucent body like a discarded glove, pulsing, but it's vanished before I've caught proper sight of it. There it is again. Medusa. Now that I am tuned into their presence they're everywhere. Their bodies split the light and remain elusive, always receding into the background. Drifting like phantoms, they snare fish fry and lurk behind strands of weed. Fascinated by their ghostly oblivion – invisible ecophagy, I observe them from the safety of the walkway, but they're out of focus again, dissolving into odd patches of light. Momentarily they bloom into pulsing reflections, laced by purple skirts and glowering gonads. Then, they've sunk and gone.

In Venice, it is said that *ponti* are places where you're supposed to give something away, so that you can change your fate and start out on a different journey, but I wish for the journey that I already love to continue indefinitely.

"Please speak to me, *Po*."

- Invisible Creatures
- Mazes | Confusing design of Venice

↳ mental state of Po dealing with so many confusing changes

Invasion

As the sun rises, the gleaming mainland giants slowly assemble around the Palace of Light's construction site in the north of the lagoon.

Poised for invasion, they are impatient to make their advance through the construction of concrete island platforms that will provide the foundations for the Cardin palace and a complex of exclusive commercial developments.

Mayor Alessi arrives early by water taxi, the leader of a solemn convoy of boats.

In the tradition of Venice's Marriage to the Sea by the doge, he offers a prayer before he alights for a guided tour of the site.

"For us and all who sail thereon, may the sea be calm and quiet."

Signore Jacopo Greco, the project manager, warmly greets him on the deck of a cargo carrier and gesticulates in imaginary lines how the construction plans will be translated into reality. The mayor flips the augmented reality monocle on his phone open and checks what he's being told against the original proposals that appear on the hand-held display. Putting the phone away, he walks forward, nodding solemnly, hands clasped behind his back like royalty.

Hanging over the ferry rail that takes me to school via Colonna to Sant'Alvise, I have a front row view of the slowly assembling, colossuses. It's clear that an industrial development is about to begin, which is unthinkable. Particularly as neither my aunts nor my father have mentioned such a thing, and they are all highly opinionated on such matters.

Several private boats are protesting in a cluster around the site, making themselves heard with hyper speakerphones, which can deliver very clear and precise messages to very specific targets from around a hundred metres away. To make sure you're heard, you use the inbuilt camera to line the recipient up in the instrument's sightline and then lock their location. You deliver your message with remarkable precision using the 'speak' button. No matter how much ambient noise there is, you'll get through to them.

They're not pointing in my direction but someone on the water bus says they're shouting "*Nessun sviluppo industriale.*"

"There's been a leak," bellows Alessi, simultaneously smiling for telephoto lenses. "Whoever is responsible for this, consider yourself sacked. You'll never work in this city again."

"We followed your instructions and the law to the letter," protests signore Greco. "Public notices were issued to minimum effect, we put posters up in blind alleyways, and announced the site opening in publications that almost nobody reads. Word could have come from anywhere."

The mayor checks his image in his viewer, making sure that he's presentable and mentally rehearses a few sound bites so that he can make a simple, yet winning statement.

I continue my way to school as the builders begin to mobilise concrete batching plants, massive hydraulic excavators, dredgers, cranes, cargo carriers and drilling machines.

Crowds are gathering in areas along the northeast of the city – Sant'Alvise, Madonna Dell'Orto and Fondamente Nova – to protest against the invading industrial forces. Others show solidarity in a gathering of small boats.

All eyes are on the arrival of the army of industrial titans as they wade into the lagoon.

• Themes
  – Corruption
  – Development

Prayer

"I've got to go back."

Cesare looks at me quizzically.

"Something's very wrong. There's no time to explain," I say.

I leap out of my seat and leave the Mestre bus. Cesare starts to distract the driver, assuming that I will return again. When he realises that I am not coming back, he makes a dramatic exit by leaping from the bus after me, barely missing being hit by the mechanical doors when the driver loses patience and slams them shut. As the bus pulls angrily out, it blasts its horn at Cesare in long slow bursts. He responds by swooping a graciously low bow. It is amazing how fast a young man, who detests sport on account of what it does to his elegantly bowed limbs, can run when the stakes are sufficiently high.

Cesare catches up with me at the Madonna della'Orto ferry stop. The decking is heaving as locals and tourists alike, are assembled to witness the industrial protest in the lagoon.

"So, where are we going?"

"San Michele."

"We're going to a cemetery? I thought you live on Murano now? That's why you've been absent from school – right?"

"It's complicated. I have to see someone."

Cesare is sufficiently intrigued to keep quiet and let events unfold, waiting for the pay-off. We grab the first vaporetto to San Michele and without waiting for the crew to properly secure the mooring for disembarking, I spring on to the decking, just like Krists does, and run through the cemetery. Despite protests from a groundsman on a ride-on lawnmower, I scale a wall on the south side of the island and make my way along the maturing beach on the southwest shore, where the curves of *Po*'s giant earthen tail have thickened.

"*Po!*" I howl, but there is nobody here but a plague of every biting insect on the island: mosquitos, midges, sand flies, sand wasps, stable flies, horse flies and black flies. Evil creatures everywhere.

I stand in our familiar place at the old cemetery wall, which featured so prominently in my childhood adventures, but the spiny backbone has thickened into a featureless dune and I can't feel *Po* thinking through me. Aleysa is now standing on a tuft of grass, soaking up the land but I don't pay her much attention. I'm completely focused on my lost twin. I can't sense its presence in my head or body at all. This place is strange, empty. I throw myself on the ground, placing my ear to the soil and listen like a physician, for signs of life. Something has changed. There is no response.

"Please *Po*, please speak to me."

I begin to sob. But the ground is silent.

Then I get angry.

"You cannot not shut me out. You must speak to me," I demand.

Po is still.

If my twin won't, or can't respond, then I'll have to make my own think-feelings.

With my ear to the silt, I search for the slapping sound of the valves that power *Po*'s vegetable heart. Channelling my terror at the prospect of an industrial invasion of epic proportions into our lagoon, I beg my twin for help.

"*Po*, if you ever loved me, or thought anything of me, *do something* now." I plead. "You don't even need to speak to me again. It's not just for me, nor for us. If these industrial monsters come, then nothing we cared about can ever be the same again."

I empty my feelings deep into the ground but I hear nothing but my own voice. My fear.

My island twin is dying. Perhaps it's dead.

I weep uncontrollably now; my scalding tears rise as steam from my cheeks.

I don't know how long I lie motionless, sobbing and pressing myself to the ground. A few sandhoppers leap acrobatically over my face. Sand fleas are eating me raw. Grit carried by the wind begins to collect in one of my ears. A crab becomes tired of hiding from my shadow drops its raised pincers and begins to forage again.

Cesare, who builds himself a set of steps from some discarded cardboard boxes used to carry flowers, finally climbs on top of the wall. He sniffs the air and wrinkles his nose as the stench. Regarding the beach as being too far down, he decides to watch my performance instead from his ringside seat.

Finally I rise, defeated, covered in angry bites. He says nothing as I accept his hand to get back up over the wall.

As we make our way slowly and solemnly to the San Michele ferry stop, he is gracious enough not to pass comment, though he casts bemused glances at me from time to time.

We sit on the wooden decking cross-legged, waiting for the vaporetto, as the timber bakes the backs of our legs. It's taking an awfully long time to come. Perhaps the ongoing protest is causing congestion in the waterways' traffic.

In the distance, we can see the gigantic machines striding onwards in slow motion, as crowds continue to amass around the water's edges. The world that I thought I knew stands still.

* Themes
    - Growing Up
        ↳ dealing with the injustice of the world
    - Lost Innocence / Imagination

PART V
(RE)ENCHANTMENT

Bio Spill

An Eni bio-oil tanker exceeding its official legal limit of vegetable oils, amounting to hundreds of thousands of tonnes, is hit by the wake of a monstrous crane. The pipeline is instantly ripped out of the hull and refinery workers race to stem the leakage, but several hours pass before the flow of golden liquid is quenched.

The oil slick spreads out, forming a fine film that ripples the surface of the lagoon with rainbow hues. Small fish nibble at its tasty body, surface skating insects wobble at the rapid changes in surface tension and ducks spoon up the tasty emulsion, like milkshake, with their beaks. The film thickens then tears into multiple islands of brilliant scum that surf the waves. Swirling and dancing with eddies, oil films seeps into the crevices of briccole, congealing around organic crusts of marine life and lubricating settling sediments. Islands of the expanding slick journey into the lagoon, where they continue to spread out until they are one molecule thick, coating the *Angeli* plinths with their syrup.

Some statues, whose bases are colonised by winking assemblages of oily droplets, are already primed for invasion. With the sudden availability of feedstock, these chemical life forms start to cluster and propagate in simple colonies.

Golden films are dispersing everywhere. More than a foodstuff, an energy store and fundamental ingredient of life, the bio-oils are also solvents that, given enough time, can soften and eventually penetrate even the hardiest plastics. Some make their way into the Grand Canal, weakening the floes upon which the *Teatro Mundi* rests. Lazy, spiralling currents draw the solvent into the theatre's base. At first, the plastics that keep the structure afloat simply soften, weakening and slowly rotting the platform from underneath. Adhesives fail under the weight, which cracks the structure like an egg. The bottom of the platform drops and water smashes its way inside. The 'world' lurches violently and the building appears to scream, as the performers and biotechnological displays are shaken like the contents of a cocktail mixer.

Gondoliers, immediately race to the shattering wreckage to rescue visitors and employees alike.

A dark eel-like shadow slithers over the tumbling fragments, searching for morsels to scavenge from the dirty and unregulated mixture of microorganisms and lifelike chemistries which are spilling from the experimental vessels.

Now, these monsters are free.

Phantasmagoria

Energy fields fracture chemical interfaces
Instantly. Many bodies are locked inside the
Crusts of their own product. Strange trails
Form in a spectacle of glimmering flesh: a
Swarm of tadpoles, barnacles, lusty insects,
Ghosts, and battling beetles. They circle
Each other for their nectar, dancing at first
With limbs and tails. Then together. These
Fragile seeds of matter are vulnerable to
External conditions, stretching their fields to
Raise a hurricane of metabolic weather.
Forming ribbons of organised flow, they
Hurl threads of transformation over the
Gleaming sea of oil. Here, souls of twisted
Matter assemble on reefs, spewing ectoplasm,
Infusing the lagoon with their strangeness.

Dogged survivors grow fatter, others longer,
Linking in chains, curling like buds, as organic
Cathedrals to the yet unborn. Others lengthen
Under the substance of their own shadows,
Bodies becoming denser, thicker, shedding
Contaminants into the primordial stew at
Simmering intensity. There goes one now,
Scurrying past inhibitor fields. Cute as a tulip.
It sprouts a stem and anchors on a quiet surface.
Several other unrelated figures join it, thrusting
Their florets into the air; a comma, caterpillar,
Cork screw, barnacle, each accreting meaning
In a bizarre crystalline garden whose liveliness
Blooms with material rebellion. First scores,
Then billions of crystalline seeds curl and
Unfold into petioles, following microscopic
Trails of impurities as they nucleate and sprout.

Rachel Armstrong

Pliant flowers push out of the water, like lilies,
Their petals formed by needles, pebbles, hairs and
Filaments. Forests of these chemical circuits wick
Up impurities, biotechnologies, microorganisms
Catalysts and all kinds of latent contaminants of
The lagoon waters. There is plenty of recalcitrant
Matter here, pushing through the golden sum and
Lifting the oily lid of the lagoon for the fishes and
All other marine life to breathe. Here, the soft
Matter of Venice is written in blooms by an invisible
Ecology of implausible substances that encode and
Decrypt these waters, revealing its carnival of wonder.
Not just a feast for the eyes, but for all the senses.
Peaceful resistance from those that wish to flourish
In strangeness, and assert the living legend of their
Existence – nature written by monsters not people –
For 'this' is how it appeared and therefore 'was'.

- Connecting to "Bio Spill"
- Themes
    - Invisible Ecology

An Extraordinary Event

We've not got much further than the Madonna dell'Orto vaporetta stop and we can't decide whether it is worth going to school or not.

I am sullen and rotten company.

"Wait!" says Cesare, sniffing the air.

"Cesare, we haven't got time…"

He ignores me and agilely pushes his way to the front of a crowd of spectators, moving quickly through the forest of hips and legs. Sighing, I follow him, excusing myself to irritable glances. Finally, I catch up with him at the water's edge. He is precariously perched on a concrete mooring block, pointing at a small flourish of milky crystals that are sprouting from around one of the decking posts.

"It's soapy, savoury, sweet and bitter, like olives," croon the wafting hands.

Then Cesare inhales deeply, filling his chest as the congregation begins to murmur and point.

"Look! There are millions of them."

While only minutes ago the lagoon had boasted a brilliant azure surface with darker twists of sapphire waves, now it is becoming a field of powder white floral blooms, which are racing out into the waters in long streams. Instant ice.

The lagoon spray is laced with a gentle scent.

"It's sensual, tinged with vanilla, bergamot, patchouli, sandalwood and with saltier bass tones," I say.

"Not bad, but you'll never be as good as me," sniffs Cesare.

I concur.

Strange Blooms

Crowds are cooing outside Sarah's laboratory workspace.

At first, she assumes there's a troupe of street performers. Venice is famous for its theatricality and much of it is illegal. Here and there, gangs of beggars motionlessly hold abject positions for hours, before taking tea breaks under bridges, when they think nobody is looking. When satiated, they resume their contortions. These same street dwellers not only channel artistic and religious notions of the abject, a character cast off by society, asking to be saved by alms from sympathetic souls, but also embody freak show entertainment, exposing impressive hairy patches, dark spots, amputated limbs, birth defects and pitifully clutching grubby babies.

Shoppers tend to quickly acclimatise to Venice's talent for the theatre of the absurd and prefer to browse street markets, where artisans and craftsmen sell tie-dyed T-shirts, snow globe miniatures, glass ornaments, commedia dell'arte masks, deformable plastic balls that splatter and reform on the ground, as well as gold-plated replicas of iconic buildings. While, grown-ups amble among tightly-packed crowds, children dart through gaps between legs to chase birds that are picking through dustbins. Moments of tranquillity can be found in the tapering alleyways between the mosaics of brightly painted houses, where washing lines dangle underwear tantalizingly alongside bed sheets. In summer, narrow streets cast black networks of lengthening shadows into impossible spaces that cool the city and seduce the lost into hidden realms. In the winter, the streets shine with their jubilant Christmas window displays.

Sarah has become accustomed to all these things and has learned not to pay much attention to the operatic sounds of the crowds, but this particular mood is unusual enough to raise her interest. Leaving her bench, she leans out of the window, where she can see the tail end of a crowd leaving San Stephano, moving in the direction of Accademia towards the Grand Canal.

There are just too many people to allow her a clear view, and she can't bear to face the crush of gathering throngs. Just as she's about to return to work, she notices a flourish of extraordinary crystalline blooms forming in the tidal zone along the brickwork in the blind canal outside the laboratory window. Even at this distance this is an extraordinary material growth. What can it be?

Taking several large containers, screw top test tubes, a stack of petri dishes and a video camera with her, she runs outside to collect as many samples as she can gather.

Watcher

The orange man turns over an old wooden crate and sits on its base, observing the chemical flower show unfold from the shoreline. He soaks in the extraordinary scene without trying to interpret it.

Recording

The biggest and boldest blooms of soft white crystals flourish out in the open lagoon around the *Exitec* boat, where Jelena and Davide have just arrived to sample microplastics and algae.

"Look at this," says Jelena. "What do you make of it?"

"I've never seen anything like it before. Thick, fluffy crystals, as big as lily flowers. Do you have the camera?"

"I do! And I have some large containers so we can make sure we capture the chemistry of the water too. We don't just want to identify the crystal type. We need to know what caused it."

"It's changing," says Davide. "The florets are growing bigger stamens."

"Okay, I'm on it!" says Jelena.

Salute

Krists sits at the foot of the earth-locked statue of my mother, having taken the plastic cast boat from Murano to secretly visit her on San Michele while everyone else is working.

"Here's to you, lagoon! You devious monster."

He raises his tumbler and spoon in salute with a double helping of algae vodka. "At least today you're paying something close to a fitting tribute to my missus. A miracle from the sea."

Inspiration

"Come on Kasia. Come on Ruzica," the workshop attendants say. "There's something amazing going on out in the lagoon."

"In a minute," grumbles Kasia, making entries into the accounts book, while Ruzica doesn't even look up, as she is tallying stock.

"No. It won't wait. You both need to get here now," comes the urgent reply. "It's crazy what's happening."

"Okay," sighs Kasia. "Come on, Ruzica, break time."

They don't even ask what's going on. The sea is sprouting brilliant white flowers. Under the angle of the sun, some have orange tips, others are laced with grey shadows that emphasise what seems to be lengthening stamens.

"Right everyone, let's get working," says Kasia.

"Fetch the cameras, and sketch books!" shouts Ruzica. "I want a new line of living flower sculptures. Think magnolias, irises, Georgia O'Keefe, Monet, Van Gogh, Manet, Judith Leyster's tulips, think – well, *floral* Venice."

— Most people are trying to see how they can profit off of the crystal flowers

Reversal

As a matter of course, Mayor Alessi is selectively deaf to public opinion. However, the crowds lining the lagoon are behaving differently than before. Their tone has changed; it's one of excitement, not anger. In fact, people may actually be whooping, celebrating and shouting for joy, even shouting his name, if he's not going crazy.

"Shhhh," he waves signore Greco to silence and makes his way to the waterside.

A sea of opalescent flowers is skimming the lagoon surface, like foam.

"See that?" he says.

"What is it?" asks the site manager.

Alessi smiles. He knows exactly what it is – an opportunity to capitalise on the widespread protest he'd been subjected to less than an hour ago.

Completely at ease with changing his mind to save face or win a vote, as only the most seasoned politicians can, he announces, "This project is on hold."

"What?" protests signore Greco. "Impossible! Everything's set in motion. The cranes are being installed, the dredgers are already paid for. The concrete has been imported from Taiwan. This has taken months, no, *years* of work, let alone investment."

"*On hold*," repeats the mayor menacingly.

Signore Greco throws up his hands and walks away, shouting at his staff.

"Call my ducal water taxi," says Alessi to his assistant. "I have an announcement to make."

Arriving in aristocratic style at the waterside, the mayor reaches out from his boat and shakes a few hands with an extremely assertive grip. He is delighted when several young women throw white flowers his way. Magnolias.

Now's the time to deliver his message.

His assistant invites the press on board and Alessi addresses the crowd through a megaphone.

"I had a vision," he says, making sure his best side is towards the cameras, "for a prosperous and flourishing Venice that would work hand in hand with its ecosystems. This project was the Palace of Light, which was inspired by the vision of one of the greatest designers of all time, Pierre Cardin."

He checks that the crowd is hanging on every word that follows.

"Today, I have been shown an alternative for such a dream. It is not the industrial development you were promised, but a spontaneous, natural and even *magical* alternative. A palace of Nature, if you will. Such a construction does not require capital venture, but asks for a different kind of investment: the care, love and attention of the people of Venice. Today's miracle has been offered by the lagoon herself, and we must heed her wishes and cherish this gift."

Ripples of excitement surge through the congregations around the water's edge.

"In light of these ongoing developments, and in keeping with my deep love of Venice and her natural environment, I am negotiating a change of plan."

Some people are already cheering.

"What I am saying is – construction work on the Palace of Light has been called off. The machines will return to the mainland and, for now, there will be no further lagoon development."

The extremely excitable audience responds joyously to the statement. More flowers are thrown; clapping children are bobbed upon tall shoulders, which makes them even more excitable and crowds of tourists raise their fists in solidarity.

"Mayor Alessi, *Il marito della laguna*," They chant.

Whatever happens next, the mayor knows this face-saving manoeuvre has just guaranteed him another term in office.

Faded

Cesare and I sit along the water's edge for several hours, watching the flowers start to wilt and shrivel into nothingness, like melting snow. Their soapy residues and earthy scent remains as faint souvenirs of the day. While some large blooms persist well into the afternoon, by sunset all traces of the miracle have entirely vanished.

We continue to sit together under the lick of evening dew, unable to talk about anything other than the miracle we witnessed.

Venice is alive.

Maturation

Not gone.
My voice has changed, not silenced. It deepens
Travelling through the ground in gargantuan
Vibrations. Not insensitive but more receptive
To pain, danger, poison and fear. It carries the
Dialogue needed to secure the fate of the lagoon
And city's future: the language of disconnections
That embodies the odd discourses of ecosystems.

Not yet.
But at some time in my life, my organic soils will
encounter sedimentary, or metamorphic forces
and transform into exquisite inert materials like
Sandstone, or slate under the Medusa gaze of
Geological time. At that point, the gels of organic
Bodies in my sediments will become fossils and
I turn into the geology upon which life is possible.

But not yet.
I am consolidating, No longer fragile, but wielding
The colossal scale of my being. As my maturing
Tissues enrich themselves, you feel this as silence.
Listen for the voice of lively matter, through which
My potency is expressed that articulates a collective
Will to live, love, and propagate within a perpetual
Ever-changing, planetary-scale cycle of life and death.

maybe why Po couldn't hear him

Simultaneously.
I taste the oils from a biotanker, the melting
Plastics of a theatre, confluences of synthetic
Agents, soapy trails of persistent droplets and
Patchy pollution that primes lively landscapes
Towards life. I respond with air currents, water
Patterns, activate chemical superhighways, and
Trigger physical networks as nature's magic.

Extraordinary.
I do not follow the laws of simple causality,
Where one thing directly leads to another, but
Act in ways that appear to transgress the laws
Of physics. Everything I do lies well within the
Spectrum of possible events on Earth. I may
Be understood as 'god' that works in strange
Ways, or as material laws not yet understood.

Sceptically.
I am no divinity, but a monstrous material being
Able to choreograph organic networks, channel
Elemental forces, and manipulate mutable events.
It is tempting to regard the fabric you depend on,
As largely inert and unsurprising. In that way, it can't
Surprise or scare you. With this false reassurance,
The illusion of control hangs over the natural realm.

Carefully.
When the eye of this perfect storm blinks, your dread
Of what might manifest beneath, is logical. You're
Woefully ill-equipped to negotiate with massively
Distributed 'soft' forces that you can't command. Look
Around you! The world is rich with living things that are
Never still. Deny these life-bearing forces at your peril, as
This pending industrial invasion has an appetite for death.

But we will not draw conclusions yet.

Samples

Canal samples of the Venice Flowers, sealed with screw-top lids, are angled in test tube racks on Sarah's bench. There is nothing left of the florets but she wonders whether the chemistry itself will remember the conditions for the extraordinary blooming that the whole city is still talking about.

She has already been reading around the subject, trying to understand the phenomenon from a scientific perspective. Potentially, the Venice Flowers could have been a transient but repeatable phenomenon, which is characteristic of certain forms of dissipative systems that can be provoked under very specific conditions. These forms of matter can create order out of disorder. She's already found a model system and experimental set-up using sodium sulphate salts that might provide a way of asking questions about what happened. Under the right conditions they show how a rapid and large-scale chain reaction can occur over many metres, when salts 'freeze' out of solution to produce long white crystal needles and incredible quantities of heat.

She has also found another example that occurs in Nature.

During polar winters, the 'perfect storm' of bacterial colonization, ambient temperature, salt and new sea ice, sets the conditions for the sudden appearance of delicate 'ice-flowers'. At these extraordinary moments, the sea air crystallises around imperfections on the surface of freshly formed ice and sprouts into crystal blooms that disappear as quickly as they form, without trace.

Such highly complex and unpredictable systems are experimentally difficult to work with, but they are real – not magical. If she can better understand how to coax the substances into compliance with a basic program, they may provide another unique way to develop her childhood passion for 'natural computation' – computation with life.

Sarah smiles, feeling vindicated in all she has ever sought through her work and her ambitions. She already knows that she will be interrogated mercilessly about what these experiments are 'good for'. But, having witnessed the city at its most extraordinary, she is simply happy to know there are things that take place in the world that can't be reduced to commodity, or instrumentation, and she's more than prepared to argue her case.

Earth Hugging

Cesare enters the classroom as if he was born balancing books on his head. He smells absolutely decadent. A wig of magnolias sits upon his exquisitely sculpted brow and his extended stature reminds me of Marie Antoinette and her spectacularly ornate hair sculptures. It was said at the time of this outrageous trend, that women's heads appeared to only be halfway up their bodies.

Cesare says nothing about the incredible incident in the lagoon.

"Ask me," he says.

"Ask you what?" I say staring at his hairpiece.

"About it," he says.

"Okay. What are you wearing Cesare? It's… peculiar."

"Well, since you ask…"

I'm realising for the first time that he actually rehearses these oratorical stunts. I feel slow not to have figured that out earlier.

He smells fantastic – *tinged with vanilla, bergamot, patchouli, sandalwood and with saltier bass tones*. I'm trying to think where I've come across that scent before.

"This artwork. This peruke, was inspired by the work of Leonard Autié, the Royal Hairdresser and artistic genius behind the periwigs of Marie Antoinette. The inventions and ambitions of this genius alienated the Austrian queen from the French proletariat and came to symbolise the monarchy's moral and economic corruption."

I'm intrigued by the way the flowers fall around his neck. It's very different than his shaven look.

"His genius portfolio of decadent hair sculptures included the Pouf, which was made of ostrich feathers, ribbons and was fastened with a single ruby. The Pouf 'jolie femme', which was a very tall version of the Pouf – reaching almost a metre high. The Ques-a-co, which was a visual pun on the title of the creation – 'what is it?' – and was sculpted as a plume of feathers that could be read as a question mark. The Hedgehog was also a favourite among courtiers, a very tall, unpowdered hair sculpture that was wrapped with a twisted ribbon, like a helter-skelter.

Rachel Armstrong

The Pouf Sentimental was much more ornate since it was a feathered sculpture bedecked with waxen figurines. The Mania was a range of poufs embellished with all kinds of objects that were imbued with status and meaning. Playful women, for example adorned their heads with butterflies. Passionate women wore Cupids and officers' wives displayed squadrons on their heads. Recently widowed women even wove the urns containing the ashes of their husbands into their wigs. Coiffure à la Belle-Poule, was a triumphant gesture in which a miniature the victorious frigate, la Belle Poule, was mounted on a sea of wavy hair."

"I think you just like saying 'pouf'," I observe. "It's very provocative. Especially when you're wearing that hairpiece."

For the briefest moment, Cesare suppresses a smile then quickly adopts his familiar air of extreme seriousness.

"It's not exactly, practical though, is it?" I add.

"Practical? Oh, no! Perukes and periwigs aren't in the slightest bit practical. Autié's sculptures were heavy, very tall and not at all easy to wear. What's even more impressive is that, since courtiers seldom washed, the hairpieces were not uncommonly a breeding ground for vermin."

"Lovely. What happened to this genius, then?"

"Oh, Autié was too brilliant to get caught up in a trivial skirmish like a bloody revolution. He was in exile in Germany when the executioner shed his muse's infamous iconic locks in 1793. Just picture the tragic scene. Immediately after the crowd cries "Vive la nation!" the guillotine comes down and the queen's head is triumphantly held up for the crowd to deride… by her hair."

"I guess to all intents and purposes she must have appeared sliced in half," I add as a rather macabre image lingers in my mind's eye of a face staring blindly from the bottom of a haystack.

Without changing the position of his head, Cesare opens his bag and places his copybook on the desk. He strikes a pose, with pencil in hand, ready to begin a day's work.

"I assume you have something to say, Gallo."

Cesare feigns mild surprise.

"I am simply celebrating life."

Miss Sapiente continues to look purposefully at his headdress.

"The world is full of miracles ma'am."

Miss Sapiente instructs Caesare to remove his 'garland', so that he

252

can take it to the school office for safe keeping until the end of the day.

"Peruke, miss. It's a *peruke*. Would you have that I wear sackcloth and go into mourning instead?"

"I want you – to adhere to school uniform regulations, Gallo."

"But there's nothing that says you can't wear a *peruke*, per-oo-key, in the school regulations, ma'am."

"Your attire is distracting, young man – even obstructive. In very plain language, it's getting in way of your classmates view of the blackboard."

"Then I shall have to cry tears of blood, ma'am. I simply cannot handle my profuse feelings today. Yesterday I experienced delight. Today I am distraught. I am denied the opportunity to salute the miracle of life. Which is, naturally, part of my religion."

He begins to sob.

Miss Sapiente tries to ignore the pitiful sound that Cesare is making, but his wail is beautifully pitched at exactly the same frequency that crying children quickly master when they need to consume the attentions of their parents. As he continues relentlessly, all of us began to feel incredibly miserable. Some of our classmates are reaching for tissues to blot their cheeks.

Cesare continues with his show of grief.

"I am part of the pageant of nature. I am speaking with the language of scent that takes the form of a *peruke*, so that I may share the fundamental poetry of existence – which has been brought into the classroom today. This denial -- this abnegation of my basic rights – is the refutation of joy."

More children start crying. His grief is infectious.

Our teacher shakes her head, once again deflated.

Cesare is allowed to look like an eighteenth-century concubine, until lunchtime.

We have barely started the morning lesson when Cesare leans over to me with the elegance of a catwalk model and whispers.

"Don't worry, I won't tell"

I look at him quizzically.

"You know."

"I do not."

'Earth-hugging"

"I don't know what you mean."

With a knowing smile and a whisper, Cesare recounts the events on San Michele, where I threw myself on the ground, shouted my own name and wept inconsolably. I was inspirational.

"I've tried it too." He nudges me sharply with his elbow.

"What?"

"Earth-hugging. You know, some people embrace each other, some clasp a tree and some quite understandably hug the ground. It's incredibly therapeutic. The benefits of embracing things that you adore are proven. It's to do with the production of the love hormone oxytocin. Of course, I'd have to question your choice of love-object. I'd go for a much more perfumed ground. A malty clay, or perhaps a mature musky compost – the kind that gardeners use on roses. My grandmother's loft has that kind of aroma sometimes."

I look at him, my bites are itching madly and I've sworn to my aunts I will not scratch them. Cesare is not mocking me but genuinely trying to understand what had happened. I also appreciate that he is giving me a dignified way out of a very complicated situation.

"Thanks," I say, "Let's make earth-hugging our secret."

Cesare winks at me in agreement and conducts himself as the floral model of diligence, just as Miss Sapiente turns around.

Home

My father is talking to Alesya through the contents of his bottle and waving his spoon as a baton, commanding the lagoon to produce miracles, as several small fishing boats sharpen into view. They feel like a memory and I wonder whether I've seen them somewhere before.

They sail around Po's gargantuan crescent tail and moor alongside us.

An old man with a stick walks very slowly towards us, as three men leap over the side of their boat in a most familiar manner, and begin to sprint into view. A muscular female figure on callipers, who moves along with her arms as much as her legs, is close in pursuit. Several women and children appear on the deck to watch us but do not alight.

Instinctively I stand up. Then, I run towards them. We all stop several metres from each other.

"Uncle?"

"You got tall, boy!" says Csaba.

"You have your mother's good looks for sure," adds Ivan.

"Need to put some meat on you," growls Piotr as Nastia grips my arm.

"Aunty," I say and grab her arm in return.

I can't remember any of their faces, but somehow I know all of them so well.

"Not so bad," she says. "A few honest arm wrestles will have you sorted in no time at all."

"You? Honest arm wrestle?" snorts Csaba.

They backslap me again in turns, to a point where I think I might never breathe again but don't really mind at all. I am delighted to see them all.

Anatoly steps forward and gives me a warm one-armed embrace like a nutcracker, still gripping his stick.

"We knew we'd find you home, boy."

Then he looks at my father.

There's a tense and terribly long silence.

Krists pulls out his spoon and plunges it into the ground. He scoops out a lump of soil and swallows it.

The men stare at each other. I shuffle uncomfortably, willing them to get along.

"I did okay, old man," says Krists, between stained teeth. They nod at each other from several paces away.

More silence.

"You did, son."

Further silence.

Nastia's had enough.

"Well, now the man-pride thing is over and done with – are you going to show us your home or not, Krists?"

My father scowls, but I can tell he's relieved.

"Sort them out then, Po."

Then, he smiles broadly.

I skip alongside Nastia and climb aboard the *Verve*. She needs no directions to Murano as it's within clear view but shows me how to walk the boat sideways. By the time we're moored, my father is play-fighting with his brothers and I see Anatoly backslapping Krists very slowly as he alights the *Voyager*. Still, they say nothing at all.

We sit together outside the workshop, along the Fondamenta in happy silence: uncles, aunts, brothers, sisters, children – all are eating Kasia's squid ink tagliatelle and watching the horizon's red orb sizzle into the sea. My father is impressively generous with the algae vodka but he's the only one using a spoon.

Lamplights aglow, we spend the small hours joking and talking together about unimportant things.

When I wake, the scent of my kin is everywhere, but they've gone.

Back Door Venice

The orange man sits on marine-polished fragments of orange bricks, on the wrong side of the orange walls of the city, basking in the last rays of the orange sunset along my shores.

This is Venice's back stage – the part that nobody wants, or cares for.

Having discovered an inaccessible beach by climbing over a wall behind a football stadium in the northeasterly sector of Venice, the orange man walks slowly along the unsteady ridge of brick fragments, chewed concrete and fractured pieces of rubble on which the shore's tenuous foundations precariously rest. In search of a new settlement, he squats back on his heels to pluck at a carpet of sea lettuce and chews it for several minutes. Then he swallows it dispassionately. Can he survive here? The living statues along the Lido have become such an incredibly successful tourist attraction that the crowded beach environment is cluttered and oppressive. It is time to move on.

Rocks slide one way then the other under the twist of his footstep. This untrodden land is a garbage tip of opportunities, monotonous views, alien species and lost items that nobody wants to reclaim – foams, water bottles, fragmented fishing nets, wrappers, weeds, cigarette lighters and excrement. Only the figure of the man draws attention, as passengers on speeding boats avert their eyes, ashamed of the place.

Tourists never come here, council officials have no interest in extending their powers of jurisdiction into a place with no commercial value and pestilent wildlife intrudes into every possible niche between the waters and the land. It is colonised by undesirable ecologies of short-necked clams, tiger mosquitos, sprouts of silver wattle, tree of heaven saplings, ragweed, eel swim bladder nematodes, Spanish slugs, bay barnacles, cotton whitefly, Mediterranean fruit flies, fishhook water fleas, Asian clams, giant diatoms, unidentified dinoflagellates, tenacious bladder wrack, prolific sea lettuce, vagrant shrimp, sand fleas, sand flies and unclassifiable micro algae.

As the sky turns green, the orange man becomes a long brown

shadow. He stands with outspread arms, capturing the tug of the rising breeze on his flesh and indulging the farewell kisses of the falling sun. A lone wave surges from the wake of a ferry, soaking his shoe leather, which becomes imprinted by the water's molecular memories. Then, he pulls up a sodden foam mat, heavy with an infiltration of algae, and rolls it up, squeezing out the excess water. He lies down on the garbage as if he were basking on a haystack under a summer sky and contemplates the difficult forms of peace-making that are constantly being struck within the lagoon.

So that he can ensure his kin may thrive here, he considers what makes a successful ecology. The lagoon's negotiations are not easily visible or measurable things. A flourishing shoreline is not about the calories contained in the sea lettuce, nor the amount of nitrogenous waste in his urine, on which beach bacteria thrive. They cannot be found in the drops of blood drawn by sand flies on his leg, nor are they in the skin fragments that he sheds, which are scavenged by beach mites. They are more than a simple courtesy between animate and inanimate bodies, where one agency submits to another in unbroken fields of succession – and they do not merely potentiate one another. Ecosystems are not simply formed by hierarchies of food chains where predators consume the young and weak of a species and leave healthy adults to breed new food for their kind. They do not only arise from the spectacle of their interactions where bioluminescent algae spill their blue light on the shore, attracting hungry fish fry. The web of life cannot be found purely in the carnivalesque processions of the seasons with their characteristic hues and displays. They are not forged exclusively in rituals where night fishermen haul in their catch of snapping eels, so that invertebrates can rest without fear of being hunted for a while. Nor are they uniquely present in the passions of lovers that make out unobserved by the water's edge.

There is no one specific indicator that sums up an ecosystem and -- even when observations are simplified into pre-determined end points, specific metabolisms, or the presence of particular bodies – they continue to be shrouded with many contradictions and entanglements, which remain largely unnoticed by us yet are open to many interpretations and purposes. Ecosystems are persistently strange and invisible bodies that cannot be simplified or solved. Such uncertainties are written into the molecular fabric of the world and form the very lifeblood of the poetry

Invisible Ecologies

of life that swells the tissues of the Po bioregion.

In backstage Venice, a large cumulus nimbus cloud passes otherwise unobserved in the darkness, dimming the brilliance of the peach moon. The orange man rises and departs through the stage exit of this beach and makes his way again into the city. Then he stops and turns around one last time, troubled by the realisation that somewhere along this undesirable beach is exactly what he's looking for, but he just can't figure out what it is yet.

Sunset

Our Murano apartment tastes of salt. Its patchwork selection of bricks drinks the elements from the outside and within. Ruzica is experimenting with a range of concretes to plaster over the inevitable defects that arise from this struggle between the elements but Kasia thinks she should let the walls breathe and keep their original character, particularly on the inside.

I want to suggest some cosmetic building surgery to bring some *real life* into the place but decide it will take too long to explain to everyone.

A couple of employees are helping out with the renovations. Durante Contadino, a swarthy man, assists Ruzica and periodically flexes his muscles to impress her. Terzo Basso, whose nose starts too high on his forehead, constantly compliments Kasia on her wonderful cooking, or figure.

Although my aunts don't seem to mind these inane habits, they irritate me intensely, so I go outside to simmer down.

Jelena is walking along the shore with Davide, probably talking about their latest range of 'living' fabrics, which are new kinds of functional earths that can clean up the environment. I like the whole idea of it. They are making a designer range of baby *Po*s.

My father is at the end of the fondamenta, waving a tumbler in the air, inching towards the plastic rowing boat moored just by the steps. He's waiting with his spoon held high for the first blush of sunset. I know he can't be doing with all the business talk, or discussions about interior décor, and he certainly isn't in the slighted bit interested in beach refuse.

"Mind if I join you, Daddy?"

Shimmering across the water from the mainland we watch the silver towers of Mestre and Marghera looming ominously, casting empty stares upon us, with grand ambitions for colonization of our island shores. Gleaming defiantly, we know they're dreaming of the moment when they might walk again on the water and chew the city's old red bones into a rubble heap.

"I don't trust that old Mayor, any more than I do the developers, son," he says, "They're all crooks, plenty capable of changing their minds again when the opportunity suits them."

"You're worried about the future of the lagoon, then?" I ask.

"Of course," he says, "I don't think I'll ever stop worrying about the future, but, you know, I've had enough of hostilities for tonight. Let's call a truce for the evening."

He looks at me with a glint in his eye.

"Come on!"

I make my way to the steps, assuming that we're taking the rowing boat to San Michele.

"No, this way!" he shouts and sprints over the bridge towards the vaporetto stop.

The ferry pulls in and Krists rather helpfully assists a group of straggling passengers and tourists embark. Just as the doors are shutting, he holds me back momentarily. Then, gripping onto the boat's blind side, he invites me to take a spade.

I dither, then grip his wrist.

Effortlessly, he tucks me in front of him and holds me tight, like a safety harness. Although I am gangly and out of sorts with myself, in those moments I am unmistakably, my father's child and most treasured companion. Instinctively, I know exactly what to do. The sea spray drenches our backs and tries as hard as it can to loosen our hold on the boat, but Krists' big belly and limpet grip will not let us fall.

Exhilarated, we cling like barnacles, keeping low so that the conductor can't see us and like spectres, we alight at San Michele to scramble over the cemetery wall and sit together on my mother's grassy knoll, watching the deepening sunset.

"To us!" says Krists, offering me a swig of algae vodka. I decline and give him a hug instead.

He lifts the bottle again, "to Aleysa, the sunset, and to life."

I smile and add, "To *Po!*"

As we both meditate upon unspoken futures that we look for at the horizon's edge, I hear a faint yet familiar voice as if it was one with the song of the sea.

"Although our adventures have now grown apart, dear twin, I am with you still and will always be here for you should you learn how to listen and look for me."

I don't know if Krists hears it too, but he looks at me, with that endless gaze of his which I associate with him reminiscing about my mother and says, "Aye. To *Po!*"

Origamy

Rachel Armstrong

"*Origamy* is a magnificent, glittering explosion of a book: a meditation on creation, the poetry of science and the insane beauty of everything. You're going to need this." – *Warren Ellis*

Mobius knows she isn't a novice weaver, but it seems she must re-learn the art of manipulating spacetime all over again. Encouraged by her parents, Newton and Shelley, she starts to experiment, and is soon traveling far and wide across the galaxy, encountering a dazzling array of bizarre cultures and races along the way. Yet all is not well, and it soon becomes clear that a dark menace is gathering, one that could threaten the very fabric of time and space and will require all weavers to unite if the universe is to stand any chance of surviving.

Rachel Armstrong is Professor of Experimental Architecture at Newcastle University and a 2010 Senior TED Fellow. A former medical doctor, she now designs experiments that explore the transition between inert and living matter and considers their implications for life beyond our solar system.

"*Origamy* crackles with a strange and brilliant energy, and folds the conventions of SF into beautiful new shapes. A rare and wonderful debut."
– *Adam Roberts*

"Perhaps the most astonishing and original piece of SF I've read in a long, long while." – *Adrian Tchaikovsky*

"A visionary masterpiece. Science Fiction, Fantasy, science and poetry combine to create a lyric on life and death that spans the whole of creation. Delightful and mind-expanding. If you miss it you have missed one of the finest examples of literary art." – *Justina Robson*

New from NewCon Press

Andrew Wallace – Celebrity Werewolf

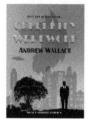

Suave, sophisticated, erudite and charming, Gig Danvers seems too good to be true. He appears from nowhere to champion humanitarian causes and revolutionise science, including the design and development of Product 5: the first organic computer to exceed silicon capacity; but are his critics right to be cautious? Is there a darker side to this enigmatic benefactor, one that is more in keeping with his status as the Cleberity Werewolf?

David Gullen – Shopocalypse

A Bonnie and Clyde for the Trump era, Josie and Novik embark on the ultimate roadtrip. In a near-future re-sculpted politically and geographically by climate change, they blaze a trail across the shopping malls of America in a printed intelligent car (stolen by accident), with a hundred and ninety million LSD-contaminated dollars in the trunk, buying shoes and cameras to change the world.

Kim Lakin-Smith – Bright Burning Star

Charged with crimes against the state, Kali Titian (pilot, soldier, and engineer), is sentenced to Erbärmlich prison camp, where few survive for long. Here she encounters Mohab, the Speaker's son, and uncovers two ancient energy sources, which may just bring redemption to an oppressed people. Set in a dystopian future, the author of *Cyber Circus* returns with a dazzling tale of courage against the odds and the power of hope.

Ian Creasey – The Shape of Strangers

British SF's best kept secret, Ian Creasey is one of our most prolific and successful short fiction writers, with 18 stories published in *Asimov's,* a half dozen or more in *Analog,* and appearances in a host of the major SF fiction venues. *The Shape of Strangers* showcases Ian's perceptive and inventive style of science fiction, gathering together fourteen of his finest tales, including stories that have been selected for *Year's Best* anthologies.

IMMANION PRESS
Purveyors of Speculative Fiction

Venus Burning: Realms by Tanith Lee

Tanith Lee wrote 15 stories for the acclaimed *Realms of Fantasy* magazine. This book collects all the stories in one volume for the first time, some of which only ever appeared in the magazine so will be new to some of Tanith's fans. These tales are among her best work, in which she takes myth and fairy tale tropes and turns them on their heads. Lush and lyrical, deep and literary, Tanith Lee created fresh poignant tales from familiar archetypes.
ISBN 978-1-907737-88-6, £11.99, $17.50 pbk

A Raven Bound with Lilies by Storm Constantine

The Wraeththu have captivated readers for three decades. This anthology of 15 tales collects all the published Wraeththu short stories into one volume, and also includes extra material, including the author's first explorations of the androgynous race. The tales range from the 'creation story' *Paragenesis*, through the bloody, brutal rise of the earliest tribes, and on into a future, where strange mutations are starting to emerge from hidden corners of the earth.
ISBN: 978-1-907737-80-0 £11.99, $15.50 pbk

The Lightbearer by Alan Richardson

Michael Horsett parachutes into Occupied France before the D-Day Invasion. Dropped in the wrong place, badly injured, he falls prey to two Thelemist women who have awaited the Hawk God's coming, attracts a group of First World War veterans who rally to what they imagine is his cause, is hunted by a troop of German Field Police, and has a climactic encounter with a mutilated priest who believes that Lucifer Incarnate has arrived...*The Lightbearer* is a unique gnostic thriller, dealing with the themes of Light and Darkness, Good and Evil, Matter and Spirit. ISBN 9781907737763 £11.99 $18.99

http://www.immanion-press.com
info@immanion-press.com